THE AVENGING ANGELS

THE AVENGING ANGELS

MICHAEL DUKES

FIVE STAR

A part of Gale, a Cengage Company

GALE
A Cengage Company

Farmington Hills, Mich • San Francisco • New York • Waterville, Maine
Meriden, Conn • Mason, Ohio • Chicago

LIBRARY OF CONGRESS CATALOGING-IN-PUBLICATION DATA

Names: Dukes, Michael (Michael Paul)
Title: The avenging angels / Michael Dukes.
Description: First edition. | Waterville, Maine : Five Star, 2018.
Identifiers: LCCN 2018004736 | ISBN 9781432846008 (hardcover) | ISBN 9781432846015 (ebook) | ISBN 9781432846022 (ebook)
Subjects: LCSH: Outlaws--Fiction. | Pinkerton's National Detective Agency--Fiction. | GSAFD: Western stories | Historical fiction
Classification: LCC PS3604.U438 A94 2018 | DDC 813/.6--dc23
LC record available at https://lccn.loc.gov/2018004736

First Edition. First Printing: August 2018
Find us on Facebook—https://www.facebook.com/FiveStarCengage
Visit our website—http://www.gale.cengage.com/fivestar/
Contact Five Star Publishing at FiveStar@cengage.com

Printed in Mexico
1 2 3 4 5 6 7 22 21 20 19 18

"There is a way which seemeth right unto a man, but the ends thereof are the ways of death."

—Proverbs 14:12

"All the world likes an outlaw. For some damned reason, they remember them."

—Jesse Woodson James

CHAPTER 1

A savage night had fallen upon the Appalachian foothills by the time Gabriel Kings and his Avenging Angels found shelter at last. Within the flimsy walls of an abandoned creek mill, the young men, fresh from their first bank robbery, slept among the horses to stay warm as a tree-bending wind howled outside and rainwater leaked in through the cracks in the roof. Despite their less than glorious habitations, they had reason to celebrate. The operation itself had been child's play compared to the games they'd all grown accustomed to over the last few years. For five of the six, as Southern-born veterans of the War between the States, going from enemy of the state to fugitive of the law seemed a welcome demotion of sorts.

At ten o'clock the previous morning, Kings, Leroy Brownwell, and Dave Zeller had burst into the First National Bank of Scarboro, North Carolina, a depository owned by traitorous scalawags and largely filled with scalawag money. The men had their hat brims tugged low but, beginners as they were, hadn't bothered to hide their faces with sacks or kerchiefs. Their unbuttoned coats flapped wide to show heavy revolvers in army-issue flap holsters. The sight was enough to make the speechless patrons reach for the ceiling without being told and move back against the walls. With so little resistance, the outlaws drew their weapons only because they felt they should.

Outside, Tom Seward and Sam Woods, mounted on fine pacing horses, passed each other along the main street. Beneath

7

their greatcoats, their hands lay near holstered guns, ready to pull and drive off curious bystanders at a given moment. One street over, Andy Yeager stood behind a hitch rail directly across from the saloon in which the town's occupying troops loitered. Against Union army regulations for former Confederates in the Reconstruction South, he openly cradled a Henry rifle, which the soldiers were thus far too busy drinking to notice.

While Brownwell held a shotgun on the bank crowd, Kings strode to the teller's cage with Zeller a step behind. The latter shoved a gunnysack across the counter as Kings leaned in with a Navy Colt and said, "I was told you're the man to see about a withdrawal."

The teller eyed the octagonal barrel of the .36-caliber revolver with a mixture of disbelief and fear. He sputtered and asked who they were and what the hell they were planning to do.

Zeller, for whom aggression came more easily, slid his own pistol barrel through the grate and leveled it with the man's nose. "Unless you wanna get shot, you'll hop to, and don't ask no more stupid questions."

Now with two guns on him, the teller glanced at Kings, who seemed the calmer of the pair, but he found no comfort in the man's eyes. "And h-how much exactly do you wanna withdraw, sir?"

"Well, now, how much would *you* say?"

"Sir?"

"How much would you say," Kings repeated, "that federal paymaster deposited here yesterday?" He paused, allowing his apparent omniscience to resonate.

Zeller crowded closer. "And just you remember," he said, jacking his gun hammer back for emphasis, "what the Good Lord said about lyin'."

The citizen's answer came slowly. "I'd say around seven . . . thousand dollars."

"We'll take the lot," Kings said. As the teller hurried to oblige, he posed another question: "Say, how them blue-bellies been behavin' themselves? They treatin' y'all like human bein's?"

For a moment, the teller forgot he was speaking to a robber and was quick to divulge to his fellow Southerner that the town of Scarboro could expect no fair treatment from the occupiers.

"You be sure to tell 'em there won't be no use followin' us," Kings said. "Not if they wanna make it back to their families up north. Tell 'em they didn't get us all. They never will."

The teller paused in the middle of transferring a portion of the money from the safe to the sack. "And . . . who shall I say you are, sir?"

Kings considered that, then, in a moment of inspiration, answered, "Why, we're the Avenging Angels of the Shenandoah."

As the teller went back to filling the sack, Zeller turned to Kings, chewing on one end of his stringy mustache and fighting a smile. "Kings?" he said.

"Zeller?"

"I think this is gonna be a pleasure."

Ninety seconds later they stepped into the leather and whipped their horses into a gallop. Although they went unchased by the bluecoats, the Avenging Angels of the Shenandoah didn't slow their mounts to a walk until they crossed the border into Tennessee. That night, by the light of a fire in the abandoned creek mill, they listened to the downpour and divided their spoils as evenly as possible. The die was cast by the passing of a bottle of sour mash.

The Wanted bills were posted two days later, on October 8, 1866, in every town, lumber mill, and general store window within a ten-mile radius. They lacked any attempt at an artist's rendering, for Scarboro contained no artists, but at the bottom of the bills the populace was instructed to contact Col. Thomas

Spooner, of the Military Department of the Carolinas, with any information that might lead to an arrest or capture.

WANTED!! IN CONNECTION WITH ROBBERY OF FIRST NATL. BANK, SCARBORO, ASHE COUNTY, NORTH CAROLINA, OCT 6. ROBBERS, CALLING THEMSELVES THE AVENGING ANGELS, ESCAPED WITH SEVEN THOUSAND DOLLARS. MADE OFF TOWARD TENNESSEE LINE. TWO OF SIX THIEVES IDENTIFIED. DESCRIPTION AS FOL-LOWS:

GABRIEL KINGS. 6 FEET. BLACK HAIR, BROWN EYES. SCAR ON LEFT CHEEKBONE, CROOKED LITTLE FINGER ON RIGHT HAND. SAW ACTION AS CAPTAIN IN 1ST VA CAV UNDER JEB STUART. ALSO WANTED FOR QUESTIONING IN MURDER CASE OF ROCKBRIDGE COUNTY LAWYER.

ZELLER, FIRST NAME UNKNOWN. 5 FEET 10 INCHES, FAIR HAIR, BLUE EYES, SMALL MUSTACHE. SERVICE RECORD UNKNOWN.

FUGITIVES CONSIDERED ARMED AND DANGER-OUS. $500 REWARD PER MAN OFFERED BY U.S. MILITARY. DEAD OR ALIVE.

CHAPTER 2

The wind picked up, causing the big campfire in the lower reaches of the Glass Mountains—a twenty-four-mile-long range located on the southern edge of the Delaware Basin—to bend and gutter. Outlaws hunkered silently about the flames, slurping bourbon-laced coffee, gnawing on jerked salt beef or corn dodgers, and waiting on their captain to finish his reconnoiter.

Alone with his thoughts and demons, Kings sat cross-legged a hundred yards out on the limestone caprock. With his back to the campfire, he took in the dips and swells of the land that lay ahead of them, searching for irregularities through a pair of old field glasses with the well-weathered initials CSA embossed along one side. It was a nightly ritual, a necessary precaution, but it had grown too dark to see anything now.

Lowering the glasses, he felt the icy caress of the wind along the back of his neck and huddled deeper into his heavy buffalo coat with a sigh. Tonight was as cold as that first night out had been, and as many years as he'd been in this hard country, he despised it still for its unpredictable weather—its brutally hot summers, numbingly cold winters, heavy rains and light snows in some places. As a whole, he thought the state of Texas held no candle to the place of his birth—by now a place he'd hardly recognize, it had been so long.

His were humble beginnings and his parents, humble people, salt of the loamy earth from which they sprang. His father, Jonathan McCauley Kings, had been the most recent in a line

11

of soldier-farmers dating back to the French and Indian War. He'd worn U.S. Army blue during the conflict with Mexico and had in fact been absent from Gabriel's life from the ages of five to seven. As soon as he had the smell of the Shenandoah back in his nostrils, though, Jonathan Kings quickly made up for lost time.

He lived by an upright and hard-nosed moral code passed down by his ancestors. Gabriel's mother, Mary Aubrey Kings, had done the best she could in her husband's absence to plant these seeds of morality in their boy's mind: to stand up for what was right and that, save one's devotion to Almighty God, nothing came before family or the home.

So when the call to arms came to those who called Virginia home, young Gabriel was one of the first to leave his family's small farm—not so much to preserve the oppression of slavery, as to resist the exploitation of his beloved commonwealth and to preserve the rights of every Southern state to rule its citizens as they deemed fit. Kings reached the Harpers Ferry district, covering three-quarters of the distance by horse, the other quarter by ferryboat, to enlist on July 18, 1861, as a member of the 1st Virginia Cavalry, under the flamboyant but tenacious West Pointer, J. E. B. Stuart.

The colonel's zeal was infectious, and a man couldn't help but feel proud, nothing short of invincible, riding with him. Among the gaggle of genteel, academy-educated tuckahoes that flocked to Stuart's command, Kings had found many of his own kind—young farmers, rough-hewn boys down from the hills and across the dark-leaf fields whom necessity would form into battle-hardened cavalrymen. Leroy Brownwell and Andy Yeager, then two-week privates, welcomed him into their confidence, and a strong bond was forged over a pot of weak coffee and a twist of tobacco.

Three days later Kings took part in Stuart's daring charge

and pursuit of routed federal troops at Manassas Junction. He also received his first wound there, in sight of Henry House Hill. It might have been his last, were it not for Brownwell dragging him from beneath the weight of the horse that had been shot from under him. The following summer Kings was singled out by Stuart himself for his efforts during the Northern Virginia Campaign and promoted to sergeant. Three months after, he made captain and was elevated to Stuart's escort, the only member who had never attended a military academy.

Stuart, by then a major general, had established a reputation as an audacious leader, garnering the admiration of his men the way a hard-working farmer garners a good crop. Kings found himself no less smitten with the general than the lowest private. The only time he'd ever questioned Stuart was when, for reasons never fully understood, the man separated three of his best brigades from General Lee's troops in July of 1863, at Gettysburg—when they were most needed.

Stuart's actions, later reprimanded and then forgiven, left their commander totally blind to Union movements, resulting in a shattering loss for the Confederacy. Kings had listened, unconvinced, to the general's side of the story and had been the sole adjutant who did not approach Stuart afterward to commiserate. He'd left Stuart's tent without a word, found Brownwell and Yeager, and thought of the men who died on Cemetery Hill.

Squatting there with his fellows, brooding on the debacle, Kings had hoped—not for the first time—that their cause would prove worth the fight. How many good Virginia boys had he seen fall since Manassas? More than that, how many good *American* boys had fallen, whatever color they wore in the fighting? Thousands, and not at the hands of a foreign-born enemy, but an enemy who worshiped the same God, shared the same history, had been brought up on the same legends and tall tales.

Although the 1st Virginia would continue to fight bravely, the bitterness that found Kings in the immediate aftermath of Gettysburg was only a taste of things to come.

Stuart's death at Yellow Tavern the following May devastated General Lee and deprived him of his most experienced cavalry commander. Eleven months later, Lee relinquished his sword. All Confederate forces were called in to surrender and, by the grace of President Lincoln, allowed to go home and rebuild what might be left standing.

So it was that thirteen long years ago, Gabriel Kings had relinquished his own sword. Following Lee's example, he forgave the North and returned to the land that spawned him, with plans to marry and work the ground till the end of his days.

When he arrived in Rockbridge County, travel-stained and half-starved, he found the farm and graves of his parents desecrated. His coon-dogs and the hired man were nowhere to be found, and where fields once stood was a railhead depot, half-constructed, with tracklayers hard at work.

He pounded on the door of Clive Parker, a lawyer and acquaintance of his father's, but even as he prevailed upon the man to bring the guilty parties to trial—on charges of land theft, unlawful purchase, anything—Kings knew it was too late. It was only when Parker told him to lower his voice that Kings ceased his supplications and started asking questions. How had the railroad gotten permission to build in the first place? Before he died, his father had made Parker executor to his will and caretaker of the land deed, to be kept under lock and key until his son returned from service.

The truth was that Jonathan Kings hadn't even been a week in the ground before Parker burned the will and sold the twenty acres to the railroad for a handsome sum. And while Gabriel could never prove it, Parker's inability to give a straight answer told Jonathan's sole surviving heir all he needed to know.

In a rage, Gabriel stormed out of Parker's office, mounted up, and thrashed the eleven miles back through the greenwood to what had once been family property, where he threatened the construction foreman with a sling blade. He gave the man and his crew twenty-four hours to pack up and git, only to be clubbed over the head from behind by one of the laborers. While he lay recovering from the blow in town, the last remnants of the Kings farm were razed to the ground.

A fortnight later, after the doctor pronounced him fit to walk, Kings was seen begging supplies off various businessmen on credit—the sort of supplies one stocks up on before embarking on a long trip. By week's end, he was gone, in search of a handful of trusted men.

At first, Kings's crusade had brought a meager sense of justification, especially when he'd looked into Parker's terrified eyes and pulled the trigger on the night of September 25, 1866. The Virginia Central Railroad executive with whom the wretch had been enjoying a Havana cigar handed his wallet over readily enough. It might have come as a surprise to the executive, given his compliance, to be promptly hurled out a side window. He broke his collarbone on the landing and was still groaning as Kings emptied a bottle of whiskey over the walls and floor of the private car, then set fire to it. His accomplices, mounted on fretting horses outside, couldn't help but shudder at the look on his face when he came down to rejoin them. Stone-faced as the Egyptian sphinx, Kings may as well have stepped on a spider.

Eleven days and a few hundred miles of track later, he and those same boys hit the bank in Scarboro for a much needed road-stake. It had all been so glorious—so defiant and bloody—but looking back, he realized that he'd never stopped to consider the consequences of his bold and violent actions. He'd only meant for there to be one job, but one thing led to another, as happens, and before any of them knew it, what began as a simple case of retribution became an addiction.

In those times of day or night when a man has no one else to turn to but himself, Kings could honestly say he regretted nothing and did not feel the need to mourn the thirteen departed souls he had to his name. At one time, he might have lamented the absence of a voice of reason, one that might have steered him down a different, less permanent path. But the only way Kings had known to settle a score was with a weapon, and he hadn't been in a healthy state of mind when he blew the top of Parker's head off.

Now, twelve years older and feeling every long month, Kings stood, a shadow among shadows, faceless in the black of night. He went down the precarious length of the craggy escarpment, half-sliding, half-creeping, boot heels scuffing and clacking like clogs all the way to where the scarp bottomed out.

He longed for a fire, for peace, for a drink of coffee to warm his insides. The first and third could be found just ahead. The second—well, he had just as soon expect the sun to rise in the west. More likely was the chance that he would die a gory death, staring down the barrels of fifty guns, or be dropped through the trapdoor of a gallows. For a dozen years he had known no peace, and with every sunset he knew his fated day was drawing closer.

At the very least, he was obliged to go dressed to meet it. Three years ago he'd traded his walnut-stocked Navies in for a pair of ivory-handled Peacemakers, which he carried in separate, crisscrossing gunbelts. The one on his right hip was holstered butt-backward and the other, butt-forward, so that it could be drawn in a cross-body or twist-draw, should the right arm become disengaged by an enemy bullet. In addition to these, he had a Bowie knife sheathed to the rear of the left-hand Colt, carried in such a way that drawing one was not an encumbrance to the other. The knife was two pounds in weight and longer than both pistols at fifteen inches, with the single-edged, razor-sharp Arkansas steel accounting for nine of those.

The musical chiming of his spurs announced his return. He glanced down and around at the men by the fire. There was Brownwell, who had ridden east from St. Louis to his uncle's home on the Potomac in 1860, just in time to join up. Yeager, still tall, lean, and hungry, squatted on his heels upwind of the coals, warming his hands. Nearby, Sam Woods lay on his back, hands beneath his head, hat hiding his face, and beyond him Tom Seward reposed upon an elbow, reading from Washington Irving.

Zeller was nowhere to be seen—answering nature's call, Brownwell explained—and the seventh, newest member of the gang, Dick Osborn, had stayed behind to stand watch over their stronghold deep within the Big Bend country. Kings knew and trusted each of these men, the five with him here in the cold of the Delaware, and the one back home camped atop the watchtower they all called the Rocking Chair. They had all been down the Hoot-Owl and back again, proving themselves worthy of the company and of the times in which they lived.

Footsteps sounded over loose shale. Moments later Dave Zeller emerged from the darkness, buttoning the front of his pants as he came back into the firelight.

His membership in the gang, while incredibly valuable, was interesting in more ways than one. As a combination scout, wagon master, and sharpshooter in the 42nd Indiana, he'd learned to survey with stealth and patience, drive horses with the skill of a lifelong teamster, and shoot with deadly precision. Zeller had served with distinction, suffering a wound at Kennesaw Mountain. He was honorably discharged but had no home worth returning to, so he headed west, making whatever money he could at the card tables.

Sitting in on a fated game in northern Virginia one night in '66, Zeller found himself opposite a small man in a short top hat by the name of Seward. Zeller was on a hot streak, and the evening's big loser had been drinking heavily. When the man lost his fifth hand in a row, he called Zeller a cheat and was shot dead for his trouble. The little fellow in the top hat, seemingly unperturbed by his financial losses, advised Zeller to get out of town before the sheriff got word. As justified as Zeller's actions might have been, the sheriff would have had no mercy on a Yankee with a hot gun. Zeller found Seward's suggestion respectable, and, after a healthy hour's ride, the two slowed to a walk. Idle palaver led to recruitment on the road, and shortly thereafter, at a Rockbridge County eating house, Yankee Dave shook hands with Gabriel Kings. Three weeks later, they hit Scarboro.

A man could wonder for days upon end as to why an old blue-belly from Indiana would throw in with a pack of former grays. Why would he fleece the pockets of the government he'd shed blood to preserve? In actuality, his motives were simple—it was the money and the life that the spending of it brought. Though it was true—he *had* girded his belly with blue during the late struggle—Zeller was a rebel after Kings's own heart, without fear and always willing to stand with a six-gun.

Back in the firelight, Zeller finished his buttoning but remained on his feet. He looked to Kings and asked, "Say, uh, how much you say that train was gonna be haulin' again?"

Kings unbuckled his gunbelts and rolled them into a bundle, placing them near his bedroll with the butts toward him. "Well, if what Andy said is true, 'bout ten thousand each run." He glanced around the campsite, speaking for the benefit of all. "Now, we've hit this line, what, twice afore? Pretty fair hauls each time and no trouble in the takin', but this time around, we should expect *some* opposition. Railroad guard, shotguns to accompany the safe, three or four at the most. Sid Dillon of the Union Pacific's tight with the green, so I doubt he'd pay for any more'n that."

"His frugality will be his undoing," Seward said, grinning. "Only four? We oughta be insulted. Give us five or six at least."

A short man with a graceful gait and ash-blond hair, Seward had preferred the prospect of adventure and easy money to returning to a financially crippled family law firm in Roanoke. Though his typical demeanor was that of an aloof, scholarly type, he was worth his criminal salt. He'd served with an artillery battalion, and what he learned had proven useful when the dynamiting of a safe or a section of railroad tracks was called for.

"Hell, he'd pay twice that many if he got wind Jesse James was comin' outta hidin' to hit his line," Brownwell remarked.

Kings stared at Yeager, who hadn't said a word in a longer time than usual—even for him. He'd been responsible for gathering much of the information needed for this venture to succeed, and it would be his job to lead the raid on the return run. Maybe he was just going over everything in his head.

"Why'n't you give us a tune, boy," Kings suggested, in the hope of improving everyone's spirits.

"Somethin' Southern," Woods said from under his hat.

Kings stabbed the kindling with a stick and looked at Zeller, showing a rare smile. "You don't object to some music, do ya, Billy Yank?"

It was said in jest, but Zeller pulled a face. "It don't have to suit me, Johnny Reb," he said, smoothing his blankets. "So long as he don't play 'Dixie.' I might have to sleep out of earshot, out of camp."

A man who didn't know Zeller the way Kings did might have taken offense, but he said, "Free country, Dave. Go on and freeze yourself."

Zeller grunted. "You forget I come from Indiana. But don't push me, Yeager." With that, he rolled over, turning his back to the fire and those around it.

A moment passed, the flames shuddering under the moaning wind, then Yeager raised the harmonica.

The first bars of "Oh! Susanna" filled the night.

Dusk was peeling away in the quick approach of darkness as they rode out of the limestone breaks. Kings led his men north, trotting for a stretch, then slowing to a walk, then back again to a trot. Eventually they would veer a shade to the east, toward a tributary of the Pecos River. From there, he calculated another two days' ride to where they would await the U.P.

His primary mount for the past six years was John Reb, a black stallion of mixed Irish Hunter and American Thorough-bred stock, seventeen hands high with three white stockings. A splendid mount, fast as a Kansas whirlwind, and though he was at times wild or aggressive enough to earn a disciplinary bite on the ear, he was as faithful to Kings as a massive dog.

Kings drew back on the reins a bit to sidle the stallion alongside Brownwell, who sat the back of a hardy chestnut gelding nearly four hands shorter. "Few more days and we'll reach the Mission," Kings remarked, then glanced up at the skittish sky. "If we don't drown afore then. Creasy said he'd be waitin'."

Brownwell was a ruddy, powerfully built man, not very tall, with sandy hair and a brushy mustache. The outlaw life hadn't changed him much from the soldier he'd once been, though Kings remembered he used to laugh more.

He never would have left Missouri by choice, never would have come to make Kings's acquaintance had it not been for a double murder charge. The first to feel the sting of Brownwell's knife was that letch of a landlord who took monthly payments from Brownwell's widowed mother in any form he could. The Mississippi washed him up two miles down from where the deed took place, and there were schools of fish nibbling at his wounds when a ferryman hauled him out. The second killing came when the town marshal tried to arrest Brownwell, which was an unfortunate occurrence, given that a few generations back a Brownwell girl had married into the marshal's family. The bond of blood, however distant, couldn't override the bond the marshal had to the law, and that bond had forced Leroy's hand a second time. Shortly after he made Virginia, the Confederate States army had been only too happy to have him, and in the company of boys like Gabe Kings and Andy Yeager, Brownwell found occasion to laugh again, though their duty was bloody.

Working a chaw of tobacco, Brownwell leaned over to scatter a swarm of red ants with a well-aimed stream. "Let's go over it again," he proposed, "how we figure to pull this 'un off."

Their horses took another half-dozen steps before Kings spoke. "We'll split into two groups of four. Only, Seward oughta ride on both hits in case the railroad comes up with a second safe for the return run. You, him, Creasy, mebbe one other, and I will hit the U.P. while the others sit tight in Refuge. They'll hit it again on the return. No matter how much we secure the first time, the U.P.'s bound to assume the return is safe and load it up. The boys'll meet us back home, we split the proceeds, and that's that."

"Sounds like a plan."

A rumble of distant thunder punctuated the statement. Though the clouds were gathering, Kings could smell no hint of rain on the wind coming from the west. John Reb, excited by the meteorological change, wanted to lope, but Kings had to restrain him to prevent the other animals from overcompensating. With a ways still to go, getting fagged out here on the caprock wouldn't do.

The arid, mountainous terrain through which they navigated had, at one point in the world's history, been totally submerged in ocean water. This was evident in the thousands of tiny seashells pressed into the hard-packed ground and the somewhat eerie graffiti of fish skeletons and ammonites fossilized in the rock faces. Heavy deposits of kettle-gray marl and pale dolomite abounded. Spanish monks, the blue waters of the Pacific their goal, had named the surrounding mountain range *la Sierra de Vidrio*, or "mountains of glass," for the way the sun reflected off the darker shale embedded in the limestone.

The following day they rode from first light clear into the afternoon, stopping only once, for nearly an hour. They started later than usual the morning after, but knew they would have to make up for the few lost hours with an extra mile or five. The horses were rested and strong, refreshed by a wet night, and seemed more eager than the men to be on the move.

The mountains and the limestone played out, and the vegetation thickened drastically. Trees sprouted up, small copses that offered a scanty but welcome amount of shade on a hot day. The healthy green of desert ferns and tall spikes of yucca stood in sharp contrast to the dull browns and tans of the broken landscape.

They were close.

From behind a heavy cover of juniper and piñon, Kings could see that some busy beavers had been at work since the last time he used this crossing. Someone, smelling an opportunity, had built a kind of trading post in the clearing across the water. There were two log cabins, one of them the store with sacks of grain or flour and water barrels against the near wall. The sign above the door read, "Samuels's Pecos Emporium." The second cabin was the home of the proprietor, made evident by the curtains in the windows.

Smoke swirled against the early morning sky from one of the chimneys. In the yard, a few chickens pecked at the barren ground, and in the pole corral yonder stood a roan mule. A man and two small boys moved in and out of the store. Kings observed them all through his field glasses with the patience of a circling hawk.

The tributary was wide, but not overswollen. Even after the recent shower, Kings estimated that, at the deepest point, the horses would be up to only their bellies in Pecos water. He decided this side of the river would be a good place to stop and rest a few short hours.

Dismounting, the Virginian tied John Reb to a nearby juniper, then planted a foot in the crotch of the next tree over, a gnarled remnant with a divided trunk. As his men watched with amusement, he took a firm overhead grip and hoisted himself some ten or twelve feet up. His hatless head surfaced in a gap in the foliage, providing a clear view of what lay before them.

This spot on the river wasn't likely to receive much traffic, save the odd traveler—perhaps someone bound for the distant border and the freedom it offered. A family on a pilgrimage might use the bumpy road to the west, but not many others.

Leaning against the branch behind him, Kings dug inside his coat for an old campaigner of a Daniel Swisher cigar. Unlit and well-chewed, it was the last of his stock. Come crossing time, he might have to see if the tradesman had any more. For now, he was content to chew and observe, slowly combing the land with his eyes, east to west.

By the time his gaze reached the trading post, the soggy cigar had come apart, and he spat it from his mouth.

CHAPTER 3

A traveling salesman was the only soul to splash across, fording a few dozen yards downriver from where the gang had stopped to rest, to approach the emporium on a slant. Kings, aloft again with his glasses at midday, watched with amusement as the salesman failed to persuade the tradesman to invest in one of his many elixirs. The transient went on his way after a few small purchases of his own, astride a hammer-headed horse over which he had little control, good for a chuckle. The man couldn't handle a loop rein to save his life and apparently didn't know his left from his right.

When Samuels went inside the cabin for lunch, Kings climbed back down to the temporary camp to find Zeller dozing and Brownwell dealing cards to the others. Kings told them to be ready to move inside an hour, then went to check his gear.

Samuels was bent over a back hoof of his mule with two nails in his mouth and a hammer in his hand when he heard splashing from the opposite riverbank. The elder of his two sons was squatting close enough to see his every move but just out of reach for one of the mule's kicks. The younger watched from the top rung of the corral with half the interest of his brother.

Samuels lowered the hoof and straightened, staring out across the water. From the thicket a man astride a black stallion had emerged. How long he had been watching them, the tradesman did not know, but it unnerved him greatly.

The rider tapped with his spurs, and the horse started to cross. He had barely entered the Pecos when another rider came out of the brush, then another and another still, until there were six in all. They came single file, army fashion, and sheets of water flew with every bucketing step.

The lead horseman approached the corral and drew up just short. He sat tall and easy in the saddle, wearing a flat-brimmed black hat over dark eyes. They were hard, emotionless eyes, circling now within a lean, strong-featured face shadowed by several weeks' stubble. His wavy black hair, strung with gray, reached down to the back of his shirt collar. There were two ivory-handled Colts on his hips, in view of all creation. Sunlight streaked formidably off the blued iron and black gun leather, and his right hand was on his thigh within inches of a pistol.

Clearly, this was no ordinary pilgrim.

It was also clear that his was no ordinary horse. The steed was enormous, one of the finest Samuels had ever seen, and looked about half-broken. A four-legged hurricane, stamping and sidling even now, it seemed scarcely controllable under a tight and skilled rein.

The men and horses spreading out on either side of this figure were not so impressive. As much as they reminded Samuels of a cavalry unit, there was something about them he didn't trust. All were armed with pistols and rifles, and one had a single-barreled shotgun forked across his saddle bow.

And here he stood, out in the open, the nearest weapon in the store yonder, with his two boys standing between himself and these strangers. Feeling like a shepherd without his staff to fend off the wolves, Samuels would tread lightly until he knew what kind of men he was dealing with.

The lead horseman lifted a hand in greeting. It was almost a salute, a gesture that solidified his past as a soldier of some sort.

"Afternoon," he said, then turned his attention to the

youngster gawking from the corral rung. Man and boy stared at each other for what seemed, to the boy's father, an uneasy eternity—the man perhaps seeing what he had once been, the boy seeing what he might yet become.

"Ethan! Come here, son."

The boy obediently climbed down and went to his father's outstretched hand. Samuels passed his youngest son to the other, saying everything with his eyes. *Get back to the house and stay there.*

"There something I can help you with, mister?" he asked, once his boys had closed the door.

The man dismounted and reached over to give his reins to a fellow with a wad of tobacco in his left cheek. "You the proprietor?"

Samuels stepped out of the corral, closed it behind him. "I am."

"Wonder if I could buy a couple smokes off ya."

Samuels started to lead the way toward the store. The stranger, who stood about a head taller, fell in alongside. "You and your friends look to be travelin' awful light," the tradesman began. "Will that be all, Mister . . . ?"

"Yessir, we *are* travelin' light."

Samuels, falling silent, held the door and waved his customer in ahead of him. By then it was nearly half past one, and the animals were anxiously nipping at one another's ears when the stranger completed his business. With four cigars stuffed into his breast pocket, he went around dispensing carrots, two to a man, before climbing into the saddle.

Samuels and his sons watched them ride away from the safety of their home. In his right hand was his trusty scattergun, and his left was filled with more coins than he'd expected for the price of the cigars and twelve carrots.

Zeller pulled in next to Kings, glancing over his shoulder as he spoke. "That tradesman's seen our faces, Kings. Let me ride back and straighten him out before he talks to anybody he shouldn't."

"No," Kings said. "He'll forget he ever saw us afore we make a mile. Besides, who's he apt to talk to out here, and what might he tell 'em? That we spoil our stock with carrots, or that we *seem* to be headed north?"

"I don't like it."

"You keep that gun where it is, Dave."

The last statement was made in such a soft tone that any other man would have laughed it off, but Yankee Dave knew Kings too well. Wasn't the sea graveyard-calm before the storm? As Zeller reined back in line behind Yeager, he thought back to a time they had robbed a bank in southern Wyoming. Kings shot a man on that job, a local would-be tough-nut who went along as a guide, for killing a stable boy—left the man facedown in the wildflowers five miles from town for the posse to find.

From the Pecos, Kings turned the horses northeast, and for the remaining daylight hours, there was no more talk. Now, under a brilliant half-moon, they rounded a bend in the lonely prairie trail. Kings caught a flicker of movement from a thick stand of piñon, followed by the faint clicking of stones.

In a move so fluid and practiced it almost looked slow, Kings's pistol was out and cocked. It caught every one of his men off guard, to say nothing of the rifleman who stepped out from the piñon to stand directly in their path.

Behind Kings, saddle leather creaked, a horse nickered, and one of the men swore. Whoever it was, he wasn't alone in his embarrassment. Of the six, Kings was the only one who had met the rifleman's challenge. The man's body was turned halfway toward them in duelist style, and because of this, no one could quite make out his features.

Kings was the first to break the silence. "Looks like we got us a stalemate, friend. What do you plan on doin' with that rifle?"

"Where you fellers headed?"

Kings let his eyes circle, searching for other crouching shadows with guns in hand. "I don't see how that's any of your business," he said.

"What's your name?"

"What the hell is yours?"

Sensing he'd crossed a line, the man lowered his rifle barrel a notch, saying, "I wouldn't be askin' if I hadn't been told to squat here and watch for a feller on a big black horse to come along. Told by one Red Howard. That name mean anything to you?"

Howard was one of Bob Creasy's aliases. "It just might," Kings said.

He started to wave his men onward, but the rifleman threw up a broad hand. It was attached to a wrist that stretched a half foot out from his too-short sleeve. He was more clearly visible now, tall and lanky, with shoulders wide and slightly stooped. His lazy drawl marked him for an Arkansas man. "You boys can hold up right there. Just *you*, partner." The strength of his voice grew as he addressed the rest of the gang. "Anybody follers, he gets a bullet."

The man wouldn't have been able to stop them, but Kings gave a little fanning motion that told the others to stand down. The rifleman, too confident for his own good, reached to seize John Reb's bridle and nearly lost a finger for his trouble.

The stallion stirred up dust as Kings regained control. "I think it's best you kept your distance, partner," he said above the snorting.

The place they called the Mission was situated down the trail in a clearing, a half mile from where the rifleman had intercepted them. It was little more than a low, brush-roofed shack with the slightest lean to the western side, and quite desolate-looking. To the rear, there were three horses in a corral—a strawberry roan, a bay, and a paint.

At one time or another, the place had been the home of a Catholic missionary, made plain by the numerous religious icons still gathering dust inside. What had become of the missionary, whether killed by the Indians or gone of his own volition, no one knew. In recent years his former home had become something of a meeting place for Kings and Creasy, and when Creasy wasn't around, God only knew who else used it.

Creasy targeted the small stuff, hitting the stages that traveled to and from the forts and halfway stations, but he was also known to lead the occasional raid on small-town banks. Sometimes, he and Charley Davis joined up with Kings for a particularly complex or risky venture, and like coyotes before a wolf pack's kill, they were only too happy to take in the considerably heavier loot. Every extra man was welcome, of course, though it had been some years since their last joint effort. The Arkansas rifleman hadn't been in on that one.

Davis was kneeling outside the open door, plucking feathers from a sage hen in preparation for supper. He looked up as Kings rode into camp, and just behind him, Creasy stepped through the shack's sagging doorway.

"As I live and breathe!" he crowed, grinning widely. He walked out to greet Kings with arms outspread. "Gabriel Kings! Step down and make yourself to home."

Bob Creasy was average in height and sturdily built, with a thatch of copper hair. His freckled, square-jawed face had a rugged handsomeness to it and was dignified, he thought, by a nose broken in a boomtown prizefight years back. On his upper lip was a scar that gave his every grin a sneering quality.

Davis was a little shorter than Creasy, almost fat but massive through the chest and shoulders. His sun-browned face was broad and weathered beyond his years, but the dimples that even his close-shaved beard couldn't hide made him a favorite of the sirens he so frequently visited.

The rifleman moved up and was introduced to Kings as Hardyman Foss. They shared a handshake and a brief word, after which Foss stood back to lean on his rifle. The pretense was to leave Kings, Creasy, and Davis to themselves, but he was actually sizing Kings up, searching for something contradictory or unbefitting of the things he'd heard. A crooked spur, a break in the seam of Kings's trousers . . . Dirt under the nails, maybe.

"Well," Kings said to Creasy, "you've had a week to consider my telegram. How 'bout it?"

Creasy crossed his arms and kicked dirt. "Matter of fact, Kings, there's a coupla questions I wanted to ask. One, why don't you tell us why we should risk gettin' shot up helpin' you take this train? I know the U.P. will have doubled security on their line, so why? When in a couple more days, we three could hold us up a stage with no trouble at all?"

"Expectin' a good-sized sum, too," Davis chimed in. "Army pay comin' in to the fort, should be upwards of two thousand dollars."

Kings chuckled. "Is that all?"

CHAPTER 4

Twin rail lines stretched from one end of the horizon to the other, breaking the monotony of the land with streaks of scalding steel and the steady chugging of pistons. The Union Pacific was scheduled to come to the end of its journey on Sunday at a quarter past two in the afternoon, and if Kings had anything to say about it, it would be with a significantly lighter load.

He and the men had anticipated the train's arrival and were waiting in the shade of the water tank when it pulled up. Kings informed the conductor, peering down from the gangway between the first- and second-class cars, that they had come to the tank for the same reason as he had—to refuel, then push on. He and his men were headed north, Kings said, and the conductor had no reason to doubt him.

Seventeen minutes later, the locomotive eased into gear and labored on toward the east, trailing smoke and echoes. Ten seconds after that, the conductor felt a complaint coming on as he leaned out a window to see the travelers whip their horses into a gallop—not north as he had been told, but hard after the Union Pacific.

Struggling to maintain composure, he announced to the first-class passengers that a robbery was about to take place. He flinched at the cries of the womenfolk and avoided the clutches of panicky men as he moved down the line to the second class. Once there, he wouldn't bother breaking stride, and he wouldn't repeat himself—by hook or crook, he had to reach that company boy in express . . .

31

By the time the conductor moved into the smoker, Kings had left the saddle, scaled the caboose ladder, and was on the roof. Finding his balance, he started along the line, headlong into the smoke. Timing his strides to match the length of the boxcars, Kings gathered speed, hurtled gap after gap, oblivious to the screeching wheels below. He covered the distance in under a minute.

Through the fumes he could see the brakeman and engineer engaged in a relaxed conversation, unaware that he was climbing down the woodpile behind them. He unholstered his gun and eased the hammer back to full-cock.

The engineer turned, blue eyes wide behind a mask of soot. "What're you fixin' to do?"

The outlaw gestured to the brakeman. "Whatever I plan to do, it'd go a lot easier if this rig was standin' still. Pull it."

Creasy and Brownwell had no problem subduing the four payroll guards bivouacked in the express company car. Pistol-whipping one convinced the others there was only one way they'd be stepping off the train alive. Brownwell moved quickly, tying hands behind backs with rawhide cords, as Creasy unloaded their carbines and stuffed their sidearms in a tote sack.

They had arrived just in time to nab the conductor, too, Brownwell jerking him in from the passage by the throat of his stiff blue jacket. He didn't need much convincing and was presently slumped in the corner, hugging his knees and wagging his head.

Once he finished with the guards, Brownwell returned his attention to the young man whom the conductor had intended to reach—an oily-haired easterner with pits on his chin. After minutes of trying, he had failed to extract the combination to the lockbox, and the boy had proven resolute in the face of

Brownwell's many threats.

"What the hell's takin' so long?" Creasy stepped over, hefting the tote sack, and took in the youth with one head-to-toe glance. "Shouldn't you still be in books, kid?" he asked with a curled lip. "What're you doin' way out West?"

Brownwell answered for the company man. "He's workin' for President Sidney Dillon himself, who entrusted him with the responsibility of seein' that this safe makes it safely from point 'A' to point 'B.' " He spat to the side. "Or some such guff."

With a sudden groan, the train lurched, staggering the men. When they'd come to a complete stop, Creasy moved to slide the car door open. As expected, Davis and Seward were waiting at the bottom of the embankment.

Creasy held up an arm against the sunlight. "We're gonna need to blow it," he said to the ex-artilleryman. "This 'un ain't no joke."

Seward dismounted and dug out three sticks from his pack. "Think this'll be enough?"

"For a start."

As Seward rummaged, Davis stood in his stirrups and saw Kings coming from the front of the train with a big, bearded man in denim close behind. Sensing danger, Davis went for the rifle under his leg and shouted a warning.

Kings spun and drew, thrusting the muzzle in the brakeman's face. The fellow stopped short, eyes crossing in an attempt to focus on the barrel.

"I just th-thought I'd watch," he managed, backing away with hands shoulder-high.

Lowering the weapon, Kings couldn't help but grin. "You're lucky we don't charge admission."

Creasy hopped down and met the Virginian halfway. The brakeman stayed where he was.

"What've we got?" Kings asked.

"Oh, we got a brave soul in there, says the bossman give him this job special, and he means to keep it. Said we'll get the money over his dead body. Brownwell's near ready to call him on it."

"Tom rigged the box yet?"

"I ain't heard any shots, so I'll venture to say no."

Kings exhaled with irritation.

"Just like old times, huh?" Creasy asked in an attempt at humor.

"Durn near brings back memories."

Creasy drew his bandana over his nose and jogged to catch up with Davis, who had also masked himself and was opening the door to the first-class car. "Well, hello there, sir!" Creasy said, swinging up and in to snatch a gold watch from a heavyset man. "You shouldn't have!"

When Kings reached the express car, he saw the guards, seated and trussed up like a brace of sage hens. He nodded at the conductor, who averted his eyes, then looked to Seward, who was kneeling before the safe in question. He was busily at work, capping four sticks of dynamite and wedging them strategically beneath the lockbox. To the left, Brownwell was holding a boy who couldn't have been thirty against the wall with a gun under his nose.

"Put it away, Leroy," Kings said. "You're scarin' the kid."

The young man seemed surprised when Kings reached out to clap him on the shoulder. "Breathe easy, son. This is just how dangerous men do business. Let's you and me take a stroll."

With an inescapable grip on the company man's elbow, Kings escorted him to a sunny vantage point forty yards north of the boxcar. They were joined by Brownwell and Creasy, who rough-housed and herded the guards with shameless abandon. Creasy in particular had never had much use for lawmen and was like a child on Christmas morning whenever he had the opportunity to abuse one or two. With a laugh, he planted a boot between the shoulders of the nearest guard, snapped his knee like a whip, and watched with satisfaction as the men banged bodies and toppled helplessly to the dirt.

The conductor, needing no supervision, had come shambling along behind. He brought to mind a peasant headed for the stocks in some medieval village, or, as far as he knew, the chopping block. Kings, Brownwell, and Creasy watched with mild amusement as the poor fellow took his position near the mess of guards, crossed his ankles, and slowly sank to earth.

Davis, shouldering a sack of valuables, led the horses to a patch of scrub grass. He moved from one to the other, scratching noses, speaking softly, preparing them for what was coming.

Within five minutes, Seward bounded out of the car and came running. "Plug your ears, gents!" he shouted, seconds before the blast.

Flashes of ignited nitroglycerin and bits of roof flew into the air. Planks and hunks of twisted shrapnel shot forth with the force of bullets, and a hot wind slammed into the faces of the outlaws and their temporary prisoners. Scraps of paper from the obliterated mail slots fluttered across the grass. There was smoke and the faint sound of screaming women. Higher still were the cries of a baby, and somewhere an engineer and his brakeman stamped and swore. Despite the cacophony, Kings knew the only injuries suffered were to their ears. In the span of his career with Tom Seward, never had a single innocent been so much as bruised from the effects of Seward's work.

Kings waited until the smoke dissipated before he left the company boy, the conductor, and the scowling guards under the guns of his men. Stepping up into the car, he was greeted by the gnarled and still smoking remains of the safe, which scarcely concealed the stacks of greenbacks and bags of twenty-dollar double eagles. Squatting in the wreckage, he began to transfer portions from the safe to the sack he'd tucked behind his belt. Before long, a dull pain began to throb in his hip. Also making its presence known was a soreness in his clicking right shoulder joint. Aches and pains, physical as well as mental, were not out of the ordinary for Kings. In the mornings he was often possessed by a weariness that made slugs of his muscles and weights of his spurs. Nighttime rarely found him asleep in his bed but wide-eyed on the porch, as if it were possible to be too tired to sleep.

He was only thirty-seven and knew it was an age that many in his line of work never lived to see. Still, Kings wondered whether his time as an outlaw had made his body that of an old man, or whether this was simply the Almighty's way of passing sentence on a man whom no worldly authority could bring to justice.

"Kings?" That was Creasy hollering. "Kings, you about done?"

He took a moment before calling back. "Just about."

Standing up, he felt the reassuring weight of the guns on his hips and liked it, to say nothing of the sack, which was not light. When he stepped down from the car, he stopped thinking like Gabriel and became Kings. He secured the sack to his saddle, conscious of the stares of his men. *Don't let no one see you sweat, boy,* his father had taught him, and he didn't.

"Wring 'em out," he shouted, and, five abreast, they wrung them out toward the horizon.

Yards behind, the company man coursed a shaky hand through his sweat-slick hair and stared across the plains after the departing outlaws. As they crested a rise, the ground seemed to disappear from under them, and for a single, perfect instant they appeared airborne, flying into the skyline on the winged horses of Greek myth.

There had been a lot of money in that safe, all of which was being carried away while he stood watching. From his periphery he saw the guards, still bound, spinning like one giant children's top as they tried to find their feet. The conductor hadn't moved. He might have passed out during the blast.

Mr. Dillon was going to be mad as a hornet, but at the present moment, the young man couldn't have cared less what the president of the Union Pacific Railroad was going to say.

He'd done all he could, after all, and how many of the fellows back home could say they'd been robbed by the likes of Gabriel Kings?

CHAPTER 5

The town of Refuge in Pecos County, West Texas, was founded four years after Appomattox by a Methodist circuit rider whose hopes for its spiritual future had long since evaporated. By no means a New Zion, much less a Salt Lake City, it was still a far cry from the Sodom or Gomorrah of the plains, largely due to the efforts of one man.

North and south of the invisible border known as the Deadline, which separated town proper from the red-light district, Marshal Asa Liddell's word was respected by all and sundry. Men could keep their guns on their person but were warned that any discharge, whether in self-defense or general rowdiness, meant walking orders. In Liddell's three years as marshal, there had been seven shootouts over cards or women, and only one of them had fatal results.

North of the Deadline, Refuge boasted multiple clothing and mercantile stores, a stable, two hotels, the marshal's office, a church that doubled as a schoolhouse, two restaurants, and an approximate population of seven hundred. The South Side consisted of six saloons, four gambling dives, three cathouses, a Chinese opium den, and a theater of sorts known simply as the Texas Dance Hall. Just a stone's throw from the outskirts of town was the cemetery with its lone sentry of a lightning-split tree.

For years Kings and his men had been paying semi-regular visits to this oasis, often not all at once. In the establishments north of the Deadline there was no place for them. South of it, there was just one where Kings and his boys could feel at ease. That was Delilah Young's Pearl Palace, the finest of the three brothels. It was a comfortable spot where a man could recline on pillows and couches, have a drink at the bar, listen to a piano that was actually in tune, and enjoy the company of some of the better-looking doves money could buy.

With its wide veranda, enameled red doors, and plate-glass windows, the Palace was a welcome sight to many a lonesome wanderer. Kings was one of the few who came there not to fornicate, though any one of Delilah's girls would have taken him into her bed without a moment's pause. His reason for letting his shadow fall across that particular threshold was to share a drink, laugh a little, and confer with the madam herself.

Hitching his horse now in the warm glow of its porch lights, Kings tried to bring to mind the last time he had seen Del and finally reckoned that it must have been two years. He draped his coat over a forearm, edged both vest halves over his guns, then stepped through the twin doors. The others had already bulled in ahead of him, eager to wake some snakes.

Just inside, a polished mahogany bar ran the length of the wall. Behind it was a garish collection of bottles below a gorgeous diamond-dust mirror. Kings lingered in the entryway, surveying his surroundings and unintentionally tracking caked mud on Delilah's expensive St. Louis rug. He saw nothing suspicious, no authority figures of any kind that could possibly recognize him or the boys. All he saw were men of his own ilk, lost souls walking the road to damnation, and hopelessly oblivious to the fact. A fellow in a black eastern hat was on the piano, while hide-hunters, muleskinners, cowpunchers, and gamblers milled, clustered, or staggered across his plane of vision, some of them with a girl or two hanging on.

A voice called from the stairwell, "Gabriel Kings, are you

gonna stand there all night, or are you gonna come over here and tell me how much you missed me?"

Kings's eyes fell upon a woman who would not have looked out of place walking the streets of Richmond with a parasol over her shoulder. She was in her late thirties, not quite beautiful, with a straight, freckled nose and a firm chin, but her figure was ample, and she was a seductress of the first order. Beaming a girlish smile, she came down the stairs in a black and silver kimono, her auburn hair falling in sausage curls to her shoulders. When she was close enough, she lifted a hand to affectionately rasp the underside of Kings's unshaven chin.

"Where do you get the nerve, makin' a lady come to you after such a long time?"

He couldn't help but smile down at Delilah Young. "What d'you expect from an ill-mannered ruffian from the backwoods?"

"Like hell, you are!" she said with a high laugh. "If nothin' else, Gabe Kings, you're a gentleman. One of the few I've known."

Delilah circled the bar and grabbed two glasses and a bottle from the shelf. Kings hooked a boot heel over the brass foot-rail and watched as she poured. They clinked rims together in a toast—what, exactly, they were toasting, he did not know, but the feeling was there all the same. Kings waited until Delilah drained hers before taking a sip. Of the many things Del could handle, one of them was liquor, and she was easily able to drink Kings, Zeller, and even Brownwell under the table. On two occasions, she'd done it to all three.

"So!" She leaned across the bar, crossing her arms below her breasts to make them bulge over the top of her bodice. "How you been keepin'?"

"Peachy," he replied, refilling her glass, then turned away so he could keep one eye on the comings and goings. "Just got in from fleecin' the Union Pacific, with plans to strike it again on the return."

"Big payoff?"

"Big enough. What about you? You seem to be doin' well."

"Oh, I am. I'm rakin' in more cash than half the other joints in this town combined. What's more, I'm doin' it without havin' to lay down with any of these yahoos."

Amused, Kings shook his head at her frank tongue. "However do you account for this run of luck?"

"I don't know, honey. I guess there must be somethin' about piano music and colored wallpaper that keeps bringin' these flies to my web."

"Longings for home, I imagine. Memories of places left behind . . . mebbe a mother played Beethoven."

"If I can give a drop of comfort to some lost and lonely soul, Gabriel, I'll have done my job."

"You're a good woman, Delilah."

"Who told you?"

They shared another chuckle. After a moment's examination of his hairy face, Delilah said, "You look tired, Kings."

He thought the same could be said of her, but kept his mouth shut.

"Seems to me like you could use a shave, a meal, a good night's sleep"—she smiled then—"maybe some lovin'?"

Kings peered down into the amber mirror of his whiskey. By design or by conviction, he'd never been one to lie with women who'd love him back at the wave of a banknote. There had been a time, however, when he might have accepted Delilah's offer. She wasn't just any woman, after all, and there was no mistaking the hope in her question, but he was a different man. Not in many areas, but there was one at least.

Another, younger lady had caught his eye in the fall of 1869, two years after he first made the acquaintance of Delilah Young. He was twenty-eight then and not yet suffering from his lean years on the Hoot-Owl. Belle Jackson was seventeen, and nature was taking its course with her body, which was pure as driven Virginia snow, but that had little to do with how and why he fell for her.

It was with her name imprinted on his heart that he looked across the hardwood now and shook his head. "We had our time once, Delilah," Kings replied, almost apologetically, "but now . . . you know I can't."

There was a pause, then Delilah put a hand to her chest and scoffed. "Honey, don't embarrass yourself! I wouldn't go back to barebackin' for all the tea in China! Mercy, no! I was referrin' to one of my new gals—fresh off the stage from New Orleans."

Her emotions reined back to their usual spot behind all the frills and warpaint, the spunk and sarcasm, Delilah came around the bar and took him by the elbow. "But even if you *ain't* interested, you can come upstairs with me anyways. Let an old girlfriend fix you a bath."

Fifteen minutes later, he was soaking in a tub the size of a dinghy in the last room at the top of the stairs. His high-topped cavalry boots stood by the door, and his clothes and gunbelts lay on the mattress of the brass four-poster. One of his Colts rested on a stool that Del had placed near his right hand, the ivory butt towards him. At the foot of the tub, the madam herself sat a chair sidesaddle, sipping more of the whiskey and hating the suds for what they obscured.

By and by, the outlaw stirred from his dreams when he heard the chair creak as Delilah got up to splash her hand across the water. "You soak in there much longer, hon, you're gonna sprout gills."

Her tone masked the almost unbearable itch she knew would never be scratched again. How she longed to hike up her skirts, join him down there in the water and listen to him say her name as he had all those years ago. When she really considered the subject, though, it was unclear, even in her own mind, whether she still harbored those feelings. Maybe she just yearned to feel like a girl again, to immerse herself in the memory of this tall rake from the hills of the Shenandoah. As if he could restore her youth . . .

Kings stood, spilling sudsy water over the edges, and Delilah handed him a towel. His sinewy form glistened fish-belly white but his many scars were as pink as the insides of a grapefruit. There was a ridged reminder that ran across the triceps of his left arm, a starburst of mangled flesh in the lower right side of his back, and an improperly healed wound in his upper right pectoral that still pained him now and again. A runaway horse had jerked him with one foot in the stirrup during the Wilderness Campaign, and as a result, if he turned it just right, his left ankle popped like a twig. His knees cracked when he rose from a crouch if he'd been down for too long. Still, he was alive.

As Kings dried himself, Del stood at the window, staring out onto the dark and lonely street below. Minutes passed, though it could have been hours. She had no clue as to how long she had been standing there, and then he was suddenly behind her in the pane, wet haired in his shirtsleeves and trousers. Gently guiding her into position, Kings took her by the waist, folded the digits of her right hand over the chevron of his thumb and forefinger, and became the illusion of her Virginia gentleman.

They glided about the room, Kings leading Delilah to the imaginary music of an invisible orchestra and regaling her with the sorts of stories he imagined he might have to tell, were he the owner of a sprawling plantation.

When her weight began to sag in his arms, he picked her up and laid her on the bed as he would a baby in its cradle. He felt sorrow lance his heart for this woman, this friend, who was adrift in a sea of troubles with no one but God and Gabriel

Kings to keep her in mind. He left her dreaming with one hand curled childlike against her cheek and her hair all about her stilled and peaceful face.

Kings spread his bedroll outside her door and spent what remained of the night with his Winchester under his palm.

Daylight broke with a lazy haze that warmed the streets and filled open windows. The sinless inhabitants of Refuge rose to brew coffee or down the odd shot of whiskey to hasten the waking-up process. It was a new day, a perfect day to further the prosperity of the respectable half of their town, and the Good Lord has no time for loafers. The sinners that made up the other half of town, by and large, still lay wherever last night's nocturnal adventure left them—in someone's bed, on the steps of some den of vice, or in the dust beneath the boardwalk. The Lord would take them in his time.

Kings checked in on Delilah and found that she had moved beneath the covers. Keeping quiet, he slipped inside to wash his face and teeth and to deposit his rifle and bedding in a Queen Anne chair. He strapped on one of his gunbelts—the one with the Bowie knife—and eased out of the room. Some patron's forgotten Prince Albert coat was hanging off the newel post, so he decided to borrow it for the morning. It was a little short in the arms, but it would do. Thus clad, and as inconspicuous as he could afford to make himself, he left the building and headed north into town proper.

He found Andy Yeager under the veranda of a café called the Blue Goose, forking eggs from a tin plate and sipping inky coffee. It was the first they'd seen of each other since splitting up at the Mission, but theirs was a wordless reunion. They stood together, watching the street and the people in it.

Side by side, Yeager and Kings might have been taken for kinfolk. Though Kings was an inch taller and slightly thicker of body, they shared the same black hair and bronzed complexion, though that was due to years under the Texas sun. Both wore facial hair, which strengthened the slight resemblance. If either had bothered to trace their family trees back further than three generations, they might have found that they shared a great-great-grandfather or two.

Yeager grew up on the slopes of Clinch Mountain on the Virginia-Tennessee border, the fourth of nine children born to a mother from Rockbridge County and a father from the Rhineland. It was upon those cobalt slopes that an old Cherokee instructed him in the ways of reconnaissance and sign-reading, talents he would go on to perfect as a wanted man. As one of Kings's oldest surviving friends, Yeager was highly esteemed and his input valued whenever a holdup was in the planning stages.

"Seen any of the boys around?" Kings asked him now, thinking that if they were to strike the Union Pacific again, Yeager, Zeller, and the others who sat out the first raid would need to ride out before nightfall. No telling how fast those railroad men had gotten running, restocked, and running again.

Yeager flung the dregs of his coffee away. "Spied Zeller and a few others sometime around one o'clock this mornin'. They was walkin' into some fancy barroom, lookin' to tie one off, all smiles."

"Fresh from the cribs," Kings diagnosed. "Looked like they'd been chasin' the dragon?"

"Didn't look like it, but who knows."

Kings squinted up into the empty, blue span of sky. "No rest for the wicked," he said, then stepped back into the sunlit street. "Think I'll go a-huntin' 'em. You watch yourself, Andreas."

Yeager watched him go. A dog barked somewhere up the lane, a cowhand trotted past on a big piebald horse, and a group of boys in overalls and straw hats were throwing rocks at one another.

He suddenly tensed with the sobering feeling that he was no longer alone on the porch of the Blue Goose. Yeager turned his head to lock eyes with a man who had come up beside him—a tall, slender man with blunt, gray eyes, and clean-shaven save for a small, neatly trimmed mustache that gave him an aristocratic look.

This was Marshal Asa Liddell. He wore black broadcloth in spite of the day's warmth, and beneath the drape of his suit jacket were the non-aristocratic ornaments of his trade—a crescent-and-star badge and holstered gun.

Yeager didn't so much as blink an eye at the abrupt appearance of the marshal but met the man's expressionless gaze with a smile. "Mornin'."

"Good morning."

This was far from Yeager's first time in Refuge, but he had never before come within arm's length of Asa Liddell. He knew enough of the man's reputation to recognize that the marshal wouldn't be easily fooled. Yeager knew a good piece of lying would have to be done here.

"I'm Marshal Liddell." He paused, not presuming to ask for a response outright.

"J. B. Walker," came the reply. "Pleased to meetcha."

Liddell's eyes narrowed slightly as he openly took Yeager's measure. "First time in Refuge, Mr. Walker?"

Here came the gamble. Should Yeager answer in the affirmative—and providing that Liddell had indeed seen him around before—there would be a handful of hell to pay. Life had made a gambler of Yeager, but he chose not to twist the truth too much this time around.

"Fourth or fifth, actually," he replied. "Last visit was about two years ago."

"Strange that we shouldn't have come across one another."

"Afraid I never stick around long enough for most folks to come across me, Marshal."

"Why's that, if you don't mind me askin'?"

"Well, it ain't that I object to fellowshippin'. Simple truth is, I'm a travelin' man. Never been one to let the grass grow under my feet."

"I've seen the time when I could have shared that sentiment."

"That a fact?"

"It is. I lawed in Dodge for a time, and before that, Casper. Didn't care for the cold too much, so I rode off in search of sunshine."

"Plenty down here."

"That there is. Don't believe I'll be leaving it anytime soon, so long as the folks around here'll have me." Apparently satisfied, the peace officer touched his hat and said, "Enjoy your stay in Refuge, Mr. Walker. Should you choose to venture below the Deadline, steer clear of the bad apples." At that, Liddell turned and walked away.

As he went, Yeager wondered exactly how he could go about steering clear when he was rotten to the core himself.

CHAPTER 6

As Yeager chatted with the marshal, Kings was steadily making his way south. All around him were the sounds of townspeople at work—the strangely comforting noise of a broom rasping over dusty floorboards, a carpenter's hammer pounding a nail, the banter passed between a friendly store clerk and a customer.

A thin young woman caught Kings's eye as she crossed from one boardwalk to the other. Taking in her flowered bonnet, her quick and graceful step, and the straight back that gently curved inward just above the bustle, he couldn't help but compare her to Delilah. The madam of the Pearl Palace hadn't carried that much clothing on her body in years, or had a home to call her own—if you didn't count a half-dozen high-dollar cathouses with girls living three to a room. While he loved her for her grit and spirit, it was refreshing to see a woman like this, glimmering with feminine finery—a rose among the grimy undergrowth. There were too few of that sort in the venues and valleys he frequented, and he was about to come in contact, yet again, with the other kind.

Back where he began his morning, Kings ascended the three steps leading up to the batwing doors of the Bull's Eye Saloon. The entrance itself was located at the left-hand corner of the building, and a paint-peeling sign along the exterior proclaimed that decently priced drinks, square games of chance, and talented courtesans could be found here.

The interior stank of tobacco, stale beer, coal-oil, sweat, and the loud perfume worn by the ladies advertised outside, and a thin coat of sawdust and wood shavings covered the floor to soak up any spills. There were two men at the bar on the left-hand wall, and about four of the tables scattered around the main room were occupied, even at this early hour, though it was coffee being poured, not alcohol. Several half-naked women lounged against the banister of the central staircase, playing with each other's hair and blinking away last night's funk.

Dave Zeller was at a table near the back, face hidden by the tipped-down brim of his hat, and there was no way to judge his sobriety. Charley Davis slouched in the chair to his right, distractedly sifting through a dog-eared deck of house cards. Tom Seward and Sam Woods were at an adjoining table. Seward sat rigidly with his hands curled around a cup of coffee—Kings surmised he was about half-sober—but Woods was slumped forward with his head resting on the elbow of an outstretched arm. Of the two, he was the more likely to have partaken of the Oriental pipe, but in that position Kings had no way of knowing.

He drew up within a few strides of Zeller's table. Seward managed a wave and Davis gave a slow nod, but Woods and Zeller didn't so much as twitch.

"Hope you boys had a good time last night," Kings said.

Zeller's reply was sluggish from beneath the brim. "How was yours?"

"If y'all still plan on hittin' the U.P., best get sobered up and pull out sometime this evenin'."

Zeller's head tipped back, and Kings was surprised to see that his eyes weren't bloodshot. "Sounds about right," he drawled, without the slightest hint of venom. "We'll meet you 'neath the livery dogtrot 'round about sundown. How'd you sleep?"

Kings half-smiled. For the time being, it seemed as if his and

Zeller's horns had come unlocked. "Like the dead," he replied.

The others had started to get themselves together. Not far behind, Zeller groaned to his feet. When he'd satisfied himself that the world wasn't tipping over, he started wading through the maze of tables. Just before he reached the threshold, a strident voice rapped out from across the room.

"Hold up there, high-pockets!"

All eyes turned to a man just emerging from a storeroom to the left of the bar. He slammed the door and stalked toward Zeller with indignant purpose, arms swinging and head thrust forward. Any regular would have recognized him instantly as Ned Spivey, proprietor, but Kings was no regular. Spivey had come from Fort Griffin to Refuge with a wagonload of prostitutes, dealers, and bartenders only last summer, and it was then that he and Zeller had had their first disagreement. They would be revisiting the same sore subject momentarily, and though the tall Indianan was well aware of the saloon man's bullying ways and penchant for knifing, Spivey had yet to bear witness to the wrath Zeller himself was capable of.

His face was leathery and unshaven, perpetually whiskered, with two permanent creases that began at the corners of his mouth and ran down to frame his chin. They deepened like two horrible scars whenever he frowned, giving him the look of a malevolent ventriloquist's dummy.

"Price for the night's eleven dollars," Spivey declared, appearing very much the dummy as he planted himself in Zeller's shadow. He stuck his hand out. "Give it over."

Zeller's eyes rolled back. "We been over this before, ya sawed-off bastard. Jeannie said she wouldn't charge me a penny, and I don't mean to pay."

"I don't give a tinker's damn what she said. She works for me, and *I'm* chargin' you for the diddlin'. Now, you're gonna pay me what's owed, or I'm takin' it outta her, by God."

"Mister, you so much as hurt her feelin's, I'll take that famous knife and make you eat it, you understand me?"

Kings feared bloodshed was imminent, and, though it might have been understandable, it was not entirely necessary. He moved quickly, wedging himself between Zeller and Spivey, but facing Zeller. "Time to get some air, Dave," he said, grabbing the man's gun arm.

"Matter of fact," Spivey broke in, "I believe you owe me from your last visit!"

"Oh, c'mon now, Kings, lemme settle my tab with this—"

"Dammit, I said, get you some air."

Zeller backpedaled slowly, never breaking eye contact with Spivey until he made the threshold. Kings saw him through the batwings and lingered there until he was sure the Yankee wasn't coming back.

"Hey! Prince Albert!"

Kings made a slow quarter-turn back into the semi-darkness. His countenance was like stone, and his voice was quiet but not confrontational. "You speakin' to me?"

Spivey came closer, assured of his own supremacy within the confines of his sordid little kingdom, until he was close enough for Kings to smell the pickled egg on his breath. "I don't see nobody else standin' there. Tell ya what, if you're partners with that shit-bird, you got two options. One, you drag him back here and talk 'im into payin' up, or two"—Spivey jabbed a finger into Kings's chest for emphasis—"you pay his debt."

Kings glared down at him. "I'll thank you to keep your hands off me."

After thirty years in the business, Ned Spivey knew how to get what he wanted from folks. He enjoyed making examples of so-called hard cases and meant to do so with this one. He reached out, index finger extended, and Kings slapped him with an open hand.

The blow knocked Spivey off balance, sent him pinwheeling to the side before he managed to right himself. With blood running freely from a split lip, he started to draw the knife from his belt but stopped short when the unmistakable sound of gun hammers rang out behind him.

Slowly, wisely, Spivey let his hand fall away and watched as Kings counted out eleven dollars from a sheaf of bills.

"I guess you must not recognize me," he was saying, "or you wouldn't have been stupid enough to try that again. My name's Gabriel Kings, and I'm walkin' outta here nice an' easy. What you intend, I can't say, but know that if you elect to keep at it, my associates are gonna have somethin' to say about that. Now, here's the eleven to cover last night, and I suggest you consider the account settled."

He let the money float to the floor between himself and Spivey, then folded the remaining bills in half and pocketed them. He backed toward the doors and waited until the others shuffled out before falling in at their rear.

Spivey was suddenly aware of the many stares he had drawn. "The nerve of that sumbitch," he growled, then added for all to hear and hopefully take for prophecy, "One o' these days, he's gonna get his."

He ignored the scattered bills for dignity's sake and barked at the bartender, who was wiping imaginary dust from the shiny surface. "Tony, put that rag away and pour me a drink."

From across the hardwood, the barkeep saw the storm clouds gathering but poured anyway. He thought he might have to use his upcoming lunch break to see Liddell about what had just transpired. The barman knew that once Spivey filled himself up with enough of his own liquor, he was liable to go looking for Jeannie's favorite boy.

"Gabriel Kings, my ass," Spivey said and signaled for another.

The rest of the day was hot and humid, and the breeze that came sweeping down from the northern plains brought with it the dust of the buffalo range. The only relief to be had north of the Deadline was to hang a wet sheet over an open window or doorway, but to the south, one had only to step inside the dimly lit interior of a saloon, where whistles could be wet, or into the Pearl Palace, which had been outfitted only last year with four double-bladed ceiling fans, powered by running water.

Kings was leaning over the railing of Delilah's balcony, watching the street below like a sentry standing guard over some valued treasure. The muscles in his jawline rippled every so often as he rotated a long, slow-burning cheroot from one side of his mouth to the other.

The northern breeze dried the lines of sweat running down his face, and he knew it was time to be heading in. Off to the west, the sun sank low, signaling the end of the work day and the start of another bawdy night.

He dipped back into Delilah's room, grabbing his hat from a nearby chair. Hearing movement, his hostess lifted herself from a mound of tasseled pillows and stretched like a cat.

"Where you headin' off to in such a hurry?" she asked, her voice husky as she ruffled her hair.

"See my boys off."

She moved to the armoire to select an evening dress and, after some inventorying, chose a pale-green floor-sweeper with an eye-grabbing cut in the front and a white sash that would hang low on her hips. "When are *you* leavin'?" she asked, holding up the dress to inspect herself in the full-length mirror.

As Kings strapped on his guns, his eyes went to the clutch of perfume bottles on the armoire, collected over the years from places as far north as Kansas City and as far east as Paris, France—or so the label said. He had smelled them all at one time or another, and he predicted there would be many a cowboy falling in love with Delilah Young tonight.

"I think it's time for me to be goin', too." He materialized behind her in the mirror's reflection and placed a hand on either shoulder. "You'll break a lot of hearts wearin' that."

"That's the ideal result, honey."

"You take care, Delilah."

She raised a hand behind her head to cup the side of his face, clenching her jaw to resist a swell of emotion. "Thanks for the dance."

"Thanks for lettin' me lead."

Delilah looked down at the dress. "See ya, Kings," she said. When she raised her eyes, she was alone again in the mirror.

Gabriel Kings took his rifle from where it stood in the corner and hung his saddlebags over a shoulder. The door eased shut behind him but his footsteps were slower than normal as he went down the steps and out the door of Delilah's Pearl Palace.

For the last time.

He couldn't have weighed more than a hundred and twenty pounds soaking wet, and the top of his head came up to about where a tall man's arm met his shoulder. He was a farm kid hoping to become something he wasn't, and nothing could make that fact any clearer than the worn corduroy overalls he tried to compensate for in the wearing of a twelve-dollar Peacemaker.

He was born John Allen Blake, but he left that name behind, choking on the dust he'd stirred up since leaving the home of his minister father on the Colorado River in search of a vision. It was not a vision of angelic choirs or the Son of Man coming on the clouds with glory, but one of blazing guns and the intrigue of easy money, of midnight rides and daylight robberies, all inspired by the resonating words of a dozen dime-store novels.

He figured it was by sheer luck alone that he happened to glance up from carving his name on a weathered hitch rail when he did. A man had emerged from a two-story parlor house and paused on the boardwalk out front with a rifle in his hand and saddlebags over his shoulder. Initial disbelief gave way to awe, which was in turn replaced by a purposeful determination. Johnny Blake could barely take his eyes off the man, even as he mounted his big roan horse—tenderly, given the early stages of saddle sores that had already started to form. Johnny edged his coat behind the twelve-dollar gun, clucked to his steed, and headed straight for the fellow who could only be Gabriel Kings.

When he reined in at the bottom of the steps, however, the man's gaze was enough to give Blake second thoughts. He'd thought to present himself bold and brash as the wanted man he hoped to become, offer to buy the outlaw king of Texas a drink, and plead his case. He'd come this far, and he knew Kings wasn't in the habit of shooting folks at the drop of a hat. What did he have to lose?

Heaving a deep breath to settle his nerves, Blake asked, " 'Scuse me, sir, but are you Gabriel Kings?"

Kings was a long time in answering. He stood straight and still as a chimney, leaking smoke, thumb hooked around the hammer of his rifle, in the hope that such a display might be intimidating enough to spook the boy out of whatever he had to say. When it became apparent there would be no spooking this one, Kings said around his cheroot, "Sometimes."

The kid grinned, but the smile appeared more a smirk. The nerves were still there. "Well, my name is Johnny Blake, and I think me and my guns'd serve you well if you was to let me join up with you and your outfit."

Kings did not reply, but the boy went on, "I can shoot and ride with any man, sir, and I'd be glad to prove it."

Still nothing.

"You sign me on, Mr. Kings, you won't regret it."

Soberly, Kings took in this over-eager youngster straddling a horse much too large for him. Farm boy, by the looks of him, somewhere between the hay and the grass, who'd ridden away from the daily toil of a sweaty, horse apple-smelling life. Had the hands of a man twice his age and that deep tan bestowed by a life of plowing and tilling fields. Kings knew the type, because he was once *of* that type. This Johnny Blake had more than a touch of the wanderlust, which wasn't exactly illegal, but he possessed a woefully misguided idea of adventure and manhood that included riding the criminal's road and raising holy hell. It was enough to make a man shake his head.

The boy opened his mouth again, unaware that the more he talked, the more he showed his bright-green color. "And if you'll excuse me for sayin' so, it'd be a genuine honor for me in my old age to say that I was once in the comp'ny of a fella like you. Fightin' the good fight an' all."

All things considered, Kings had to admire this pup for the backbone it took to walk his horse on over and introduce himself. He removed the cheroot and turned his head to spit before delivering his curt reply.

"Go home, Johnny Blake. Put that pistol away, find yourself a pretty little gal and spend your days chasin' her 'round the barn. Texas needs more good, brave boys like you."

The young man raised a hand in protest, but before he could get a word out, the big red horse between his legs sidestepped sharply to the left, almost as if he'd understood Kings's instruction and was keen to start for home.

The outlaw decided to take advantage of Johnny Blake's present distraction, but before starting down the boardwalk, he paused to advise him one thing more.

"As to them dime novels you no doubt set such store by, the

pages you don't set fire to, stick 'em in the privy." He stuck the cheroot back in his mouth. "You'll get better use of 'em there."

John Allen Blake watched Kings go, walking five doors further and then looking one way before stepping onto the street. There, his tall, black-shrouded form met another of his band in the shadow of a saloon flying the Texas flag. The other man was carrying his shotgun over one shoulder, his pistols cinched in crossed holsters over his duster. He offered what Johnny correctly guessed to be a chunk of tobacco, which Kings refused. The man with the shotgun bit off a wedge and rolled his jaws until he'd tongue-packed the tobacco in place. After a brief exchange of words, both men headed for the livery.

Blake's gaze dipped against a sudden, warm breeze, and he found himself looking at his hands, gathered over the horn of his old saddle. They were big in comparison to his sinewy forearms and thin wrists, with palms rough to the touch—hands he was sure the Good Lord had not intended for the hoe or plow.

He examined his gun hand. The little finger, broken by a ruckus at the milking bucket when he was ten, was curled permanently at the second joint like a brown caterpillar. The break was nearly identical to the one that angled the same finger on Kings's right hand, only Blake was sure that injury had come from something a great deal more impressive than an agitated Jersey cow.

Whatever the cause, Johnny took it for an omen that he would soon be riding the Hoot-Owl alongside the man who'd just turned him down.

"Ain't that right, Red?" he said to his horse, who replied by spreading his hind legs to release a spattering yellow torrent.

It was reiterated that Zeller, Yeager, Woods, and Foss would intercept the westbound Union Pacific sometime around high noon the next day. Seward would ride with them. And while Yeager played hell trying to prevent Yankee Dave from pistol-whipping the daylights out of a mulish company man, Kings would lead Brownwell, Creasy, and Davis southwest. Their destination was their stronghold in the Big Bend—over a thousand square miles of long shadows and winding ravines in which an inexperienced rider could easily get lost.

They rode double file onto the thoroughfare, Kings and Yeager leading each short column at a walk. Yankee Dave Zeller rode in the drag of Yeager's column, staring trancelike between the ears of his dun mare. His mind's eye was filled with fleeting images of bare flesh and unbound hair. It had been a long, dry spell for him on the trail, in the canyons, and he sure was going to miss Jeannie. The fact that she thought him the moon-hanger and never charged him a red cent was beside the point. Hell, he would have doled out as much as $200 if she was of a mind to charge that much. As a matter of fact, if he had been in any other business, he might have asked her to marry him as they lay in each other's arms the night before.

Some kind of outlaw, he chided himself, even as the nine-strong cavalry shifted from a walk to a soft Sunday jog as they closed on the town limits.

Before his time on the other side of the law, Zeller spent three years in service to the Union. More than once, he'd had occasion to wonder whether he'd been blessed with a sort of sixth sense—a sense with which he could smell danger as easily as any pilgrim smelled rain. Whomever he had to thank for this knack—whether God above or the graybacks of Mason-Dixon below—Zeller was glad for it.

Else he would have taken a load of double-ought buckshot, courtesy of a shotgun-wielding Ned Spivey, right in the back.

"Time to pay the piper, boy!" was the cry that yanked Zeller back to the here and now. He wheeled the dun hard to the left, raising a high-pitched horse scream as Spivey's sawed-off belched flame. The spot where the saloon man stood at the edge of an alley was too far to do any more damage than kick up dust, but Zeller felt confident he could make up the difference with one of his Colts. He was just bringing his muzzle to bear on his wide-legged target when his mare backed into one of the other horses. His shot went wild.

Spivey edged further into the street and triggered the second barrel at Zeller—*missed again*! As a water trough across the street disintegrated, the saloon man swore and flung his spent weapon to the ground. He pulled a pistol from his waistband and drew a bead of his own. Zeller, locked in a battle with his own horse, had lost sight of Spivey.

At the far end of the commotion, Kings reined his stallion around and slapped with his spurs. Spivey's aim was spoiled for a third time when John Reb's right shoulder slammed into him. The collision sent the man reeling, legs tangled, until he lost his balance and pitched to the ground.

The Virginian whirled the black again. Spivey rolled over, bringing his gun up, but Kings was faster, firing down at him with deliberate precision. His first bullet smashed into Spivey's right shoulder. The second hammered into his left thigh. Then he was gone.

Regrouping, the horsemen drummed down the street and swung west, leaving the saloon man writhing in the dirt, vowing, "Gonna get his. That sumbitch is gonna get his."

CHAPTER 7

Kings led them west for two days before he was able to suppress the feeling that he'd left a loose end back in Refuge. Brownwell, Creasy, and Davis rode along pleasantly enough, as men who have the luxury of following often do. They dozed for stretches of time and passed short topics of conversation back and forth like a bottle. Every so often, Yeager would raise his harmonica to play a bar or two of "Good Ol' Rebel" or "The Bonnie Blue Flag."

It was just before noon the fourth day out when they came in sight of the Chisos Mountains, a twenty-mile stretch of rock-edged ridges, bluffs, and plateaus that ran along the edge of the horizon. As the riders' shadows grew longer, the Chisos reared ever higher. The closer they drew, the more apparent it became how green the mountains were with foliage, their craggy faces dotted with the trees that gave the range its name.

It was getting on to sundown when they passed beneath the Rocking Chair, that massive, vaguely chair-shaped formation that told the outlaws they were almost there. A figure was barely visible at the highest point, crouched with a rifle that caught the dying light of the sun along its barrel. A second flash winked at the encroaching horsemen as the sentinel held up a telescope to discern their identity. That was Dick Osborn.

Kings took off his hat and waved, and Osborn returned the gesture before ducking from sight. He would be starting down the long ridge to the clump of honey mesquite about a hundred feet below. There, he'd collect his trail-wise mount and let it pick its way down.

Kings and the others rounded the base of the Rocking Chair to enter a valley between the steep cliffs. A shin-deep creek lined with desert willows wound down the middle, running deeper into this sanctuary. Cottonwoods, live oaks, and *huisache* abounded in a sea of *grama*, strong and green with their bluish-purple flags aloft at the stems, and bright orange Mexican poppies mingled with bluebonnets and yellow rabbitbrush. Sage hens scuttled through the grass as the outlaws passed, too lazy or too frantic to take flight, and a small herd of mule deer grazed on the opposite creek bank. A few lifted their heads at the sound of approaching horses, then went about their business.

The moon was high when at last they saw the log cabins—two long structures flanked by a stand of cottonwoods. With a breezeway between them, the cabins had two doors each, front and back, and nearby was a corral that led back into a pasture, enclosing a barn and a water trough constructed of piled rocks.

Kings reached the corral first. He dismounted and touched aching feet to earth, then loosened the cinch to give John Reb an easier and well-deserved breath. For a moment he clung to the horn with both hands, murmuring words of encouragement that only his horse could hear. The men dismounted around him, then turned their horses into the corral and trooped with Kings into the first cabin.

Only Charley Davis lingered by the corral. He let his body sag against the gate, let his saddle raise dust as it slipped from his grip, and watched the horses crowd about the big trough. Submitting only to Kings's giant black, they banged bodies and nipped at one another. Davis's bay gelding had not yet watered but was rolling its sweat-stained back and sides in the grass. Despite his exhaustion, he smiled, having always found pleasure in observing four-legged life.

"Glad to see another human bein' again."

With a hand on his pistol, Davis rounded and peered into the darkness. He made out the short, bowlegged shape of Dick Osborn standing just a few yards off, holding the reins of a rangy *grullo* horse. The fellow's ammunition belt sagged with the weight of two heavy pistols, but Davis's eyes were drawn to the stubby shotgun resting in the notch of Osborn's arm, its twin barrels sawn down six inches short of the forestock. It wouldn't have taken much muscle to swing the weapon up into action.

That wasn't good, Davis told himself. A man leading a horse shouldn't have been able to catch him unawares when mountain sheriffs and possemen had never been able to. As it had to Gabriel Kings before, the thought occurred to Davis that maybe he was approaching that proverbial hill.

"Who're you?" he asked, hoping to disguise his chagrin. Davis was the only one who hadn't noticed Osborn atop his station.

Osborn was the sole member of Kings's crew who hadn't served in the war but spent much of the decade hiding out in Mexico, leaving two dead bodies behind him in Brownsville. The primary role he played in a job—if the gang planned to rob a bank—was to ride into town ahead of the rest, scout it out, locate the target, and size up the type of law enforcement that would have to be dealt with. He then passed that information on to Kings, who put it to good use.

Osborn kept coming, more amused than peeved at Davis's challenge. "Don'tcha think it oughta be *me* askin' that question, *amigo?*"

"Who're you?" Davis said again.

"Well, so long as you ain't got a warrant in hand, you stubborn bastard, I got no problem givin' my name . . . or one of 'em." Osborn offered his hand and a crooked smile from behind a thick black beard that pointed at the chin. "I'm Dick Osborn."

"Charley Davis."

"I ever see you ride with this outfit before?"

"First time."

"Thought so," Osborn said. He stripped the rig from his horse and swung with his toe to hustle it into the corral. He then motioned with the shotgun toward the cabin nearest the corral, where lantern light shone through the windows. "Let's head inside, Davis. My keister's sore from crouchin'—yours, no doubt, from ridin'—and I reckon we could both stand a cup."

Davis's pride was still smarting from having been crept up on from the flank, but he found himself taking a liking to the diminutive Texan.

When Osborn lifted the latch and nosed the door open with the shotgun, Creasy and Brownwell looked up from passing a cloth pouch between them. There was water boiling for coffee, a pleasant sound.

Across the puncheon floor, Kings sat with his stocking feet extended toward the fireplace. His eyes were closed, and his breathing was even, but there was a tautness to his face that made it clear he wasn't fully relaxed. The thumb of his left hand was hooked over the handle of his Colt, the fingers steadily drumming the holster. Over the years, it had become almost impossible for Kings to be totally at peace—one part of him was always either at play with itself, seemed like, or tense as a spring wound too tight.

Brownwell hauled out chairs for the late arrivals. "Have a seat, Os. You remember Bob Creasy."

"Sure." Osborn nodded, dropped into the chair beside Brownwell, and turned his head toward the sound of coffee.

Creasy patted himself down, searching for a match. "Them others should be ridin' in by tomorrow night, right?"

"More or less," Brownwell answered.

"Leavin' soon, Crease?" Kings asked from across the room. It was hard to tell from his tone what he thought about it.

Creasy nodded. "Yeah, I think me an' the boys'll just take our share an' pull out. I've a hankerin' to see Acuña again."

"Acuña," Kings repeated, as though tasting the sound of the place. Shadows leapt and moved weirdly across the room as he got to his feet with a wince and made his way over. "Might be a good idea, that. Make yourselves scarce, let things blow over this side of the river."

"That's what I had in mind."

"Keep a lid on it, though, wouldja? That's a lotta dirty money you're gonna be wavin' around down there, and where there's filth, there's flies. Buy one too many whores, too many drinks . . . Folks're liable to take notice."

"I ain't no greenhorn, Kings."

"No need to get ruffled. I just know you an' your boys like your women and your drinks, and I might need y'all again."

Over the past several days Kings had gathered little sleep, and the light of the lamp on the table gave his face a ghostly cast. His advice was sound, though, there was no denying that, and it punched holes in the bravado of a man who, for all his talk, lacked restraint when cash was in high supply.

Shortly after Kings turned in, Osborn leaned close to Brownwell and whispered, "What the hell's eatin' him?"

"Damn if I know, but he's gotten worse since we left." Brownwell drew on his cigarette, the tip glowing a dull red. "I ain't about to ask him, though, not afore he volunteers the true source, leastways. Had to shoot a fella back in Refuge—get to that in a minute—but I don't think he's frettin' too much about that."

"He's shot fellas before," Osborn said.

"He ever said anything about hangin' 'em up?" Davis asked.

"Might have, here and there," Brownwell said, "though I can't remember one p'tic'lar instance. Then again, I've seen the time I thought about that m'self." He took another drag before continuing. "We've been doin' this a helluva while now, had some narrow scrapes but always come out okay. More'n likely, he's just tired. Tired and not wantin' to press his luck with the U.P."

In spite of what he'd seen, Osborn was skeptical. "Think so, huh?"

Brownwell looked down the hall. "Possible, but I been wrong before."

Creasy, Davis, and Foss stayed on two days more before they rode out for their base at Ciudad Acuña, south of the border in Coahuila State.

The canyons were quiet all summer. The men came and went as grown men are free to do, but like young sons, they obeyed Kings's strict order to behave, as given by a father. Those who went out gambled, drank, and whored, but otherwise behaved as law-abiding citizens. Kings himself rarely left. Once, in July, he'd gone to post a letter to the town of Floral, which was just a day's ride north of the Jackson spread, and the second time, in early August, he rode northeast and was gone for a week, simple isolation his desire.

Frank Wingate rode in on a mid-September morning. Kings was out in the yard, chopping wood in his shirtsleeves, and was halfway through the pile when he heard Sam Woods's voice behind him.

"Kings? We've got company."

Wiping sweat from his brow, Kings swept the landscape until his eyes lit on the objects of Woods's attention. Four horsemen advanced from the west, still several hundred yards off but in no apparent rush to reach the compound. The easy manner with which they rode meant one of two things. Either they were friends—and those were few and far between—or they were strangers, tentative in their approach. Like coyotes drawn by the scent of a smokehouse, their presence was unwanted, maybe even dangerous. And Kings had only Woods to stand with him.

As far as he knew, Osborn was still asleep in the second cabin. Yeager and Brownwell had taken off early to comb the brush in search of meat for the stores. By now, they should have reached the Santa Elena Canyon, where a leg of the Rio Grande separated American soil from Mexican.

Zeller and Seward had pulled out three days prior, each with a portion of their cut from the U.P. job saddlebagged. They didn't say when they'd be back or where they were going, and that was fine with Kings—just as long as it wasn't Refuge. Kings knew Zeller still felt he had business there. He'd threatened to settle it multiple times over the last few months, but every time, his words proved hollow. Surely, he had more sense than to ride back. No, they wouldn't have gone there . . .

Sam was in the breezeway, arm across his chest to the inside left of his coat, gripping the handle of a pistol. "I'm with you," he called out.

Kings planted the ax in the cutting stump, then tightened his gunbelts. "Glad for it," he said over-shoulder, and the words were not uttered lightly.

Their acquaintance extended back to the latter half of '63, when Woods came north from Richmond to Harpers Ferry with a depleted cavalry unit. Although he was immediately mustered into General Stuart's command, he never formally met Kings until eight months before the surrender.

A slim, dark man who curled the tips of his mustache with wax, Woods, like Dapper Tom, spoke with a particular tone and possessed enough of a vocabulary to suggest an above-average education. He was the surgeon of the bunch, with a rudimentary knowledge of the human anatomy and how to stave off infections. He could pull from Shakespeare and Milton quickly enough, but he was, thankfully, a little quicker with a gun, which counted more for men in their line of work.

Finally, the riders drew rein with scarcely ten yards between them and Kings. The second fellow on the left was Wingate, lean and hawk-faced, given to coarse language and outbursts of violence. As a direct result of those famous outbursts, he could lay claim to eleven murders, some of which had been committed over the slightest aggravation.

Smiling amiably under the shadow of a dark-brown slouch hat, Wingate did not speak until his companions had fully assembled on either side. When he opened his mouth, out came an unusually deep and gravelly voice that never failed to make an impression. "Been a long time, Kings. I'd say, what, three years?"

"Four, to my count."

Their last meeting was at a trading post up on the Canadian River. Kings had been on his solitary way back from scouting out a Kansas bank, and though he had crossed paths with Wingate once or twice before, most of what he knew of the man was based solely on his reputation. And Wingate had quite the reputation. He was a road agent and bank robber, an occasional killer-for-hire, and master of a pack of wild dogs just as mean as he was—clearly, the men with him now.

They hadn't been with him that night. If they had been, Kings might not have intervened against three men whose leader shouted that a debt was about to be paid. When the smoke cleared, it was the gunman and his cronies who had gone to their Maker, and Wingate and Kings lit out together. Ten miles down the road Kings went his way and Wingate went his. Hats had been tipped but no invitations extended, as far as Kings could recall.

"Mind if we step down?" Wingate asked now, starting to swing his leg up and over. "Got me a powerful damn cramp."

"You wouldn't have brought trouble to my door, would you, Frank?"

Kings's question was tainted with a quality that held Wingate off for the moment. "I shouldn't be expectin' a posse to come whoopin' in here after ya, should I?" Kings persisted. "Or bluecoats out of Fort Davis?"

"Now, Kings, you oughta know me better'n that. You done me a mighty big favor once, and though I suppose there's some would call me evil, I ain't in the habit of doin' evil unto my friends."

A quiet settled over the yard. One of the horses stamped, shook out its mane, and somewhere in the trees behind the cabins a dove called. Finally, Kings spoke again. "Who've you got with you, there?"

Wingate grinned again and gestured to each man in turn, starting with the tall, broad-chested fellow on his right, whom he introduced as Dan Carver. Kings had heard the name, not attached to what was necessarily a compliment. Word was that he had killed more men with a knife than with a gun, that he could pick a fight as easily with a scarecrow as with a troop of soldiers—quite the reputation for a man who couldn't have been more than thirty-two. He met Kings's gaze through a pair of sleepy eyes, his mouth half-twisted in a sneer below a heavy mustache.

To Wingate's left was Jack Lightfoot, a slender man with milky-blue eyes that stood out against his dark complexion. His straight, hard features, shoulder-length hair tied in a knot, and mismatched manner of dress cast him as some sort of halfbreed.

The last of them, Henry Coleman, was a wiry, strong-looking Negro, with sprigs of black hair jutting in all directions beneath a felt hat with a rolled-up brim. His jaws worked slowly around a cold cigar stub. Sitting his horse two arm's lengths away from Lightfoot, Coleman appeared bored, distant in more than the literal sense.

At Kings's approval, Wingate and his men turned their animals into the corral and ambled through the door of the first cabin—all except Coleman. Instead, he squatted by the corral, seemingly content to watch the horses. Woods, distrustful of the Negro, stayed in the doorway, watching him.

Inside, the three visitors seated themselves and accepted a glass of whiskey poured by Kings himself. Wingate sipped his at first, then squinted with pleasure at the high-quality taste. He downed the rest in one clean motion. "Nice little hideout you got here," he remarked, examining the room. "Never did find us one, did we, boys?"

Kings let a moment pass before trying at civilities. "I thought you mighta settled down somewhere in Old Mexico by now, Frank. Got yourself a pretty little *mamacita* and got baptized, but I guess you're still pluggin' along."

Wingate chuckled broken-glass laughter. "Pluggin' along and pluggin' away, that's right!" He reached for the bottle Kings had left uncorked. "I figger if it keeps bread on the table, ain't no reason to call it quits. Honest gun work yields an honest dollar, Kings. Oh, sometimes we hold up a depository or two, same as you fellers, and sometimes we don't do much else but live out the back of cathouses, but we keep busy. Yes, sir, it's a wonderful life."

As Wingate helped himself to another drink, Kings decided to take the measure of his companions. Aside from the silver-studded gunbelt he wore, there was really nothing about Light-foot that would have made him stand out in any *cantina* or hash house in the state. Of course, if this was the same Jack Lightfoot that Kings was thinking of, then he could track an eagle through a clear sky.

He could still feel Carver's eyes on him and was aware of what the big man was trying to do. Kings saw Carver for the schoolyard bully he'd probably been, and though his means of intimidation had assumed a more dangerous shade since then, Carver still wanted to play kids' games. A staring contest was the last kind of game Kings wanted to cash in on, though he hated to admit, the man was beginning to agitate him. Five years ago, Kings would have backhanded the look from Carver's ever-following eyes and booted him out the cabin door, but he suppressed the urge. He reckoned the best way to get Carver's goat was to deliberately avoid any and all eye contact.

As to the Negro hanging around outside, Kings knew him for a killer—a heartless, stone-cold killer, made that way, no doubt, by a more brutal life than the others had lived.

"What sorta misdeeds have y'all been occupyin' yourselves with?" Wingate inquired, handing the bottle back. Although he usually limited himself to one drink, Kings poured himself another.

"Well, we struck the U.P. this side of the last rainfall, both runs." He decided to conserve his whiskey this time around, content with only one sip for the moment, before adding offhandedly, "Had to shoot me a fella up to Refuge."

"Ya don't say," Wingate said, straightening with interest. "What fer?"

Kings shrugged. "Threw down on us with a scattergun on our way outta town."

"Just wanted a piece of that five-thousand-dollar bounty, more'n likely."

"Could be."

Carver leaned forward, elbows on his knees. "You kill him?"

Kings was looking at Wingate when he answered. "Put two

slugs in him, wing and thigh. I reckon he'll remember me the rest of his born days." He paused for another sip. "Other'n that, it's been an uneventful summer."

An hour later, as the visitors were saddling up outside, Kings went over to Wingate and asked, "Where you boys headed?"

Wingate looked at him, then finished tightening the latigo. "Who's to say, *mi amigo*? We's conversed a little on catchin' a train to San Antone. Been a dog's age since we was last in them parts. Jack heard tell there was a troupe in town, and seein' as none of us is wanted there, we thought we'd catch us a show and kick our boots up fer a time. Either way, I don't expect we'll be back thisaway anytime soon."

Wingate swung aboard but waited until Lightfoot, Carver, and Coleman rode past before reining away. Kings bristled at the notion that the man would go without as much as a parting word and took several steps beyond the corral gate after closing it. "Be seein' you, Frank," he called after the departing horsemen.

Wingate did not look back but tossed a casual wave over his shoulder. "*Adios*, Kings," he had to shout. "*Muchisimas gracias* fer the whiskey."

Kings watched them go until they were nothing but specks on the land. After a while he sensed Woods at his side.

"A gentle riddance," Woods remarked. Wingate had hardly acknowledged him, but that was just fine. "You ever met any of those others?"

"Heard of Dan Carver . . . nothin' good. Lightfoot's supposed to be the best tracker come down the pike. But that colored fella . . . can't say as I ever seen or heard of him before."

"Wingate mention why they came through here?"

Kings had wondered that himself. "Just passin'."

"Well, I'm glad their stay wasn't a long one," Woods said. He paused to offer Kings a cigarillo, then lit one of his own. "Say,

71

what day is this?"

"September fifteenth," Kings replied, then snorted in amusement.

"What's funny?"

"You realize what's just around the corner?"

Woods looked at him curiously. "Should I?"

"September twenty-fifth, eighteen hundred and sixty-six," Kings said, sounding as though he were reciting from memory, "I put a bullet in the man who sold my father's farm, and, come October sixth, it'll be a dozen years to the day since the Scarboro job."

"Been that long, huh?"

They smoked in silence for a minute or two before Kings, spitting shreds of wet tobacco, turned back toward the cabin. He emerged some moments later, a clanking burlap sack in his left hand, and started off through the grass to the northeast. "I'll be back shortly," he said in parting.

To which Woods replied, "Watch yourself, brother."

Brownwell and Yeager came loping back to the compound a little past noontime, each with game dangling to one side of their saddle bows—Brownwell with a brace of rabbits, Yeager with a wild tom turkey. Osborn came out with his shotgun slung over his left shoulder and took their horses. Contrary to what Kings thought, he hadn't been asleep after all but, along with Woods, had been keeping an eye on Coleman from the window of the second cabin.

Woods was waiting inside, reading from Seward's weathered copy of *The Last of the Mohicans*. He told Brownwell and Yeager of the four visitors he and Kings had received and asked whether either of the two knew Frank Wingate.

Yeager didn't, but Brownwell said, "I met him once before on the Hoot-Owl, but I recollect me and him crossin' paths back in St. Lou, 'fore the war. He was all fire-and-brimstone, gettin' loud and pointin' his finger when the barroom talk would get political. Most of us thought he was full of it, till he up and shot a man on Independence Day. All for sayin', 'God bless the Union.'

"Now, I was still a kid, more or less, and I hadn't yet run afoul of the federal government. When Wingate popped that poor fella in the windpipe, it was the first kill I'd seen. It was only a year after that when I took a knife to that piece of trash we rented from. And that sheriff, not long after. Believe he was a second cousin of mine.

" 'Course, Missoura bein' comprised mostly of future Secesh, what Frank Wingate done to that Union-lover was looked at as an act of simple patriotism. Hell, they made a hero out of him, at least for a night. Might've made *me* a hero, too, if it hadn't been for that damn second cousin."

Kings extended his right arm and aimed at the line of cans and whiskey bottles set up in a row along the horizontal trunk of a rotted cottonwood. Turned sideways in a duelist's stance and balancing the Peacemaker lightly in his fist, he centered his sights and squeezed the trigger.

The first can launched into the air, and, before it landed, Kings notched his gun barrel a tick over. He centered on a large peach can and blasted it off the trunk, too. He did the same to the remaining three targets, and from the first shot to the last, only five seconds had gone by.

He ejected the empties and reloaded five chambers, leaving the one under the hammer empty. He lowered the hammer and holstered, then shifted his feet around, left shoulder forward. On the twist-draw, Kings brought his second Colt into action, firing rapidly, and the last five bottles shattered. He drilled for another forty minutes until finally, after thirty targets and zero misses, Kings left his guns holstered. *Good enough,* he told himself.

On the walk back, he had a lot of time to think. Generally, his mind was clouded with thoughts concerning the next job. There were occasions when he needed to dunk his head in a pail of water to relieve the headaches that came with the meticulous planning. He used up boxes of matches some nights to keep the candles lit, and he'd awakened with many a stiff neck after falling asleep with his face on the table.

Earlier, Kings had been ruminating on a bank a few days' ride to the east, but at the moment, his thoughts were nowhere near the town of Agave Seco and the bank he expected to find there, fat with cattlemen's cash. No, his thoughts were out on the Frio River, where *she* awaited him.

Nine years had passed, but things hadn't changed much. Belle Jackson was still independent, still strong-willed, and, to his eyes, even prettier. He was just as lost a cause as that terrible war had been, and he still pined for her.

He'd sworn himself to stay true to Belle and had never strayed from his pledge. Their romance was a forbidden thing—as much by her parents as by the way things were—and so they had to tread carefully. They had spent precious few nights together, and, fortunately, their passions hadn't yet produced a son or daughter to shame them both and end the alliance he held with her father.

He would have given back all he'd stolen if he could walk away tomorrow—yield control to Brownwell or one of the others, and marry Belle. He had kept the woman waiting long enough. How much more time would she be willing to spend on him, if she hadn't given up already?

He couldn't even recall how long it had been since he'd last laid eyes on her . . . a year, was it, or more? He had yet to receive a response from that letter he'd sent. Of course, he told himself, if she ever *did* decide she'd had enough of waiting and worrying, she would be justified in whatever course of action she chose.

Did she still stare out over the prairie, hoping to see him crest that last rise, or had she turned her attentions toward a dashing Yankee cavalryman, or some good-looking Texas horse trader in business with her father?

And even if the day *did* dawn when Gabriel Kings hung up his guns and adopted one final alias, to what sort of existence would that consign the woman he loved? He'd hoarded away just about enough money to settle into a comfortable and civilized existence elsewhere, and, when it came to making more, he could always pass himself off as a cattle buyer or horse breeder. He had the inclination; Belle had the eye for four-footed flesh. As to keeping up outward appearances, no doubt the local preacher would welcome any collection plate contribution Kings chose to make.

But, putting aside all these outward changes, what would be different? No matter how far he and Belle ran, and no matter how many children they matriculated through Sunday school, Kings could never stop looking over his shoulder—never stop seeing Pinkertons on every street corner or mounted lawmen on every horizon.

Bogged down and floundering, his thoughts turned quickly back to Agave Seco.

CHAPTER 8

Stirrup-to-stirrup, they rode down Congress Avenue toward the imposing bulk of the capitol building. The two riders were nearly identical, mounted on matching bay horses, and although they were not in uniform, they had a distinctly military air about them. If a passerby had thought to look, he might have noticed the star-in-a-circle badge each man wore on his chest, identifying them clearly as Texas Rangers.

Under the eyes of two neatly dressed men idling on a bench, the rangers swung down and, in the absence of a proper hitch rail, tied their horses, one to a side, to the black wrought-iron rails that led up the capitol steps. The larger, gray-haired ranger paused a moment, then bent backward at the waist and groaned as he heard something crack like a handful of twigs. *Caleb,* he thought to himself, *you're getting to be too damn ancient for this.*

Caleb Stringer was a captain in one of the state's six frontier battalions. Though he was a Tennessee man by birth, the siren call of Texas lured him away from home over thirty years ago, and he'd been a Texan ever since. He served under Captain Jack Hays in the twilight of the '40s during the Mexican-American War, but, unlike so many others who flocked to the Stars-and-Bars years later, he chose to stay behind and defend against opportunistic Indians and bandits. He had spent most of his life in the saddle and, more than once, nearly perished in it. However brittle he might have felt on this overcast October day, he could still outride and outshoot many a man half his age.

The other fellow, Paul Leduc, was Stringer's sergeant. An eight-year man, he was a foreigner to Texas as well, a fourth-generation Louisianan—not a Cajun, as were most of his neighbors growing up, but the descendant of a French Huguenot who crossed over in the last century. A stalwart six-footer, habitually clean-shaven, he was younger than the captain by twenty years. Unlike his superior, he had indeed felt the call to go off and serve his country, but, because of Louisiana's treasonous leanings, he traveled to Kentucky to enlist in a Union-allied regiment. After the war, a short stint as a shotgun guard for Wells Fargo polished his marksmanship. By the time he handed in his resignation, whatever misgivings he'd had of being shot at were gone. When his wanderings brought him to Texas, Leduc found a ranger force in desperate need of fighting men, and himself in need of funds.

The rangers ascended the steps, passing under American and Lone Star flags hanging forlornly in the still, late evening air. One of the two on the bench looked up from his paper as they passed and raised his eyebrows at the sight of their dusty boots and jangling spurs.

Once inside, the rangers had only to identify themselves and were promptly directed to the governor's office. Neither had a clue as to what Richard B. Hubbard wanted, or how long their audience with him would last, but each man burned with a private curiosity.

The double doors opened after a quick knock, and the governor received them with the warm handshake and winning smile of a true politician. He was tall and heavyset, his bushy brown beard streaked with gray, and clad in a black Prince Albert coat tailored to suit his girth. Leduc thought Hubbard projected a sense of dignity appropriate for a man in his position.

"Hel-lo, gentlemen, and welcome," Hubbard boomed. "I hope y'all had a pleasant ride in."

"Pleasant enough," Stringer replied.

"Can I offer you boys a cigar?"

Stringer accepted one from the proffered box but did not light it, planning, instead, to smoke it on the journey back to headquarters. He was a man who believed that matters at hand came first, leisure second.

When the governor extended the cigar box to Leduc, the younger man shook his head, saying, "Believe I'll pass, but thank you, sir. I can't abide the devil-weed."

Hubbard shrugged, selected one for himself and struck a match against the edge of his mahogany desk. After a few puffs, the stuffy air filling the large room was permeated by the rich scent of Virginia tobacco. "If this is what's considered devil-weed, gentlemen," said the governor, waving out the match, "I'd love to see what angel-weed is like."

Hubbard had been a commander of the 22nd Texas Infantry during the war and afterwards practiced law. He was elected lieutenant governor in '73 and again three years later, just before assuming the office he held now. Over the course of his term, Hubbard had done a decent job of continuing the previous governor, Richard Coke's, task of reconstructing postwar Texas, reducing the public debt, promoting educational reform, and stabilizing the state prison system.

Now, in what would be his last few months as governor, Hubbard had apparently decided he owed the state of Texas one last duty.

He motioned for the two lawmen to have a seat opposite his desk, across which were scattered various leather-bound books, sheaves of paper, a walnut metronome, and—perhaps to make an impression—a well-kept but somewhat out of place Colt Dragoon in a flap holster.

As they seated themselves, the governor gave them a good once-over. Both men were dressed in simple garb—homespun shirts and worn leather vests under heavy coats, woolen trousers tucked into the tops of tall boots that had seen better days. Curiously, Leduc had a black silk neckerchief knotted loosely about his throat, the ends tucked down into the collar of his vest for protection. Each carried a knife and a pistol on their belts, the pistols chambered so they could use .44-caliber rifle shells interchangeably. Both men had been deeply tanned by the sun, their skin toughened by harsh *llano* winds, and they possessed builds that testified of strength and endurance, though Leduc was slightly shorter and leaner than Stringer.

Hubbard cleared his throat. "Well, as you know, gentlemen," he said, "our fine state suffered greatly in the wake of that ruinous damn war, and, like my predecessor, I've had only the very best interests in mind movin' forward. Governor Coke helped get us up off our hands and knees, and I daresay I've helped get us to where we can walk without Yankee hands to guide us.

"We're doin' fairly well, for the most part," he continued, "and the only way left to go is up. You men down on the border have near about got the Indians and the Mexicans whipped back, as I understand it."

After a short pause, Stringer, sensing that Hubbard was awaiting some sort of reply, said, "Yessir, but we've lost many a good man in the doin'. Taken an arrow in the hip and right arm, myself. Sergeant nearly lost his scalp to a Comanche buck one time."

He wasn't sure if that was what Hubbard wanted to hear.

Leduc shifted in his seat, wishing the governor would get to the point. Like Stringer, he was ever mindful of his duty, but he appreciated a more direct approach.

"Well, I'm glad to see you both alive and well," the governor was saying. "And, gents, as good as it is to know the tide's turning our way, it's been my continued experience that as soon as one obstacle is taken care of, another springs up in its place."

He leaned forward, folding his large hands as they came to rest on the desktop. "That's why I've called you men in here."

They started down the steps nearly an hour later, but not a word was said until they'd seated themselves at a corner table in the local chili joint.

With his back to the hustle and bustle of the kitchen, Sergeant Leduc held a cup of black coffee to his face with both hands, letting the steam warm his cheeks, then smiled as he sipped. There was no color or smile to be found on the captain's face, though, not even as he carved into his beefsteak. His mind was devoted solely to the commission they had just received—to exterminate the last remnant of Jeb Stuart's cavalry; to run to ground Gabriel Kings and his Avenging Angels, who had been a plague on this state and others for far too long. That was no small thing to ask, even of lawmen with their accumulated background and experience, but the governor had promised them something well worth the risk. In addition to the government footing the bill for any expenses they required, the state reward of $5,000 would be theirs to split—his and Paul's—and it didn't matter if they brought Kings in dead or alive. Texas Rangers made little more than forty dollars a month in state scrip, so the sum was as good as a million to them.

Kings's most recent heist had yielded a payoff of $20,000. Apparently, that was the straw that finally broke the camel's back. And so, after a steamier and more financially strenuous summer than usual, the governor had finally been given permission by President Hayes to organize a force fit enough to bring the outlaw gang to justice.

Hubbard had informed Stringer and Leduc that they couldn't have come more highly recommended. Their names had been touted by Major John B. Jones himself, who was ten years younger than Stringer but a trusted friend, and, coming from such a source, Hubbard said he felt as sure as the Second Coming that no one else could handle the job better than they.

A telegram had come in that very morning from Allan Pinkerton, the renowned founder of the detective agency that bore his name. They had been in communication for some time, these two important men, and the telegram informed the governor that Pinkerton was sending two of his best agents "out West" to lend a hand in the operation, an offer that was only too welcome.

The telegram stated that the Pinkertons would be arriving in Austin tomorrow, on the noon stage. They were to meet Stringer and Leduc at Smith's Hotel at the corner of Sixth and Congress, and from Austin, they would head out. The guns of the outlaws had been silent since their last big haul, and the word from Refuge, Texas, was that they stopped there for a short time before riding southwest, presumably to their headquarters somewhere in the broken ridges of the Big Bend.

That, then, was the path the lawmen would trace.

Marshal Liddell of Refuge had wired Austin with this information. Apparently, Kings and his men had kept hands in pockets and guns in holsters for the majority of their stay and would likely have passed through unnoticed had it not been for a brief and bloody shooting scrape on their way out. Liddell's details were sketchy, but the gist of it was that a local saloon owner had fired upon one of the gang with a double-barreled shotgun. Liddell had not informed them of any motive, but the saloon man had been wounded, shot twice by none other than Kings himself.

Leduc was presently shoveling potatoes, steak, and black beans past his teeth with exuberance. He did not once look up at the captain, knowing the time to talk would come. That's how it was with Stringer—if he wanted to discuss something, he would open his mouth and start. If he didn't, then a team of oxen couldn't pull the words from him. The sergeant was happy to let Stringer mull for the time being and hailed the waitress for a refill.

Dishes clattered in the kitchen, and a man at a nearby table roared with laughter.

"Paul?"

There it was. "Sir?"

The waitress appeared, and Stringer kept his thoughts corralled until they had the table to themselves again.

"The governor's askin' us to corner seven of the meanest, fightin'est, unreconstructed criminals there is. We're only two Texas Rangers, and our ranks are stretched thin enough from here to the border. Two Pinkerton men straight off the train from Chicago, Paul, makes four, to tackle this assignment."

Stringer wagged his head as he drew the cigar from his vest pocket.

"*Four* guns . . . ridin' against *seven*," he repeated. He popped a match head off his thumbnail and lit up. "We could mebbe look around and muster some extra hands, get a posse goin'. I guess the governor's offer'd cover it, but, all things considered, I'd say the Spartans had better odds at Thermopylae."

Leduc took a minute to chew on that. "Well," he said slowly, "I don't know much about the Spartans at Thermopylae, but hell, Cap, ever since I've been a ranger under you, we've always bucked a stacked deck. I don't see these odds as much better, but they ain't much worse."

Stringer considered the glowing tip of his cigar. "Well, then," he said with a shrug of sober resignation, "what are you gonna do with your half of that state *reward*?"

The Pinkerton men stepped off the stage onto the streets of Austin a half hour late, the only passengers to have their bags tossed down from above by a bellhop who rushed from the lobby before the dust had a chance to settle.

The rangers—well-rested after a rare night on feather beds—were reclining on the long, whitewashed bench on the hotel veranda, arguing as they had a dozen times about the pros and cons of the newer, lightweight, rimfire model of six-gun that Leduc preferred, versus those of the older, heavier, cap-and-ball model once favored by Stringer. Out of practicality, the captain had been forced to give up the Dragoon and now carried an unassuming 1875 Model Remington, blued and walnut-handled, which again put him at odds with Leduc, who wore a pearl-handled Colt with a nickel finish. Some arguments are never to be won, and Stringer decided this was one of them.

It was he who first noticed the two new arrivals disembarking from the four-horse coach. The first was a somber-featured man of about forty years, just under six feet tall and stoutly built, with turkey-tracked blue eyes and a close-cropped beard. He was dressed like a dude, his checkered coat, waistcoat, and trousers rumpled and dusty from the long trip. To all appearances, here was a fish that had swum too far downriver, but the formality of his suit concealed two service wounds, and his coat was unbuttoned at the bottom for faster access to his side-arm.

By contrast, his partner was short and slender with a dark coat-hanger mustache and a much younger face. Though his expression was vacant, his eyes carried a faint light of amusement as he took in his surroundings, as though he found it amazing that places like this still existed. He was dressed almost identically to the first man, though in pinstripes, and he did not appear to be heeled.

Stringer stood to meet the pair as they started up the steps.

The newcomers halted as their eyes came to rest on the ranger badge, and, though there was no need for him to ask, the captain did. "You the Pinkertons?"

"That's right," the older of the two replied in an authoritative but strangely high voice. "You the rangers?"

"That's right."

"My name's Mincey. This is my partner—"

"Patrick Delaney," the dark-haired Pinkerton offered, shedding his straight face for a disarming smile. "Pat, better known. How d'you do?"

"Howdy. I'm Captain Stringer; this is Sergeant Leduc."

"Glad to meetcha both," Mincey said. "Pat and I need to see to our rooms, but maybe you'd wanna wait for us in the lobby. We should be down directly, then we can get to work."

Stringer nodded and a short while later found himself and the others gathered around a table at the chili joint wherein he and Paul had taken supper the night before.

Walter Mincey was an Illinois man, formerly a cooper, and had served briefly in a short-lived organization known as the Union Intelligence Service. After learning the tricks of the investigative trade from Pinkerton himself, Mincey assumed various roles, ranging from barroom Confederate sympathizer to uniformed soldier, collecting intelligence deep behind enemy lines. Following the surrender, he joined the newly formed agency of his now close friend, the aforementioned Pinkerton. Many years and some dozen assignments later, Mincey held the rank of senior agent.

Delaney, the son of Irish immigrants, had been too young to serve in any military capacity but was, fortunately for him, born in the same city that served as Pinkerton headquarters. He had been in their employ for the last seven of his thirty years, seeing investigative action abroad in Missouri and Kansas. By nature, he was affable, the last one anybody would expect to wear the

84

badge of a Pinkerton detective or carry a pistol in a shoulder holster. He knew how to wield the respect that came with both.

Once their lunch had been set aside, the four lawmen talked through the day and into the evening, the rangers informing the Pinkertons as to whom they had been charged with apprehending. Each man realized that the fugitives were essentially the ultimate outlaw band—war veterans, hardened by years of living and fighting with cannons booming and bullets whizzing in their ears. They knew every canyon, arroyo, ravine, holler, nook, and cranny in which to hide, from the Mason-Dixon all the way to the Rocky Mountains. They were known to ride some of the best horses ever foaled, these so-called Avenging Angels, better than the average posseman could afford. Dozens had tried and dozens had failed to apprehend them. Tough lawmen went pale at the idea of pursuing the gang into the Big Bend, and even the small details of soldiers that patrolled the neighboring area fought shy of the Chisos foothills.

They were the very best at their trade, having stolen an estimated half-million dollars from the pocket of the U.S. government. It was an amount to rival any sum stolen by their peers, the now defunct James-Younger gang.

Stringer was looked upon to assume command of the small bunch of lawmen, as he was not only an officer in the rangers, but a man who knew best what Kings was inclined to do, where he would be inclined to go. He suggested they ride west to Refuge, have a word with the local law, round up all the facts they could, and see if a posse could be rousted into saddling up with them.

The four parted company around seven o'clock that night, the rangers bound for the general store, where they stocked up on supplies—not too light but not too heavy, either. They would be traveling hard and fast, and a pack mule or horse would only slow them down. Only the bare essentials were procured and added to the state tab.

Simultaneously, the Chicago lawmen secured for themselves a pair of horses—a lineback dun for Mincey and a seal-brown mare for Delaney. They also purchased two cast-off saddles, paid the hostler with a check, then took a trip to the local armory. From a rack on the back wall Delaney and Mincey hefted Winchester carbines and signed over what was asked for them. And so, cradling these weapons, the detectives retired to the hotel for the last good night's sleep they would have in a while.

Before the morning sun broke, the rangers were met at the city limits by the Pinkertons, astride their new mounts. Wordlessly, the four horsemen strung out in a single file line—Stringer riding point, followed by Mincey, who was in turn followed by Delaney. Leduc brought up the rear.

They rode west.

Four men trooped through the front doors of a certain Refuge saloon, dusty from travel and with an air about them that narrowed their line of work to a handful of seedy options. Ned Spivey watched them head to the bar from a corner table. His bandaged left leg protruded to the side, propped on a chair and causing him no end of grief. His left hand was filled with a tall glass of local, and his right arm hung in a sling.

The men—two whites, one who could have been a breed, and a john henry—leaned their rifles muzzle-up below the counter and ordered four drinks. The bartender poured three, hesitating when it came to the john henry. One quick look and a nod from Spivey filled the glass.

He waited until the barkeep served them once more and until the last of them swallowed before clearing his throat. Raising his good arm, glass still in hand, Spivey called out, "Could I have a word, gents?"

As one, the four turned to see who had hailed them. Only after they'd taken his measure, seeing he was virtually half a man, did they begin their approach.

The first one was just below average in height and slight of build, but, even so, he gave the distinct impression of being the head man. Flanking him was the half-breed and the big, scar-faced tough-nut who looked like he could bring steers down by the horns. The john henry was positioned a little ways apart from his companions, hinting at a certain intolerance, that the only reason he put up with them was to have three extra guns on his side. Not that he looked like he needed them.

They would do, he decided. They sure as hell would.

"You Spivey?" the head man asked in a gravelly voice.

"That's right. You Wingate?"

"That's right." He drew himself up, nodding to each of his men in turn. "These are my associates—Carver, Lightfoot, and Coleman."

"Telegram took long enough to find you fellas."

"Well, it found us."

"Uh-huh. Y'all come highly recommended."

"And who done the recommendin'?"

"Friend of mine. Pete Hooker."

Wingate thought a moment. "Cardsharp outta Jacksboro?"

"Fort Griffin."

Wingate grunted. "What can we do fer ye, Mr. Spivey?"

The saloon man left Wingate's question hanging for a moment. He took a drink, set the glass down, then flicked an ant from the tabletop. He stared up at them.

"You can set down and tell me what you know of Gabriel Kings."

CHAPTER 9

"Texas Rangers, eh?"

Asa Liddell sat up and reached for the piece of paper held out by the big, gray-haired man who said his name was Stringer.

It was late afternoon in Refuge, and Liddell had just returned from the Rancho Grande Saloon on A Street, where the monotony of the day had been shattered by the blast of a double-barreled shotgun. Warned he would be shot if he again spat tobacco juice on the gambling hall's well-kept floors, a local nuisance and grifter had defied the bartender's challenge and was cut down just as he was gathering spit.

Liddell had dismissed the matter, viewing the act as a service to the community. As far as the marshal was concerned, the deceased had been deserving of such a disposal. He wondered, though, what had caused the rate of shootings to spike so drastically within the last month. First Ned Spivey's scrape with the Kings gang, and now this.

He had returned to his office and newspaper only a short while ago. Walked in at around four o'clock, and the men standing before him now had walked in at around four fifteen.

"Texas Rangers, eh," he repeated, but this time it was less of a question.

"Yessir," Stringer replied, "and these two fellas in the city hats are Pinkerton agents. The four of us've been given the authority to hunt the Kings gang to the ends of creation. We answer only to Governor Hubbard, and him to President Hayes,

88

as that paper there says, and it'll hold up in any court of law."

Liddell nodded. "It would seem so," he said and handed back the commission that declared Stringer and his party, quite literally, all-powerful. The other ranger was leaning a shoulder against the north wall and staring at the marshal with expectant eyes. The Pinkertons stood by the door, somber-faced and silent, wearing rough and weathered frontiersmen's coats and patterned trousers. The contrast was interesting, not just between their own mismatched wardrobes, but between the agents and their indigenous companions.

At length, Liddell asked, "And what can I do for you, Captain?"

The man's reply was brusque. "Just answer a question or two, I reckon. The governor told us you sent him a telegram not too long ago, reporting a shootin' here in town. Guess somebody got wounded pretty bad, and you think it might've been Kings started the trouble."

"Can't say that he started it, but he sure as hell ended it. I believe there was some sort of quarrel existing between him and the man he shot. Man name of Ned Spivey. Now, Spivey's not exactly a good Christian—or a good *man*, for that matter—but he said he'd swear on a Bible it was Kings. On top of his testimony, I had a talk earlier that same day with a fella who bore a striking resemblance to Andy Yeager, a known associate of Kings, so to surmise it *was* the aforesaid miscreant would be . . . more than reasonable."

"Any idea where they might've gone?" Leduc asked.

"Well, I wasn't present at the time of the shooting, but witnesses said they rode southwest. We all know what lies to the southwest, but I hear there's no way to be certain about *anything* with this bunch."

Stringer took a deep breath and glanced around the room. Paul, he knew, was itching for a concrete plan, to be pointed in one direction. The man was like a coonhound in that way. He would sleep little, ride a lot, but Stringer wouldn't hear so much as a single groan or complaint from him. Neither would he hear any pleasantries—not until the task was completed. The man was a soldier, a stayer if there ever was one.

Those Pinkerton agents, now—he had to give credit where credit was due. For a couple of city boys, they'd proven themselves to be made of the same stuff as the hardiest Texan. First day out, Mincey had informed Stringer that he and Delaney both were already acquainted with the trail and its hardships but went on to admit that this current assignment would, in all likelihood, challenge them more than any of their previous jobs. Comforts were few and far between on the hardpan through which they were trekking, but these eastern men grumbled less and rode with more determination than half the ranger recruits Stringer had known over the years.

The previous night, the four of them had revisited the subject of forming a posse here in Refuge but were uncertain as to what they could promise any potential volunteers to compensate for the risk. Uncertainties aside, the lawmen knew they had to add a few extra guns to their small arsenal if they wanted to swing this assignment in their favor.

Stringer offered his hand, and the marshal got up to shake. Every minute spent here was a minute that could have been spent looking for men, and every minute spent looking for men was a minute lost in their search for Kings.

It was almost as if Liddell had read the captain's mind. "You're gonna need a few more bodies in the saddle if you plan to ride on the Big Bend," he said.

Stringer kept a straight face. "Now that you mention it, it *had* crossed my mind to see if I couldn't put a posse together here."

"There's some might could be persuaded," Liddell allowed. "Only this bein' the Kings gang, I don't know how many you're likely to get. I've had to wrangle a posse or two in my time here, and the men were eager enough, so you might have some luck. Most of our boys can ride, and there's a decent amount of good shots among 'em."

"Couldn't say for certain how much we could pay 'em," Stringer warned. "The state'll only put up so much on the barrelhead."

The marshal nodded, knowing how that sort of thing went.

"I'd like a chance to talk to that saloon owner, too," Stringer said.

"Spivey and I've never been on what you'd call good terms, but if it means gettin' back at Kings, I'm sure he'd be willing. I was you, I'd hide those badges for the time being and head on down to the red-light district. See if you can glean anything from that crowd."

There were four men at the center table in the Bull's Eye Saloon, and half that number was comprised of Avenging Angels. Dave Zeller sat with his chair squared to the wall, his expression stony and shrouded by wispy plumes from the cigar in his teeth. His right-hand pistol was out and on the green felt, within reach. To his left sat Tom Seward, dapper as ever in a red brocade vest, tipping back a stirrup cup two fingers full of Old Eagle whiskey. His chips were neatly arranged in separate columns, segregated by color—white twenty-five-cent pieces, blue one-dollars, red tens, and yellow fifties.

Across from Zeller was a long-faced man with a droopy mustache, sipping rye. With what looked like a well-used gun on his hip, he was something of a badman, but his reputation had yet to reach beyond the borders of Mason County. His name was John Peters Ringo, and he'd recently been turned loose from the hoosegow, his hands washed clean of the blood he'd spilt during the Hoodoo Range War of '75. Five months of freedom under his belt found him here, in Refuge, in the middle of an all-out, thrill-seeking tear through West Texas, with the Arizona Territory in his near future.

The fourth player was a lanky cowhand, nobody famous and destined for anonymity except on whatever ranch he could find work. Clearly in over his head, he was down, judging by his stack of chips, fifty dollars or so.

Tom Seward, unreadable behind his cards and his chips, was well ahead of the others, but Yankee Dave was more than a little distracted. He was no cardsharp anyhow—not really—and his primary purpose was to ensure that his dandy companion stayed alive. He played halfheartedly, making careless bets, tossing in chips at random. Either way, whatever Seward won would be split between them.

Zeller had come back to Refuge to do just what Kings hoped he wouldn't—to settle the score with Ned Spivey and take Jeannie away from this pit. He had intended to execute his plan earlier in the evening, but so far had seen neither hide nor hair of Spivey, and Jeannie wasn't in her room. The game had been going for three hours, and he'd sat through every one of them with the patience of a cat, but that patience had run its course. He glanced up every five minutes, it seemed, hoping to catch a glimpse of one or both of the people he sought. The thought had crossed his mind, in the second hour, that maybe one of Kings's shots had killed the saloon man, but that didn't seem likely. Zeller remembered where Kings's bullets had landed—arm and leg—and neither had looked like death wounds.

No matter. He could wait a little longer.

Outside, a sudden wind called to Seward, who was now more than $300 ahead of the rest of the players but sweating heavily. He went to the window and tried to raise it, only to find it wouldn't budge. Seward listened to the howling, contemplated folding and getting out of this sauna of a saloon. It seemed as good a time to walk away as any.

When he turned back to the table, though, Seward found that the cowhand had dropped out of the game and another gent had taken his seat. This man—sun-browned and dressed in trail clothes—smiled and said, "Evenin'! Too late for another hand?"

For a moment, Seward remained standing, for, despite his hot streak, he very much did not care to play another. In the end, though, his craving for cash won out as the newcomer, still smiling, dropped crinkled U.S. greenbacks on the felt. Zeller dealt the man in.

Over the next half hour, it became apparent that the stranger was anything but strange to the pasteboards. Tom Seward would have caught on and cut him down if he was able to, but by and by he noticed a semblance of a pattern emerging. The stranger would bluff nearly as often as he folded, and he had a poker face to rival Seward's. He would raise the limit when he had good cards, then play more conservatively until the pot had been built up before calling. Of course, he turned up the winning hand—four of a kind in nines.

After another hour of losing, John Ringo had had enough. He knocked back one last shot before shoving away from the table. He got up, shuffled across the floor, and disappeared into the dark beyond the batwings, moving ever onward toward his destiny in Tombstone, Arizona.

"Guess tonight was my lucky night, gents," the newcomer said, sweeping chips into his hat. "I'll be hanged, though, if I let a man walk away without standin' him to a drink. Come on to the bar."

Seward hesitated but collected what remained of his winnings and followed the stranger. Still seated, Zeller took one last look about the room. Nothing, by damn! Every other girl, it seemed, was working the late shift tonight, every girl but Jeannie.

And *still* no sign of Spivey.

Up against the hardwood, the stranger, who introduced himself simply as Smith, paid for two drinks a man.

"You boys frequent this dive much?" he asked.

"Not all that much," Seward replied, keeping his eyes forward. "We're just passing through here, truth be told."

"Where you headed, if I ain't pryin'?" This Smith was just full of questions.

Seward, for his part, was full of answers. "Not sure exactly where, Mr. Smith, just driftin'. Itinerant, I suppose you could call us."

"What about you?" Zeller asked.

"I'm driftin' south, more or less," Smith replied, "if I don't find a reason to stick around. You boys know of any action here?" He explained that the cattle outfit he'd been working for had gone bust at the end of last season, and he was again living out of saddlebags.

"I hear the faro dealer a few doors down took sick with lead poisoning so the house is lookin' for a new man. You know the game like you do five-card, I'd ask around there," Seward suggested.

"Oh, that kind of work ain't quite for me."

Smith didn't drink whiskey like Zeller and Seward, but beer, and he was in no hurry to finish. He was friendly enough, sure, but Zeller stayed on his toes, listening close for the slightest hint that this character was more than he said he was. He'd bet a bundle that Smith wasn't the name marked in the family Bible. On the other hand, who was Dave Zeller to be building crosses for a man who enjoyed the convenience of an alias?

Seward extended an unlit cigar. "Smoke, Mr. Smith?"

"No, thanks. I can't abide the devil-weed."

By now the Bull's Eye was mostly deserted, with only a handful of scattered women and their clients mumbling sleepily to one another. The barman was stationed at the far end of the counter, polishing a glass and humming a tune.

Standing out from the remaining hangers-on were three unkempt, rough-looking types in a tight knot near the storeroom. One of them, a heavy-shouldered, sandy-haired hulk of a man, looked down the length of the bar at Smith. He grumbled something to the others, who did not hold in their laughter.

Smith stiffened a little at the sound but did nothing—only raised his glass for another sip. Zeller and Seward watched him closely, curious to see how Smith would handle himself. The men were types well-known to the two outlaws—troublemakers, easy to anger. They were easy to outsmart and easy to whup, too, when it came down to it. Still, there *were* three of them, and this was neither Zeller's nor Seward's fight.

The sandy-haired man rolled a cud from the right side of his jaw to the left before calling out to Smith. "Hi-dee! That su-uu-ure is an adm'rable bandana you got yourself, mister. Silk, ain't it?"

Smith swallowed his beer, said equably, "That's right."

"How much that set you back, fancy man?" one of the others asked.

"Whoa, now, Joe, ain't no call to insult the gentleman!" The big fellow turned to Smith with a hangdog look. "He didn't mean nothin' by that, mister."

"No offense taken," Smith said. He was breathing calmly through his nose. His mouth, or rather, one corner of it, was lifted ever so slightly, and his gaze was steady upon the three—not locked on anyone in particular, but avoiding none.

"Say, mister." That was the sandy-haired man again. "Where in the hell didja come by that pretty little pistol? Don't that nickel just shine like the *stars*, fellas? And that pearl?" The man honked drunken laughter, but it was a hollow sound, with no feeling behind it—he was testing the waters, trying to see what he was dealing with. And then he pressed his luck. He leaned forward and extended one huge hand. "Can I touch it?"

"You must be touched in the head, mister."

The big man's face went still, the grin no longer there. "What'd you say to me, huckleberry?"

Smith may as well have reached out and slapped him. Zeller prodded Seward with an elbow, signaling that now was as good a time as any to step away.

Smith's voice was loud in the sudden quiet of the room. "I'm just havin' a beer, mindin' my own, and here you're startin' in to cause a fuss. Now, you can do the smart thing, and have one on me, or we can do the stupid thing. Come on, mister. Let's have that drink."

The big man's eyes went again to the pretty pistol on Smith's hip. He was sober enough to recognize that before him was no tenderfoot, but there were too many witnesses, too many people who had heard the insult, for him to swallow his pride and accept a free drink. He came around the end of the bar, closing the distance slowly. The angle of his neck and the stiffness of his shoulders showed what he was thinking—he was going to rip Smith apart with his bare hands.

He'd done it before, to what he'd taken for tougher men.

"Suppose," he said, finally stopping, "I don't wanna drink with no mother-lovin' dandy like you?"

Too fast to follow, Smith planted his left fist in the big man's gut, sending him to his knees. Sucking wind, the big man looked up, shock showing in his eyes just before Smith drove downward with his right. Knuckles to the temple will put out the lights of even the most seasoned bare-knuckle champion, and the big man was no champion. He hit the ground cold, and, before either of his friends could react, Smith jerked his pistol and had them covered.

One of them wobbled, in the midst of going for his own gun but thinking better of it. The pair hesitated, suddenly uncertain, and stared dumbly when Smith asked, "What do you wanna do, fellas?"

"What if we wanna keep pushin'?" said the taller fellow.

"I'd advise against it," Smith replied. He didn't lower his gun, and he didn't blink as he said it.

Eventually, the shorter man nodded and said, "Hell, I don't fancy meetin' St. Peter tonight. If you're buyin', I'm havin' red-eye."

Before following through on his offer, Smith bent at the knees to disarm the felled Goliath. He sent the pistol across the hardwood to the barkeep, then produced two coins from his pocket with that same hand. "Sorry this happened, friend," he said. "I'm buyin' drinks for those two but leave that sleepin' beauty thirsty."

When he turned around, Yankee Dave Zeller and Dapper Tom Seward were nowhere to be seen.

Three figures came together under a corner streetlamp, their collars turned up against the cold of the new day. Three more were approaching from the direction of the marshal's office—a man, a woman, and a shorter man using a cane. Once they'd crossed the invisible border of the Deadline, the hobbler and the woman branched off without so much as a parting word to the other. They started for the Bull's Eye Saloon a block away, unaware that, had they left the marshal's ten minutes earlier, the man would have been dead and the woman, in the arms of the killer.

The sky to the west was blue-black, a slightly lighter shade to the east as the sun continued its long climb up the curve of the globe.

Features illuminated as matches cracked. Smoke wafted and gathered in cancerous patches above the circle of four. A passerby would have heard them conversing in low voices. Every now and then, one took a look around, as though trouble lurked around the nearest corner.

"You boys have any luck?" asked Caleb Stringer, just back from the marshal's.

"Better than expected," said Pat Delaney.

"How many'd you get, Walter?"

"Five men, only two of whom are bachelors, but they're dyed-in-the-wool believers in law and order. They want Kings brought to justice just as bad as us."

"Bully. How 'bout you, Pat?"

"Three, Captain. Each of 'em swore they can sit a horse and shoot with any man in Texas."

"That makes twelve. Twelve is good."

A short distance up the street, a stray dog bayed, and somewhere out beyond the city limits, a coyote answered.

"You manage to learn anything, Paul?"

"Not so you'd notice. It seems like there's an epidemic of lockjaw takes hold of folks around here, you so much as mention the Kings crew."

"Lot of 'em have prob'ly crossed paths with some of them fellas. Some have mebbe even done a little bit of ridin' with them. You never can tell."

"They seem to have an awful lot of loyalty to one another, don't they, for a bunch of low criminals," Delaney observed.

"Some do. But there's enough who'd gladly tell what they know for a share in the reward money, if they knew anything. Only thing that keeps their mouths shut is the fear of Kings himself comin' down on 'em. Whatever else can be said about him, our boy's been known to bring the wrath of God."

Mincey grunted. "You get him alone, strip away all the guns, he's just one man."

"That's what I aim to prove to this country."

There was a pause, then Leduc said, "Did run into a couple of men, though, who I've reason to suspect run with him."

"Who, for instance?"

"Tall fella, kinda edgy. Played a hand of cards with him and a smaller gent wearin' a black city hat. Talker of the two, sounded book-learned. Dave Zeller and Tom Seward, mebbe."

"Twenty-five-hundred-dollar reward for that first one," Mincey said.

"Union man, wasn't he?" Delaney asked.

"That's what the warrants say."

"Whaddayou suppose he's doin' runnin' around with these graybacks?"

"Money," Mincey replied. "Politics don't have one thing to do with it."

"What about them two fellas, Paul? No prisoners?"

"No, sir. I looked away for a minute, and they'd taken their leave of the place. Tell you somethin', though—I been walkin' these boards since midnight, and I ain't spotted 'em in any of the other dives. I wouldn't know what their horses look like, but somethin' tells me they ain't in town anymore."

"No?"

"My guess is they already lit out. With daylight comin' on, I say we can track 'em without much trouble."

"There'll be plenty of trouble waitin' for us when we find them," Mincey said.

"*If* we find 'em, you mean," Delaney grumped.

"Gents, out here, all a man can hope for is a fifty-fifty chance."

"Well, Cap, I say we better the odds."

The baying up the street stopped, and the land lay quiet and still around them, around Refuge.

"All right. You men go pack up, get your things set. How

soon those volunteers say they could be ready?"

"Hour, at the most."

"Tell 'em we ride in thirty."

Two thousand dollars, silver coin, split four ways came to $500 a man. Two-fifty up front and they would be paid the other half when the job was done.

"Dead or alive," the saloon man had said, "don't mean a speck of owl crap to me. I just want that sumbitch to know it was Ned Spivey had him killed. You tell 'im that, when you got 'im bleedin' out, stuck-hog, in the dirt. You tell 'im Spivey sends his regards."

"Oh, yessir, Mr. Spivey," Frank Wingate had sworn, "you can count on that."

And so, for a meager $500, he shook hands with a man who wanted Gabriel Kings dead as Julius Caesar. Spivey's very words, and Wingate would see to it.

Kings was a wizard with a six-gun—not exactly the speediest, but definitely one of the nerviest gunhawks Wingate had ever seen—and he'd ridden with some of the most madcap killers ever to come out of Dixie. Sure, he may have owed the man for the time he saved Wingate's hide from a permanent tanning up there on the Canadian, and Wingate fully intended to make good on that debt. What better way, after all, than to pay Kings back with a bullet, do him the ultimate favor? Ease that sodbuster's pain and send him down. Lay down a cactus flower, drink a little whiskey, and pour some onto the grave—*Vaya con el diablo* and count your pesos for the boatman, Kings—then beat for the border with the money in hand.

He'd buried bona fide *amigos* with less ceremony.

Always wanted to fight him, Wingate did, to pull back and throw down for all the cards. Never really got the chance, though. But here it finally was—the chance to see if there was any truth to all the stories, the chance to call the legend out, so that he, Frank Wingate, could shoot him dead.

It was high noon, two days' ride out from Refuge. A west wind howled, shaping and herding the blanket of clouds through the sky and casting clots of shadows upon the plain below. Dry brush rattled, thorns clicked like talons tensing for a kill.

Ahead of them lay over sixty miles of desolation and emptiness, sixty miles they'd only recently crossed and were now inclined to relive for the second time in as many weeks. Though this crossing had proven more lucrative than the last, it would be anything but easier this time around. No matter which way it was navigated, no matter how wide one rode around one thicket of mesquite, hoping to avoid the knifelike cut of the groping thorns, around the next bend was another thicket just as impenetrable.

Wingate felt his white-shouldered bay horse shift beneath him and watched as Lightfoot continued to examine the ground. He'd been at it for minutes now, shifting like a crab, sniffing, licking the fingers he stuck into one depression or another, and mumbling freely even as he refused to answer any questions.

Carver scratched at his neck-beard. "We dally here any longer and Kings'll die of old age." He glared down at the long-haired tracker. "You been starin' at them tracks long enough to write a book, professor."

Ignoring him, Lightfoot walked back and swung aboard his gelding without the use of stirrups. Seeing that, Wingate had to remind himself the man was half white.

"We about ready, *professor*?" Carver said, watching the breed's every move.

Lightfoot fanned Carver's flames a little more by taking a long pull from his canteen. It took him as much time as a man does to pull on his boots. Then he swallowed loudly and gave a big sigh of satisfaction, just for the hell of it.

Henry Coleman looked on, his features betraying a deep annoyance at the way these peckerwoods were carrying on.

Lightfoot, making no attempt to hide the fact that he was enjoying himself, offered his canteen to Carver, who slapped it out of his hand with an oath. Wingate, quick to react, kneed his horse between them, barking at Lightfoot and waving Carver down. "You got our attention, Jack! Start talkin'."

Lightfoot chuckled as he got down to retrieve his canteen. "Well, seems like there's a good-sized bunch headin' in the same direction as us."

"Reckon we oughta ease up a little," Wingate asked, "so we don't step on their heels?"

"I'd recommend it," Lightfoot said, "just to be on the safe side."

Wingate nodded and got down from his horse. He began to rummage through his saddlebags for the bottle he bought off Spivey. He turned back around with the cork in his teeth and spat it into his palm. "Well, now, let's get outta these saddles for the time bein'. Jack? Dan? You fellas wanna settle your differences right here, you just have at it."

Carver, caught off guard by this unexpected offer, looked down at Lightfoot, at Wingate, then back again. He swung down with a calm that belied his eagerness to box Lightfoot's ears.

"How you want it, breed?" Carver asked, face split by an ugly grin. "Fists or knives?"

Lightfoot answered by flinging his big skinning knife handle-up into the hard-packed earth. Although he was forty pounds lighter and much wirier than Carver, Lightfoot was apparently confident in his ability to handle himself in a bare-knuckle brawl.

This seemed to amuse Carver like nothing else. He chuckled as he deliberately mimicked Lightfoot's gesture—knife in the dirt—then moved in, pumping his fists. Lightfoot slid into a half-crouch, arms out, elbows tucked in close to the sides, his fingers curled like claws—more in a wrestling position than the stance needed for what Carver had in mind.

When the bigger man seemed a breath away from taking the first swing, a blast from the barrel of Wingate's gun kicked up dirt at his feet. Wingate fired again as he walked toward them, over Lightfoot's head this time, and lifted his voice in a roar that could have come from Satan's own mouth.

"Enough!" By now he stood between the two and alternated holding his gun on Carver, then Lightfoot. "I can't hardly believe this . . . When this is all over and done, if either of ye got enough steam left, you can go ahead and eat each other's livers, for all I care. But fer the time bein', cool *down*!" He paused, and when he saw that neither man wanted to continue, he said, "Now, I want you damn fools to shake hands."

When they had, however reluctantly, Wingate shoved his pistol back in its holster. "And get your asses back in the saddle," he growled. "A few more miles won't hurt us."

CHAPTER 10

The sunlight of early afternoon drenched the sheer rock face to the left of the horseman and diamonded the dewy embankment of the creek beside which he rode. He was dozing in the saddle, the steady rocking of his animal putting him to sleep. Though the sun was shining, the air in the ravine was cold, and sweetened by the presence of the nearby water source. The rider had his coat buttoned all the way up, and the holster that usually rode against his thigh now rested in the V of his crotch.

Somewhere up in the limbs of a desert willow, a mockingbird sang, further deepening the rider's doze. As pleasant as it was, it was unfortunate for Johnny Blake. If he had his head up and his eyes peeled, he would have noticed the shadow moving stealthily through the brush on his right.

In strides that could have been leaps, that shadow was on him, clasping the back of his gunbelt with one hand, shirt collar with the other, and jerking the boy from the back of his shrieking horse.

Johnny found himself spread-eagle on his back in the grass, pinned to the dirt by a knee belonging to a man holding an enormous Bowie knife. In the silence, the bushwhacker and the bushwhacked stared at each other, trying to place faces. Johnny didn't dare speak, as the blade was less than two inches from his jugular. At length, the man withdrew his knife just a hair and broke the silence.

"You a long way from home, boy. You lost?"

"No, sir, I ain't lost."

The blade moved a tad farther back, but the pressure of the knee did not relent. "Oh! Well, that's mighty good to hear. If you ain't lost, then I guess that must mean you know where you're headed. Where might that be?"

"I'm bound for the hideout of the Avengin' Angels."

"And just how would you be knowin' the way to that?"

Johnny cleared his throat. "I don't, exactly, sir, but ever'one knows y'all headquarter somewhere hereabouts."

"How's a kid like you have the sand to come here when every lawman in the state don't?"

"I 'spose it's 'cause I got the ingredients, sir."

"Well, what's your name, Mr. Ingredients?"

"John. Johnny Blake." He hesitated. "And—and you're Leroy Brownwell, formerly of St. Louis, Missoura, who shot and killed Asa Grant in Tascosa in July of 1869. Knifed the U.S. marshal up in Fort Griffin back in '72, and along with only Gabriel Kings and Dave Zeller, robbed the Wichita savings bank in '73. Shot your way out of a hornet's nest. Twenty-five-hundred-dollar reward on your head, alive or dead."

Despite himself, Brownwell was impressed—and just a touch flattered. There seemed to be no high-and-mightiness to the youth, so he decided to hold off on dispatching him then and there. With a narrowing of his eyes, the Missourian sat back on his haunches but did not let Johnny Blake adopt a more comfortable position just yet.

"Take a breath, there, John," he said, "unless, o' course, you've come a-callin' after that bounty." Again, he lifted his knife point, fixing it like a pistol sight on Blake's nose. "You didn't, didja?"

"Hell, no, sir," Johnny replied, having fortified his tone with as much strength as he could. He inched up to the props of his elbows—it was as far as Brownwell let him—and said again,

"Hell, no! My intention was to ask, and if it comes to it, *beg* Gabriel Kings to let me ride alongside of y'all. I can shoot with the best," he went on, "and I'm as darin' and courageous a soul as you'll ever come across. I know I ain't exactly seasoned, but if I was just given the chance—"

Brownwell stopped him. "Whoa, whoa, whoa. Don't go makin' your case to me, kid. Save it for the chief." He got up, slapped the dust from his knees, and watched as Johnny slowly did the same. As soon as the kid was on his feet, Brownwell moved with surprising quickness and plucked his gun from its holster.

"Hey—!"

"Hay's for horses, sonny." The outlaw casually examined the Colt, testing the action, spinning the cylinder. He listened with an approving ear to the buzzing noise it produced and was glad to see that there were no notches—genuine or otherwise—disfiguring the wooden grips. When he saw the weapon was fully loaded, he took the liberty of ejecting one slug, then lowered the hammer on the vacant chamber. He flipped the shell into Johnny's open hand.

Smiling, Brownwell shoved the gun behind his buckle. "All right. Let's go see Kings."

He was seated at the head of the long table in the main cabin, staring at the door as if he'd been expecting Brownwell to haul Johnny through it that very second. It was more than a little alarming, though he didn't look quite as striking as he had on the boardwalk in Refuge. As placid as he may have appeared in his shirtsleeves and suspenders, the look in Gabriel Kings's eyes was no cooler than the tip of the smoldering cigar in the fingers of his right hand.

Kings appraised Johnny in such a way that Johnny couldn't tell whether he was more likely to shake his hand or shoot him.

He'd shot men before, Johnny was sure, for much less than trespassing.

Johnny allowed his eyes to pull away from Kings's cat-still form and piercing gaze—no easy thing—and as they ventured about the place he saw enough guns to arm a small detachment of soldiers. They were on the table, standing in corners, hanging in belts over chairs, suspended over the fireplace. Johnny's intrigue outweighed his anxiety for a fleeting moment, as he thought of what Kings must have had planned to have such an arsenal out in the open. He glanced about for the crates of explosives Tom Seward must have had stockpiled, but beyond the revolvers and repeaters, all he saw was Kings's personal guard.

Andy Yeager was at the table with Kings—Andy Yeager, who in 1875 shot dead the nephew of the mayor of Eagle Pass and was nearly hanged for it but sprung himself from jail the night before.

Turning around from the fire with a coffeepot in his mitted hand was Sam Woods, and Dick Osborn was in a rocking chair to Johnny's immediate right, running a cleansing rod down the barrel of a shotgun.

And there Johnny stood, hat in hand, with an empty holster on his hip, unsure of what to say or how to say it.

Brownwell made the introductions, pounding Johnny's shoulder and announcing with a one-armed flourish, "Fellas, allow me to introduce Mr. Johnny Blake, who's got a brain like an almanac and his heart set on throwin' in with us."

Blake wouldn't have been willing to lay a bet on it, but he thought he saw a light of amusement flicker briefly, then die in the eyes of Gabriel Kings. The outlaw slowly raised the cigar to his lips, sucked until the tip glowed like a ruby, and streamed smoke. Finally, he said, "I expected to see you a lot sooner, Johnny Blake."

"You—you did?"

"Been a long time since Refuge. You get halfway home afore you decided to turn back?"

In fact, the worsening condition of his saddle sores had delayed the mission longer than expected. Now appropriately medicated and having dispensed with his overalls in favor of tighter, duck-canvas trousers, Johnny realized that owning up to such a thing would hardly lend itself to a favorable impression in the eyes of these men. Instead, he merely stated, "It's just that I come a long ways with one thing in mind, and I didn't fancy goin' back havin' accomplished nothin'."

Yeager looked up. "You won't accomplish much gettin' your head blowed off by some spectacled posseman."

"There's nothin' big in knowin' how to shoot a gun," Kings said. "In takin' life. In stealin'."

Johnny could do nothing but stare. What were they carrying on about? How could they talk like that? Their guns had gotten them everything they had: money without working, freedom in the face of infamy, legendary status in their own time.

Kings's voice turned colder. "You got no woman to come home to, no children to carry on your name. You're lucky to have one safe place to lay your head, count your blessings if you got two. I hear the softest footsteps, even when there ain't a soul around."

"This kind of livin' ain't cut out for everybody, kid," Brownwell said solemnly from behind. "You ain't got the guts God gave a razorback, you're apt to get swallowed up. And there's no goin' back once you start."

The world seemed to grow smaller around Johnny Blake. The bleakness of their words confounded him. The way of living they'd described, these heroes of his, was a far cry from the tales he knew so well. He'd expected to bite an apple, to be welcomed wholeheartedly to the barrel, in fact. For what were these men—these veterans and Southern loyalists, heroes who'd rallied to the call while his cowardly father stayed home in the pulpit—but Robin Hoods misunderstood? Shouldn't they have been eager to increase their numbers with likeminded souls?

After a time, Brownwell spoke again. "Well, Kings, whatcha want me to do with this tyro? He's found and seen a good deal of our little hideaway, and I doubt he's losin' his memory, sprout like him."

Johnny imagined being taken around back and laid low with that big knife, but Kings did not pass judgment straightaway. The man stood—slowly, as was his practice—and approached, not stopping until an arm's length separated them.

Even as Kings towered over him and searched every inch of his beardless face, Johnny sensed he had crossed some threshold. With every creeping second that passed, he allowed the spring wound tight around his body to loosen. He even raised his left hand to hook a thumb in his pocket. He settled onto his heels and willed his breath to leave and enter him more smoothly.

Finally, just as he got his breathing level, Kings made a ruling. "Give the boy back his gun, Leroy. Sam, get 'im a drink, will you?"

Brownwell frowned but pulled the pistol from his belt and tossed it back. Kings reached across the open floor to accept a cup of coffee from Woods, then transferred it to Johnny. The kid accepted the drink with a nod and waited until the man he hoped to follow pointed to the door he'd only just come through.

Kings did not speak immediately but walked out ahead of Johnny, then kept walking as the kid followed close behind, ignoring the coffee in his hands. Kings stopped at the fringe of the yard, just where the cleared ground met the scrub grass, and the kid dared a few steps more until he was nearly shoulder-to-shoulder with the man.

Johnny felt the stares of the others crowded in the doorway

but allowed himself the fleeting fantasy of standing with Kings as an equal. He imagined himself sharing in the details of an upcoming heist, of being confided in with some entrenched worry, some tactical concern, and envisioned himself reassuring Kings that all would go according to plan, as they almost always did. He pictured another gun on his left hip and a full beard wreathing his face.

With his eyes on the looming Chisos, Kings said, "Been a while since some would-be confederate came along, wantin' to get in the gang, but I will say not a one of 'em ever knocked on our door like you have. Now, if you've studied my escapades as close as you make out, I reckon you know I've never been much for takin' on hands I couldn't swear by." He paused to fix Johnny Blake with a look. "Every one of them ol' boys inside, they know me and I know them."

Johnny nodded, mumbled, "Yessir."

Kings went on. "I can't weigh the truth that's in them dime novels about Gabe Kings and his Avengin' Angels, but we go back to the same skirmishes, most of us, same blood-lettin's of the late war. We can turn our backs to one another without fear of catchin' a ball to the spine. That kind of trust ain't cheaply bought."

He took a crunching step into the grass, and Johnny strode to keep up. "I admire the sand it took for you to ride in here, Johnny, but don't you think of this here as two friends walkin' down a promenade, sippin' whiskey and talkin' 'bout the old days. That ain't what this is."

Kings rounded on him then, and his next words sank deep. "This here's the last we ever speak on the subject of you joinin' up with us. One way or t'other. Understand me?"

"Yessir."

"What I said in there—what we *all* said—still stands. What in the hell makes a kid like you wanna twist John Law's tail and ride with men like us? Life on the farm that damn dull? The gals that ugly where you come from?"

Johnny scuffed his toe in a patch of dirt. "I reckon it was, Mr. Kings, damn dull. And tell you the truth, I can't say as I ever figgered myself for the settlin' down type. Not if it meant turnin' into the man my daddy become. Domesticated. Gutless. Couldn't put his Bible aside to give the Yankees what-for, not even after they burnt down the home place and hanged Uncle Jim from the rafters."

"It wouldn't have brung him back," Kings said.

Scared and feeling condescended to, Johnny Blake summoned a spark of temerity. "No more'n killin' Clive Parker would've got back your birthright, Mr. Kings, you'll pardon my sayin' so."

Kings arched an eyebrow, but it wasn't anger that showed in his face. What it was, Johnny could not suppose, but no bullet came, and he continued, adopting a deferential tone. He spoke of rejecting the future his father intended for him, of lighting out before he could be packed off to the seminary, and of one afternoon in Refuge's Los Toritos Cantina when he'd overheard a regular say that a man with a striking resemblance to Gabriel Kings was known to periodically take up residence at Delilah Young's Pearl Palace.

"So what'd I do but rent out a room and wait. Wait, wait, and wait, till the day I saw you come out the front door. And not a moment too soon, Mr. Kings," he grinned then, "as I'd durn near run outta coin."

Johnny's attempt at charm was lost on Kings, who appeared perturbed. "You could've had a hell of a wait on your hands, boy," he said dryly, dragging on his cigar. "We don't water there all *that* often."

"Hell, I'd've waited till the census, if that's what it took, sir. You're all my daddy wasn't."

Kings frowned at that. "No need to run your pa down any fu'ther, son."

"Well, could ya understand, Mr. Kings, why I weren't too keen to turn back, even after what you told me on the steps of the Pearl Palace?"

"I reckon so," Kings granted. "But I still ain't heard a good enough reason to give you a bunk in one of my cabins. You already proved you got the grit to brave these canyons, and I recall you said you can shoot. Hell, most boys in Texas can."

Johnny shrugged. "I got no place else to go."

"That don't mean you belong here!" Kings's voice rose to a rough pitch as he flung the cigar into the dirt. "You stood where I'm standin' now, boy, you'd know how true that is. Now you best think up a better reason than that, or this conversation's spent."

The words stung. Johnny kept a tight grip on himself but could not meet the outlaw's eye. He had an eerie feeling that his next words might be his last. Spreading his hands, he spoke resolutely. "I've none to offer, Mr. Kings, save that I ain't goin' back, and I ain't settlin' for anythin' short of my purpose. I reckon you're gonna have to kill me here to get shed of me. I only ask, sir, that if that's what you elect to do, you oblige Mr. Brownwell to keep his knife where it's at. Gun me down proper, nice and clean."

The next sound Johnny heard—and it did not come quickly— was not the clicking of a well-oiled gun hammer as it was thumbed back, but a dry snort, followed by an even drier chuckle. "Would that be the same Leroy Brownwell who shot Avelino Duarte from a second-story window down in Presidio?"

Johnny lifted his gaze. Though he'd sounded amused, Kings was not smiling. Would *these* be his last words? "No, sir," he said cautiously, "you can pin that on Dick Osborn. And if I may, I don't believe he could rightly boast about that. Everyone knows that *pistolero* called him out fair and square. What's more, that he could shoot the eye out of a bird flyin', and he didn't see Osborn's shot comin'."

"He should have," Kings said, "but I wouldn't mention that to Dick when you bed down next to him tonight."

Johnny gawped, stunned to silence. Kings stepped on the cigar he'd discarded, then turned and started back through the grass toward the cabins.

CHAPTER 11

The posse arrived at the location of the outlaws' vacated camp by four in the afternoon. Last night's fire, kept small so as not to pinpoint their position in the dark, had been snuffed out by having dirt kicked over it, and nothing but cold ashes remained. Several cigarette stubs were stuck in the sand like white grave markers, and a bottle had been smashed over a nearby rock.

Mincey waited with Delaney while Stringer and Leduc, the more experienced trackers, spread out to assay the landscape. The townsmen congregated together, not fully at ease among the professionals who had recruited them. Under a dark Refuge sky, Stringer had administered the oath, and, while there had been no badges to distribute, each man was required to sign his name at the foot of the crinkled federal commission Stringer passed around. The last of them scarcely had time enough to dot the *i* in his name before the freshly formed posse was in the saddle and riding.

It didn't take long for Stringer and Leduc to discover where the outlaws had picketed their horses. They deliberated for a minute, then walked back to Mincey and Delaney. Only after things had been discussed amongst themselves did Stringer turn to face the civilians. "Surprise, surprise, boys," he said. "Seems our quarry is headed south."

The appointed headman, a heavily bearded freighter named Job Kullander, spoke up. "That mean they're headed for Mexico, Captain?"

"All it means is they're headed south. For now, anyway. They could eventually change their minds and head west for the Big Bend, but we hope to catch up with 'em 'fore they reach that no man's land."

The posse pulled out, with Stringer and Leduc riding point. Even with the dying light of day, the several-hours-old trail was yet discernible. They were able to deduce, by the length between tracks, that the outlaws had galloped their horses steadily for most of those hours, slowing only to a canter before once again resuming the pace. Eventually, and unsurprisingly, the south-bound trail swung—some would say corrected—hard to the west.

Since last night, there had been no moon. It would be the same again tonight, and Stringer wouldn't risk misreading even the clearest sign, no matter how bright the stars. It behooved the men, therefore, to make camp and wait till sunrise.

They dined on jerky and hardtack and washed it down with sugarless coffee. A few of the deputized men, unfamiliar with the sometimes grueling demands of a lawman's work, were heard to mutter and grumble, but, for the most part, pride kept their teeth grit.

After the dregs had been tossed away, Leduc walked off from camp, stopping at the very edge of the firelight. The others were bedding down, but he was soon joined by the captain, who caught his signal. After a moment of contemplation, Leduc posed a question.

"What're you thinkin', sir?"

Stringer studied the tip of his cigarette, his second of the night. "They're runnin' them horses awful hard," he said. "They'll either have a plot to swap for remounts somewhere between here and the Bend, or turn and make a stand. If they decide to fight, we'll shoot it out with 'em, take prisoners if we can, and go from there."

"Hope they decide to fight."

"We'll see about that *mañana.*"

"Who the hell are they?"

Dave Zeller, peering through a worn brass telescope, breathed the question to Tom Seward. The two renegades were perched on a brush-grown rise in the land, Zeller on his belly and Seward kneeling by his side. Their horses were ground-reined several yards down the slope.

The Yankee had caught sight of the dust cloud yesterday. He thought nothing of it at first, but when it reappeared this morning, a wavering dot on the horizon, sweat broke out on his forehead. With the strong prairie wind blowing the way it was, there was no question. Those boys were riding straight up their backsides. Not gaining ground, but not losing any, either.

For the moment, he and Seward held a good enough lead—something like three or four miles. They zigzagged across the land, switching directions every hour or so, testing the path of the distant riders. The pursuers seemed to mirror the outlaws' movements, never once breaking formation.

Now, as he watched them lope ever closer, Zeller squinted through his glass . . . as if squinting harder would define their features any more. It was no use, and he was not about to risk letting them get close enough to see if he could identify any of them. He couldn't make out much—next to nothing, actually, except animal color. Sunlight glinted off what was probably a concho-studded saddle, and, once, he thought he saw a flash of sunlight on one of the men's shirts.

"Damn . . ."

"What is it?" Seward demanded. "What do you see?"

Zeller lowered the telescope an inch. "Looks like one of 'em's wearin' a badge. If one of 'em is, the rest prob'ly is, too."

"Who's got any call to be following us?" Seward said angrily.

"We kept our noses clean in Refuge, didn't we? You didn't even get the chance to even the score with that saloon man."

Zeller couldn't say for sure, but his backbone tingled with a haunting suspicion. The same suspicion had torn at his gut two nights ago in Refuge and forced him to postpone his plan to waylay Spivey outside his joint.

Seward now seemed to suspect the same thing. "Dave? Can you tell if any of 'em is packin' a pearl-handled gun?"

"No, but I'm startin' to get a bad feelin' about that very jasper."

"Hell, it's no wonder he was so interested in us. Damn that I can't resist the offer of a free drink."

"We best get movin'."

Zeller lingered a moment longer, spat an oath, then withdrew.

Alone on the bluff, Seward shook his head. "Satan's fire . . . who the hell are they?"

Stringer and Leduc were on their stomachs at the edge of a drop overlooking a watering hole. The gradual slope to their right led down thirty or forty yards, down to where the water lay with a thick growth of mesquite and cactus all around. The desert was quiet with the coming of night, save for the calling of an unseen dove.

As the rangers examined the scene below, the others kept watch on the perimeter. All was absolutely still, but the tracks leading down the grade were clear as day. So, too, were the imprints of the hooves and boot-soles down by the water's edge.

Stringer broke the silence. "Looks dead as a Christmas goose down there."

"Reckon they're onto us?"

"Men like these don't last long without some kind of sixth sense. 'Course, with a posse this size, you'd be hard-put *not* to notice our dust."

"One thing's for sure—*some*body's been down there, and there was only two of 'em. Question's whether they still are."

"Yep."

"Wouldn't bet they stuck around, though," Leduc reasoned. "We got 'em outnumbered, and, nine times outta ten, this kind would rather run than fight."

"You never know."

They waited a few minutes more, searching for any other signs, any movement in the thicket beyond. Finding none, the rangers retreated.

"We're on the right track," Stringer informed the team. He turned and made a halfhearted gesture in the direction of the seemingly peaceful watering hole. "No sign of life down there, but they could be layin' low, waitin' for us to get comfortable and ride into a bushwhack." He shot a line of spittle into the dirt. "Then again, they could still be kickin' it for their hideout. No way to know for certain."

Before mounting up, the lawmen selected three self-professed crack shots to accompany them down there, and the rest would remain atop the bluff until they received the signal to come ahead. These crack shots were Kullander the freighter, Jensen the liveryman, and Thompson the shopkeeper. Sitting lightly in his saddle, Stringer led the way down the slope, followed by Leduc, then the Pinkertons, and, finally, the townsmen. Every man in the company was exhausted, but even as Stringer steered toward the watering hole they held themselves alert, conscious of the fact that they could, just as the captain said, be riding into an ambush.

The riders halted at the edge of the watering hole but fanned out so as not to cluster and offer better targets for whomever might be hiding in the mesquite. Guns at the ready, the posse-men watched as Stringer got down, Winchester in hand, to more closely inspect the marks left behind in the hard-packed earth. He squatted, looking down and sideways at the hoof-prints, with the barrel of his rifle trained on the grove.

"Cap!"

He heard Leduc's shout a split second after he caught the glint of gunmetal from the thicket. Two heavy reports echoed, one on the heels of the other, and Stringer felt the air pop as an outlaw bullet snatched his hat from his head. The second shot, snapped in haste from his side of the firing, gave the captain enough time to plunge face-first, rifle and all, into the muddy-beige water to his left. Holding in a shallow breath, Stringer kicked blindly for the other side.

The others dismounted quickly and scrambled for cover. Leduc threw down behind a shoulder of rock, and the Pinkertons managed to find room behind a snarl of rotted timber and scrub. The townsmen hung back, hugging the ground as the firing intensified from within the grove. Though caught in the open, the lawmen made it through the first barrage in one piece and were soon returning fire.

Leduc kept his eye on the water, concern for his captain outweighing his instinct to join the fight. The only movement came from the near side, the ripples and roiling mud showing where Stringer dove in. Leduc wondered if he might have hit his head on a stone below the surface, but then, like some aquatic monster, the hatless shape of Caleb Stringer breached, flopping onto the far embankment with rifle still in hand. He might have been a sitting duck if the outlaws had the luxury of ignoring the larger force directly before them, but Stringer was instantly on his feet, falling into some brush at the far edge of the thicket. Then he was up again, like a jack-in-the-box, levering three rounds from his Winchester on the diagonal. The outlaws were as good as surrounded.

The fight wore on, the possemen now firing steadily into the trees from two angles. After a few more minutes of gunplay, the area fell silent as both factions paused to reload. There was the strangely calming sound of rotating cylinders and fresh cartridges clinking into place. Somewhere in the background, one of the scattered animals whinnied in fear and was echoed by another.

Leduc took advantage of the brief ceasefire to call across the water. "You all right?"

"I'm good!" Stringer shouted back and then hushed up. Wouldn't do to mark his position too neatly . . .

Darkness was encroaching, visibility worsening, and with it, the accuracy of every combatant. From experience Leduc knew a stalemate could last hours. Just as easily, and perhaps more likely, those rascals could abandon their plinking and slink off before he and the others had a chance to rally. Inching toward the edge of the rock face, he decided to risk a peek and was almost immediately blinded by the muzzle flash of a man who stepped out to the side of a Y-shaped tree trunk.

From his side of the firing, Leduc heard the unmistakable, meaty sound of a bullet striking flesh, followed by a scream. Leduc didn't have time to look and see who had been hit—he had an opening and had to take it.

He swung like a gate, sighted down the barrel, cranked off two quick shots. The renegade forty yards away jerked left and right from the impact. A third bullet, fired by Stringer at a forty-five-degree angle, blew him clean off his feet.

As suddenly as it had commenced, the fighting was over. First it was quiet, then the possemen heard the pounding of outlaw hooves, one horse and one rider, fading into the closing night.

As it turned out, it was Jensen who caught the bullet. A shoulder wound was no laughing matter, but the way he carried on, he may as well have been gut-shot. When the time came to dig out the lead and cauterize the injury, his friends got him good and drunk. The liveryman promptly passed out anyway, and it was a relief to everyone involved.

Water was warmed for coffee and a fire lit. Crowding close with a blanket about his shoulders, Stringer joked that, in view of the state of his hat, things would be getting drafty for his old scalp. Kullander and Thompson were treated as heroes by their fellows, and, despite the fact that one of the renegades had made off, there was a feeling of accomplishment in camp.

They had shown two members of the Kings gang that, as opponents in the game of death, they could not be taken lightly, and by the glare of a match the dead man in the thicket was positively identified as Tom Seward.

Stringer and Mincey agreed that, although the remaining outlaw, who could only have been Dave Zeller, had a good head start on them, he couldn't get far, mounted as he was on a winded horse.

The trail would be fresh as dew come the morning.

With the watering hole miles behind him in what was now full dark, Zeller dismounted under a lone tree to let his lathered mare blow. He wasn't faring much better, but would have happily traded what he got for a pair of flaming lungs. Midway through the exchange of lead he'd taken a bullet in the right thigh. Luckily, it had missed the artery, penetrating mostly fat. As it was, the bandana he'd used as a temporary tourniquet was soaked through. He was glad for the coolish night—the colder it got, the harder it was for him to feel anything at all, but the blood that continued to stream down his leg and into his boot was an uncomfortable reminder.

Turning up the collar of his sheepskin, he sat down to think. He didn't figure those lawdogs would pursue him now, with no moon to light the way. He was willing to bet they would camp till the morning, cocksure of themselves in light of their victory.

Hell of a victory. Seven on two. Zeller spat with disgust and hit his own boot.

Seward was dead, and he was going to miss that sophisticated little cuss. Kings would take the news hard, no doubt.

As he washed the blood from his leg with canteen water, he muttered aloud, perhaps to his mare, perhaps to himself, "I don't plan on gettin' stretched."

Another fight was out of the question. Taking a detour would be the best thing. Come first light, he would mount up and lead these boys on a wild goose chase for as long as he could. Take them far away from Kings and the others, and, if possible, give them the slip.

Zeller drew a hip flask from his pocket and muttered, "I know this country, dammit." He threw a little whiskey on the wound, inhaled sharply, and cursed the posse to the hottest hell. When he caught his breath, he drank deeply, wincing from the pain as another wave surged through him.

Zeller thought back to the minute before the shooting started, as he and Seward watched the lawmen ride into their hastily planned and poorly executed ambush. Tom had turned his face, drawn and burnt by sun and wind, toward Zeller and, for the first time in twelve years, abandoned his book-learned grammar.

"These ain't exactly the best odds, Dave. Gotta hope for some kind of damn miracle."

Ten minutes later, he was dead in the dirt, never again to see the green lawns and apple orchards of Roanoke.

Yankee Dave stared into the darkness. Any man could have the wool pulled over his eyes. He just needed to work a little miracle, like Tom said, and those boys would be chasing dust devils to God knows where.

CHAPTER 12

The waning crescent moon hung like an empty, silvery rocking chair above the rolling scrubland that encompassed the town of Agave Seco. Spawned and supported by cattle and sheep ranchers, the settlement lay smack in an area once thought inhabitable only by scorpions, coyotes, and the Comanche. Tonight it lay quiet, dimly lit with streets sparsely populated.

As the small hours of this balmy Sunday evening crept toward Monday, two riders walked their horses east through the scrub. An observer might have thought they'd swapped horses somewhere back along the trail, as the rider on the left seemed almost a child in the saddle of a large roan gelding that dwarfed his partner's lean-hipped *grullo*.

Three others had already entered town limits from the north—three riders, four horses—and were presently passing a carpenter's on their way down Main Street. The trio consisted of Brownwell, Yeager, and Woods, who led John Reb by the reins. Brownwell, riding between the other two, let his eyes roam, seeking out movement but finding none. All was quiet, all was well. Now, if Kings had gotten where he needed to be, ascertained what he needed to ascertain, then the job was halfway done.

Finally, the three reached the depository. Brownwell swung down first but paused a moment to look around and ensure that they had gone unnoticed. It wasn't common, after all, for three men to be stopping by the bank so long before opening.

Down the street a ways, Brownwell saw that Osborn and Johnny Blake had taken their positions on opposite sides. Dick was on the left, huddling with his horse between a shoe shop and an apothecary, and the kid was on the right, between a wheelwright's and a smaller, boarded-up building. One thing Brownwell couldn't quite discern was the cast of Blake's features. It was just as well—he didn't want to contemplate what-all might happen if the kid let his nerves get the better of him.

Brownwell still wasn't anywhere near at ease around Johnny Blake, but he wouldn't go so far as to fathom that all that buttering-up had been done just to make a name for himself by putting a bullet behind Kings's ear. A man could lie like a rug to achieve whatever ends he sought, but the worshipful light that came into the kid's eyes when Kings reined in alongside him the first day out, or when he'd reached across the fire last night to refill the kid's coffee cup . . . Well, there weren't many outside a Memphis painted lady who could counterfeit that.

And yet, even as Brownwell finished hitching his horse outside the bank, the rankling thought came again—why the hell had Kings let the boy come along? This was a job for men, and he'd never been one for taking on disciples before.

Brownwell had been unable to get a straight answer. The old Gabriel Kings, who would have let light shine through a challenger for a look he didn't like, might have tied this kid to a tree or whupped him till the homestead seemed like New Jerusalem, then sent him a-running. Not so long ago, he might have had the stomach for that sort of business. But, as Kings had noted and as Brownwell had to allow, there was something to be said of a fellow who would ride blindly into the labyrinthine canyons called home by the Avenging Angels, just to repeat a question that had already been answered . . .

"Trouble in here."

Spooked, Brownwell whirled, hand on his gun. He saw that the left-hand door had been eased open from the inside, and it was Kings speaking from the darkness. "Let's go."

Brownwell decided he could puzzle over the acceptance of Johnny Blake some other time. Leaving Yeager and Woods to stand guard, he unlimbered a sack from his saddle horn, which clinked and rustled faintly as it moved. Though he was by no means a safecracker of Tom Seward's caliber, Brownwell possessed enough basic knowledge to feel confident wielding the sundry tools presently in his care. But what was this, now, about trouble?

Mounting the raised platform, he shuffled past Kings into the bank, crossed the lobby, and vaulted lightly over the high counter. The door to the narrow closet that served as a vault in the rear of the building stood ajar, Kings having broken the hasp minutes before, and as Brownwell moved in he made out a black, stove-sized safe.

Even in the poor light, something about it made him hesitate. He extended a hand and ran it down the side of the durable cast-iron frame, the action almost reverential, but Brownwell's brow creased as he realized this was not the lockbox he had expected.

Kings's cautious footsteps were marked only by the faint chiming of his spurs. "I know," he said, reading the set of Brownwell's shoulders as easily as a man reads a face. "It's a beefy sonovabitch."

"And it's new," Brownwell said shortly. "I don't think I brung enough sticks to blow this door off."

Kings scraped a match along the underside of his boot, then removed the globe from a lamp he found on the counter. He touched the flame to the wick, let it catch, and set the lamp beside Brownwell to be positioned at his convenience. The light glittered over the raised lettering of the manufacturer's stamp, playing off the dull gleam of the safe door and its blunt, resolute dial. It veritably mocked the men who knelt before it.

"I can try and crack 'er," Brownwell suggested, speaking to himself as much as to Kings.

Kings turned his head, spat on the floor. "Get to it, then. Failin' that, we're gonna have to blow it. Door doesn't come off all the way, we can use our guns to do the rest of the negotiatin'."

"Dick failed to mention this after his reconnoiter," Brownwell said, unknotting the throat of the sack.

Kings was frustratingly calm. "Said they kept the vault closed, remember? Four hours of watchin', and not a one of them tellers ever needed somethin' from the vault."

On the street, Dick Osborn thought he heard something. He bent an ear to the stillness of the air—straining, willing the noise to sound again. When it finally did, he identified it with confidence as nothing more than an old tomcat, yowling halfheartedly as it slunk along the boardwalk opposite. Dick let his breath slide free, and the tensed muscles of his face relaxed in the faint glow of his cigarette.

Across the way, Johnny Blake's knuckles were white from gripping his carbine so tightly. His eyes, having failed to locate the true source before it disappeared into a cluster of crates, darted to and fro like minnows, covering every dark corner, every false front, and every window for witnesses that weren't there.

Watching him, Osborn shook his head. The nerves were finally getting to the kid. Jittery as he was, if his horse so much as farted he was apt to squeeze off a shot, and that was one thing Osborn didn't need. He hissed at Johnny, went unheard, then tried waving an arm to get his attention. Johnny's head and shoulders turned, and for an instant Osborn thought he might be on the receiving end of that accidental shot. When no bullet came, Osborn exhaled and motioned for the kid to breathe easier.

Within the bank, Brownwell had started the work. The Missourian sat cross-legged, shoulders forward, with a binaural stethoscope in his ears and one hand steadily, imperceptibly moving the dial one tick this way, then that, then back again. No one knew how Seward had first come by this instrument, which had not yet been universally fine-tuned and was hard enough to come by in the Old South of a decade past, let alone the Hoot-Owl. It seemed fitting, however, that the scope had been made by Fergusun's, London, and that it would be used to crack a safe made by Edward Tann & Sons, London.

The work was tedious, not for the faint of heart or short of patience. Every passing second elevated the threat of discovery, but this was the only way. There was no bank teller on duty to whose head a gun could be pressed and no manager to open the safe for them. Though far from ideal, and not a feature of the original plan, this method was preferable to a full-fledged dynamiting. Brute force, with the type of attention it drew, would be their very last resort tonight.

Kings was by the door, keeping an eye on the street and the men in it. He had passed through here once before, more than a year ago, studying, noticing, sometimes sketching the physical layout of this place, its dimensions, its geography. Just as importantly, he had taken stock of the population. As a general rule, the citizens were a hardened and rawboned bunch, and many of them good shots. Most folks hereabouts were like that—by necessity, if nothing else—and so Kings had been obliged, prior to arrival, to enlighten the boys as to this truth.

It was one of the first lessons he'd learned, having veered off the straight and narrow—that when a man does that, he marks himself, oftentimes for life, as an enemy of the people. And in a place like Texas, the people were to be respected, if not feared. Only a handful had not turned their backs to him and his men, and he intended to pay that handful a visit very soon. Provided they made it out of here in one piece . . .

Brownwell sat back suddenly with a bitter oath. He rolled his shoulders, cricked his neck, then leaned back into it. That wasn't a good sign. The task required discipline, precision, and already, not even an hour in, the cussing had started. The bank clock ticked slowly, and Kings sighed. He caught an inquiring look from Yeager through the glass and signaled that it wouldn't be much longer.

Light began to break over the rooftops. By now, even Kings's inhuman composure had weakened a bit, though one would have to look hard to see it in him. He'd twice had to rub the slight dampness of his palm on his trouser leg, but otherwise, his expression was stony, his eyes lifeless. Brownwell had cursed twice more, and twice Kings had stepped over for a closer look. Despite his aggravation, the Missourian was working deliberately, but that was the nature of safecracking. The clicks on the other side of the heavy door were faint, and the mechanisms anything but precise.

Glancing at the bank clock, Kings estimated that Brownwell had been working for nearly ninety minutes. Another thirty and the sun would be up. He looked to the vault, saw his man stretch one leg out to massage a cramp, and decided it was time.

"Leroy?"

Brownwell looked over his shoulder, still rubbing.

"Blow it."

Brownwell used all he brought, and, when the sticks had been properly situated, the fuses joined, Kings tapped on the front window. He gave Yeager a thumbs-up, and the gesture was returned. Kings waited until Woods had stepped down to ensure the security of the tied horses before he gave Brownwell the go-ahead. The Missourian raised the lamp and lit the fuse, then sprang over the counter and lay flat, eyes level with Kings and the dust motes.

The peace of earliest morning was shattered in the explosion. Dull echoes spiraled across the street, trailed closely by the sound of glass raining down from window panes broken by the uncontained blast.

Brownwell was right—it hadn't been enough to take the door completely off its hinges, but he and Kings fired a round each into the right spots and watched with satisfaction as the door tumbled loose. Coughing harshly, Brownwell stood to one side, holding the tool sack open as Kings squatted to peer in.

All he saw were four banded sheaves of greenbacks, probably no more than $3,000, and six coin trays, mainly in silver. He wasted no time filling the sack, then went through the drawers. What he found, he took.

From farther up the street there was the sound of return fire. The kid had mounted, but his big red horse was frantic, fighting the reins, which meant that Johnny's carbine may as well have been a cork-gun. Woods had spurred off to lay down cover fire for Osborn, who was fumbling with his stirrup. When Osborn finally swung aboard, he turned his *grullo* back into the welcoming maw of the alleyway. Woods and Blake followed.

The criminals branched off in two separate directions. Kings, Yeager, and Brownwell charged down Main Street, attracting most of the civilian gunfire, while Woods, Osborn, and Johnny skirted the buildings by way of the alley, drawing fire only once.

They regrouped once they cleared town and rode east. A few more shots rang out after them, but the distant puffs of smoke were as threatening as dandelion tufts against the lightening sky.

To preserve the strength of their animals, the gang slowed to a canter. After a bit of riding Kings twisted in the saddle to do a head count and saw that Brownwell and Yeager were close behind. Woods followed by a few lengths on the right wing, and Osborn was on the left. In the rear, Blake was slowing, his posture slackening. With a frown, Kings reined to the side and saw the kid's shirtfront darkening with blood.

It was then that the men witnessed a heretofore unseen sight. Gabriel Kings, with a look of dread, kicked free of the stirrups, practically leaping to catch the sagging body of the dying youth and ease him gently to the scrubby ground.

The bullet had entered just below the right shoulder blade, probably tearing through the lung before exiting out the boy's chest. Kings said his name, was forced to repeat it, and Johnny's eyes focused on him. The corners of his mouth raised in one last smile.

"Mr. Kings," the boy said as a line of blood ran down his chin. He groaned. "Oh, God, what—? Why does it hu—hurt—?"

"Don't talk so much, kid," Kings told him. "It'll pass soon."

The column had done an about-face, horses rearranged in a defensive semi-circle. Some of the townies were sure to pursue, at least for a few miles, so the men sat their mounts with eyes and guns at the ready. For the moment, though, there was no sign of life from Agave Seco.

Woods dismounted to kneel beside Kings and Blake. As the band's de facto surgeon, he felt he ought to at least examine the back-shot youngster, but, like Kings, he recognized immediately that all was lost. The blood told the story, and it wouldn't be worth the agony to unbutton the kid's shirt and turn him over. Frowning, Woods shook his head at Kings.

He may have been dying, but Blake caught the silent exchange. He looked up at Kings and managed another few words. "Sh-shame I'll never get to see them canyons again. They was some sight."

As the boy bled out in the sparse grass, Kings could not but wonder at the clench in his gut. He had looked down on the face of many a dead man—and many a dead *young* man, torn and shot to doll rags on the field of battle. But this was different. This time around, it had been Kings himself who put the pen and paper in the hand of another, not some tasseled-and-starched, pencil-pushing officer. He couldn't answer for those good Virginia boys, whose faces, in the end, had gone grayer than the uniforms they wore, but he knew that ultimately, the blood on this particular boy's shirt belonged where it was—on his hands.

Before Kings could find the right words, articulate the right apology, the familiar sound of a death rattle rose from within the chest of John Allen Blake. His eyes slowly widened, his pupils unfocused, and life left him in one long sigh.

For a moment, the boy looked to be at peace, and silence settled over the scene. Even the town that lay behind them, roiling in chaos minutes before, had fallen quiet. There were no shots, no shouts, no galloping horses. At the moment, there was absolutely nothing.

Nevertheless, Kings heard Brownwell's anxious pitch. "Gabe, they'll be gettin' themselves together. We gotta move."

Kings spoke flatly into deafened ears: "Agave'll bury you better'n we can, kid." Then he stood and returned to his waiting stallion. He gathered the reins, and, in the time it took for him to sweep his leg up, over, and into the stirrup, he reverted—once again stoic and unfeeling.

He was a man acquainted with death, after all, and his inner voice echoed Brownwell's—tracks had to be made; they oughtn't to dally.

As black ants began to speckle the hands of Johnny Blake, Gabriel Kings gave his horse the spurs and loped ahead into the new dawn.

CHAPTER 13

The East Frio River country was an area with which a man like Arthur Jackson could fall madly in love. He left the South twenty-four years ago, seeking to build a new life for his young family on an unclaimed stretch of land on this branch of the Frio, but it would be three more years before the Jacksons finally settled in the truest sense of the word. At the time, the Mexican government and its people were still reeling from their territorial and economic losses at the hands of the U.S. Army—an army from which Jackson himself had only recently been discharged—and Indian raiding parties kept the oncoming wave of settlers more or less at bay. Strong men had withered and died in that country long before the Jacksons ever set down wagon-tracks there, and of the five children born to Arthur and his wife, Martha, they'd buried three between 1857 and '61. But Jackson was one of those who preferred to look his problems in the eye, and against the odds, he came out a winner.

He'd had a mind to breed and sell horses in the land of Texas, and with him he brought a hearty stallion and three spirited mares of good stock. Within a year, his small herd had multiplied to seven. Another year passed, and the number increased again. The next year, a clan of nomadic Irish horse traders supplied two mares and a tall black stallion of Hunter blood to the ranks of Jackson's remuda, and so it had gone.

That encounter with the Irish had been over twenty years ago. Now, the herd numbered upwards of three hundred animals—some of American blood, some of Irish, some of Indian mustang ancestry—all of them free to roam and graze on over five hundred acres of grass, drink from the cold waters of the Frio, and rest under shady copses of pecan and live oak trees.

It was the closest thing to heaven Jackson had ever seen. The Comanche threat had by now been handily subdued, thanks to the combined efforts of the Texas Rangers and the army, with frontier ranchers like Jackson doing their small part as well. There were still periodic brushes with American rustlers and Mexican bandits, but since long before the Civil War it had become common knowledge in that part of the country that if you had your sights set on thieving Jackson horseflesh, you better be able to shoot. The men he employed certainly could, and they shot to wound, because Jackson preferred to settle grievances in the old-timers' fashion—by hanging.

As a major in Zachary Taylor's Army of Occupation, Jackson had slung a saber through a mass of Mexican infantry, screaming like a man possessed. He had held and aimed a rifle that brought down stock thieves on the fly, and he had plaited the rope that sent a good deal of those thieves kicking into the next world. But as hard and unforgiving as he could be, Major Jackson was proud of the fact that he had done a fair job in raising his children.

His youngest and only surviving son, Titus, was a handsome man of nineteen who could have ridden into Austin and had his pick of any of the pretty women there, like apples from a tree. A first-rate horseman, a fine shot, and with a sharp mind, he would be ready to take a more prominent role in his father's business in another year or so.

The Old Man's success in raising such an admirable son came from the practice he'd had in raising an admirable daughter, although his wife had objected—more than once—to the style of her upbringing.

Taught the way of the horse and bridle before the way of the needle and loom, Belle could ride like the wind, and, if it came down to it, she could shoot just as well. Whenever she took her early morning ride down to the banks of the Frio, her prized Winchester rifle went with her. With that same rifle she had consistently proven herself a finer long-distance shot than even her brother.

Yet withal, she was as much a lady as her mother. There could be no question, given the number of promising young bachelors who had darkened their door at one time or another, but all of Martha Jackson's hopes for grandchildren had been dashed time and again as the major scared each of these suitors away. None of them had been good enough for his daughter, and, apparently, Belle was of the same mind. She'd never shown much interest in any of them and had turned down more secret proposals and offers of elopement than either of her parents knew.

Recent years brought the major to the realization that he might have turned away one boy too many. Belle was now cresting the ridge on twenty-seven, was unmarried, and had a mother convinced she was doomed to perpetual spinsterhood.

The one man Martha had ever caught Belle looking at with any admiration was the one man on God's earth with whom she could never be partnered. But those had been glances cast on the sly, the kind seventeen-year-old girls were apt to cast on much older, intangible, and handsome men. Thankfully, Gabriel Kings had never acknowledged or returned those glances . . . so far as Mrs. Jackson knew.

Her husband's time- and battle-tested friendship with Jonathan Kings was what garnered his sympathy for Gabriel and his desperate band. For a criminal, Gabriel Kings was a damned fine man. Jackson always thought he would have made Belle a fine husband, had he entered into another profession.

Unfortunate, is what it was. One night, Jackson had said as much to his wife, and, although she gasped at the moment, she went on to wonder at how beautiful their grandchildren would have been.

Unfortunate . . .

Even more unfortunate was that as each day came to an end, Belle Jackson went to sleep praying for Kings's safe return, in full knowledge that her prayers were unlikely to receive an answer. Every time he rode away, she knew she might never see him again. The thought that calmed her enough to let her sleep was that, like a bad penny, Kings always turned up, and she clung to that promise.

Funny thing was, she didn't recognize him when he did turn up again.

A year and three months had passed since she last saw his face, and *still* she didn't recognize him.

She was watching, on horseback, at a distance of three hundred yards from the cover of a small grove, as five horsemen meandered through the hills toward her very location. Even through her daddy's old spyglass, Belle couldn't make out any of the men's faces, but by the slump of their bodies they appeared to be dog-tired. Their horses moved at an uninspired walk, heads bobbing level with their shoulders, showing they had put some miles behind them. She waited uncertainly, reins drawn tight in her left hand and murmuring words of comfort to her fussing sorrel mare.

The Winchester was in its scabbard, beneath her right calf, its stock canted upward in the perfect snatching position. But to draw the rifle now, even as a precaution, would be mighty unwise. Who could say what the horsemen were apt to do if they happened to glance around and catch a flash of light off the dark steel?

There was no wind and no obstructions before her. With her sights raised and a bead on, she was confident she could ventilate a tomato can from a hundred yards. A man on a moving horse was another target entirely, and she didn't know what breed of man these might be.

Belle decided she had lingered long enough. She turned her horse, slapped heels to flanks, and went tearing down the path for the ranch house.

The mare was young and loved to run and carried her rider back along the curving trail to their destination in no time. Lounging by the holding pens were Belle's brother and the two ranch hands, smoking cigarettes. The hounds, Dauntless and Peerless, prowled nearby—lazy sentries—but at the sound of galloping hooves, they loped back to the pens, barking as they came.

John Bevans was the foreman, a native Texan and seasoned rangeman who had helped the major transform a stretch of hell into a second Eden. Rawboned and gray-haired, he glanced up as Belle pulled in her mount. Bevans hurried over, helped her down, and demanded of the girl who was practically his niece, "You all right, Sis? What's the matter?"

"*¿Bandidos?*" asked Fernando Elías, the stocky *mesteñero* from south of the river.

"Doesn't look like it." Belle shook her head, out of breath. "Five men, look like they've covered some country."

"Seem like a threat?" Titus asked.

Again, she shook her head. "Looked like a strong wind could put 'em all in the dirt, and their animals didn't look much better." She paused to frown. "Didn't look like they were hurtin' for weapons, though."

Titus kept his eyes on the horizon, backpedaling toward the house. "Awright," he said. "Belle, you come with me."

She held back to unlimber her Winchester, then started ahead of him as he turned to the others and said, "You boys stay out here and watch for 'em to come in. Y'all got your pistols with ye?"

Bevans's belt was hanging on the post of the main gate, and Fernando's was located not far off. They quickly buckled them on, loosening the rawhide thongs that secured the pistols in their holsters. Bevans was no gunman, Fernando even less so, but they had fought off enough adversaries to call themselves survivors, and could stall, if they had to, until reinforcements came.

Titus knew better than to shoo his big sister into the house, but he didn't want her exposed too much in the yard. He went in to fetch their father, while Belle took up a defensive position on the wraparound veranda. Resting her rifle across the railing, she knelt behind its long barrel with the butt tight in the nook of her shoulder.

"You still there, Sis?" Bevans called out, without turning around.

"I am, John, and I ain't goin' anywhere."

"That's the way I'd have it," the foreman called back.

Thus encouraged, Belle felt the ten pounds of untested steel and wood in her hands lighten considerably.

Inside, Titus cleared the parlor in three bounding strides and charged up the staircase to his father's study. There he found the major bent over his desk, nose inches from the pages of his business ledger. Jackson was a lean but large-framed and striking man who, if so inclined, could intimidate like the Angel of Death, but when he twisted in his seat to peer over the rims of his spectacles, the Old Man looked no more intimidating than the average notary.

"Titus," he said. "What's got you lathered up?"

"Got riders comin' in, Pa."

Off came the spectacles, and the man behind them seemed transformed. Pursing his lips to draw the fringes of his elegant tawny mustache together with the top of his Van Dyke beard, Arthur Jackson stood up and was suddenly six inches taller than his son. "They seem friendly or foe-like?" he asked, heading for the stairs.

"Belle reports they look well-armed," Titus replied, "though she mighta been hasty in thinkin' they could mean trouble. Still . . ."

As father and son traversed the parlor, Martha Jackson emerged from the kitchen. She was flanked by two small, sloe-eyed girls, daughters of the Spanish-looking Fernando and his *mestiza* wife, Oralia. The lady of the house motioned for them to stay put, then gathered her skirts and traced the course of her menfolk as far as the doorway.

Bevans and Fernando were waiting at the foot of the steps, facing outward, and Jackson strode out between them with Titus close behind. The hounds were farther out in the yard, pacing and huffing at the scent of the newcomers. From the threshold, Martha noticed her daughter and hissed at her to put her gun away—for God's sake—and get inside immediately. But Mrs. Jackson's authority went unacknowledged today. Belle didn't so much as flinch at her mother's command, much less lower her sights.

If he had felt any of the apprehension his people evidently did, the Old Man would have been relieved when his eyes touched on the lead horseman. As it was, he was surprised that no one had recognized Kings. At the very least, they should have known his horse—John Reb had been foaled in their very barn.

Moments behind the major, John Bevans chuckled, "Aw, hell," and reached out to good-naturedly slap his Mexican coworker on the shoulder. Fernando, nearsighted as he was, kept his hand hovering above his gun. Only when he recognized Kings's all too familiar saddle-posture did he relax, and the fluid dismount drove in the final peg.

Por cierto, aquí era un amigo. If nothing else, Fernando admired the way Kings sat a horse.

Belle recognized that dismount as well, and her heart leapt. Standing, she looked on as her father received the incomers, calling off the hounds that obediently retreated to the veranda steps. Kings came foremost, and the two tall Virginians met in the middle of the yard to shake hands. Neither were particularly sentimental men, but by the hold of their shoulders, the strength of their grips, it was plain to see that they were genuinely glad to see each other.

There was an unintelligible exchange of words, and then Kings looked toward the veranda. Their eyes met, and Belle—who had done her growing on an untamed prairie, done things few women of her day had ever done, and had the gumption to rival any man—felt her knees turn to jelly.

Nearby, Fernando's oldest daughter, Teresa, was tugging on Mrs. Jackson's dress, crying with excitement, *"¡Es el Señor Reyes, el Señor Reyes!"* It wasn't long before Sofía, the younger, picked up the chant.

It was a suitable enough distraction for Belle, who feared that her feelings would be found out if she stayed on the veranda a second longer. Resting her rifle against the railing, she swept past her mother in the doorway and took both girls' hands in hers. *"Vamos, chicas,"* she said, then shifted back to English in a way that was common for that region. "Why'n't you go upstairs and practice your weavin'?"

Disappointed but taught well by her mother to mind her elders, Teresa led her sister upstairs. Belle waited until she heard the door close before moving again. Hands at her waist, she steadied herself, breathed deeply, then stepped into the kitchen.

Oralia, olive-skinned and lovely, was spreading flour for tortillas. She looked up with a gentle but knowing smile at the clicking of *la Señorita* Belle's boots.

"Let's move, Oralia," *la Señorita* said. "We've got hungry men comin'."

The Jacksons' masterfully crafted cherry-wood dining room table had survived a bumpy trip out from Lexington, as had the missus's china and silverware, and out of a household of nine, it sat ten. That night, the Elías family hung around long enough for Oralia to finish laying out the settings, then retired to their separate quarters, partially to make room for the five extra mouths, but also to quietly nurse their youngest, who had suddenly complained of an upset stomach.

With the hounds circling the table, hoping for morsels to be tossed their way, the Jacksons and their guests ate well, and the conversation was pleasant enough, though it moved at a rather halting pace. The major had the run of it but never dominated or talked down at anyone who might not have been as knowledgeable as he. He was by nature a quiet sort of man—very similar, his daughter had come to realize, to the man she loved. The discussion turned from horseflesh to Indian matters, skirting around the recent bloodshed in Lincoln County, New Mexico, then settling on the patenting of the phonograph by Mr. Edison. How fascinating and strange it would be, they thought, once the invention went into mass production, for a family to hear a brass band or string quartet in their own house.

"Way I see it," Brownwell said from the far end of the table, "you can keep your phonographs. We never needed none of them back home for some fine music."

Talk was then given over to the yellow fever epidemic that was wracking the Mississippi River Valley and had thus far claimed over twelve thousand lives, a statistic that caused Mrs.

Jackson to cover her mouth with her napkin in horror and implore the menfolk to abstain from such talk at the dinner table.

Her son loudly overruled her in the next breath, saying, "The Quarantine Act's got everythin' south of New Orleans sealed up good and tight, but it's them blamed mosquitoes they got to worry about. They seem to be doin' more damage down there than anything."

This statement elicited another shudder from his mother and a balled-up napkin thrown in his face by his father.

"Was there much threat of contractin' that particular affliction in the war?" Bevans asked, looking across the table at Kings. "Reason I ask is, I had a cousin who died of—well, I had a cousin who died of disease in '63, but it weren't yella fever."

Kings looked up from smearing butter on a biscuit. "Not so much as catchin' typhoid or dysentery," he said, then added with a sideward glance, "but I believe that's all I hafta say on that, John. Like to turn my stomach, and I wouldn't want to waste this fine meal."

From his seat at the head of the table, Major Jackson studied Gabriel Kings closely. It occurred to him that although the man's exhaustion showed clearly in his face and bearing, he was better-looking than his father had been, and Jonathan Kings had cut a fine figure before pleurisy sent him to a premature grave the third winter of the war. His wife, Gabriel's mother, followed within a month—of grief, it was said.

After the dishes were cleared away, the men repaired to the veranda to smoke. Yeager, Woods, and Osborn did not linger but made a beeline for the barn and its loft, where they would all be bedding down. Brownwell humored Kings for half an hour but kept quiet, content to pick his teeth and spit. He excused himself when Titus started to speak of how the railroad barons were making money hand over fist, and what a grand thing it was, to see that sort of progress being made.

Eventually, the men of the ranch said their good-nights and turned in, leaving Kings alone to burn down his cigar. After just a few hours, he was already beginning to feel better. Looking out into the darkness, coat buttoned to the collar, he allowed his mind to empty and his spirit to become saturated with the lovely peace of the late hour.

Wind blew in gently from the south, carrying with it the smell of the Frio. A bat fluttered by, chasing insects. In the outlying darkness, Kings heard corralled horses moving. He imagined the ghosts of Stuart's magnificent cavalry racing across the moonlit plain, galloping toward an unseen enemy.

Inevitably, painfully, that conjured charge into a fantastical field of glory came up short against the memory of Yellow Tavern. Then Yellow Tavern melded like blood and water with Agave Seco, and Kings saw Johnny Blake's sparsely whiskered face graying by the second all over again.

It was not an image he wished to cling to, but neither did it grieve him beyond bearing. He simply saw the dead boy's face, clearer than the gnarls in the wood of the railing before him, and made no effort to force it from his mind.

Who knows how long it would have stayed there had Belle Jackson not crept onto the veranda shortly after midnight, gentling the cloth-screened door shut behind her so as not to wake the house. She had a patchwork quilt about her shoulders, the edges of which trailed down to shapely white ankles that disappeared into lavender slippers. By contrast, her heart-shaped face and slender neck were flushed from the girlish thrill that came with biting the apple, and her bright-blue eyes—china-blue, to be exact, with flecks of brown ringing the pupil—were a dazzling, mystifying mosaic.

"Good evening, Miss Jackson," he said. It was the second time he'd addressed her directly since his arrival.

"Good evening, Mr. Kings."

With what her mother would have scorned as shameless audacity, she went and allowed him to take her onto his lap. She felt a tremendous security there, a greater ease than she had felt in over a year and could never experience anywhere else.

Their affair was almost a strain, the kind that makes both lovers, at their weakest, regret ever speaking to one another. It brought pain when miles separated them, but perhaps an even greater pain when they were as close as they were now.

Belle had a smart head on her shoulders. She knew the major would never approve of her taking the name of Kings, and when she let herself dream, she realized that, if by some miracle she and Gabriel ever *did* enter into holy matrimony, she would be forced to live as no loving wife should. He himself had told her that more than once. She would exist with the constant dread of assassins peeking through the cracked doors of her own home and pace the floor with worry if he ever stayed out later than usual. After a time, their children would take notice. And, of course, those children would never truly know their father.

And so this was all they had, this intimacy on the sly. They creaked back and forth in each other's arms, pushing reality from their minds and listening to the sound of each other's breathing, wishing they had met before the war.

As a young girl, she'd not heard of his endeavors down in Dixie. Or in Texas, for that matter. She never put much stock in reputations anyway, and his was no different. Instead, Belle chose to unearth the real Kings firsthand, and, in spite of herself, she liked what she found. She was intrigued, but she let him do most of the work. In the years that followed, it had taken him many a compliment, countless tips of his hat, a private chat if he was lucky, and, eventually, a secret walk down by the river to change her first impression of him—that he was an aloof, haughty young man, invested in his own small legend.

The U.S. government had had a harder time finding a chink in Kings's armor than this woman. In the face of death, he might have been cold, unflinching, and totally fearless. Staring into the eyes of Belle Jackson, he was shy and reticent, all the while living out the definition of a gentleman.

After more than a quarter of an hour, it was Belle who broke the silence, though half-whispers have never broken anything. "I dreamt on you, Gabriel," she said. "A few nights ago, I saw you in my sleep."

She nuzzled deeper into him, her hand suddenly a clamp on his upper arm, and he was surprised at the strength of her grip. He stopped rocking. "That a fact?"

"Didn't like what I saw," she went on. "I was outside of myself, watchin' it all happen before my eyes. Like a play. I saw myself dressed all in black and standin' in the middle of this crowd. Must've been hundreds of folks gathered about, and it was the strangest thing. They all seemed to be . . . swayin'. Like wheat in the wind, like they wasn't even alive.

"I couldn't quite make out any of their faces, but they were all lookin' in the same direction—lookin' up, as though struck by a vision. The 'me' that I saw turned to see, and I turned with her, and that's when I saw you, hangin' from a scaffold. I saw the other me open her mouth to scream but"—she seemed to choke, took a moment, then resumed—"no sound come out. I understood it then, the black. I woke up sweatin' like a winded pony."

"Belle—"

"How am I s'posed to say for certain where you are or how you're faring?" she broke in sharply. "Whether you're still above ground or below it . . . how the hell am I s'posed to know? Am I s'posed to wait for it to come out in the papers? 'Gabriel Kings, the notorious bandit, killed by a hundred sheriffs!'"

Her tears finally brimmed but she kept charge of herself. Kings gently smoothed a hand over her hair, murmuring to her as if he were speaking to a spooked horse. "It's all right, darlin'. You oughta know by now it's some difficult to kill me. Haven't I always turned up?"

"Yeah," she said, almost grudgingly, "you have."

"No hangman's gonna rob me of spending the rest of my life with you, don't you know that?"

It was the first time he had ever used those words when speaking of their future. Before, it had variously been "the time we've got" or "as long as I can." Belle did not fail to notice the change in phrasing. She caught her breath and said with bitterness, "Your *life*? My God, how much longer is that apt to be, Gabriel? My daddy thinks highly of you, but you know as well as I do that he'd never walk me down an aisle with you at the end of it."

"Let's cross that crick when we come to it," Kings said in a way that put an end to the subject. He started rocking again. Gradually, when the fever had passed, she lowered her head to its resting place on his chest and again found temporary comfort.

She closed her eyes, and the words drifted from her lips. "I love you, Gabriel Kings."

He sighed deeply through his nose, and that was enough for her. Not a man of flowery speech, her outlaw. In the silence she felt his body begin to respond to the press of her weight. Then, "I always thought you looked mighty fetchin' in black."

She clapped a hand to her mouth to stifle her laughter, and to him the sound was more than worth the hard ride it took to get there.

The following morning found Kings walking down by the corrals, attended by two little girls who clung to his fingers like leeches. He dodged a swarm of marriage proposals, saying that he did not imagine their *papá* would give his blessing. And then Teresa, who was sharper than most her age, pointed out that their mother had gotten married when she was only fourteen. The outlaw laughed and swore that in another five years or so, he would ride back and see if they still wanted to marry him then.

Both girls assured him they would.

Well-rested and lethargic from a large breakfast of tortillas, beans, and *chorizo con huevos,* he felt like a new man. This ranch's gate had always been open to him, and every time he splashed through the shallows of the slow-running Frio, it felt like coming home. The Jacksons had been friendly to him when friendliness was not expected, and the daughter of the Old Man had been a point of light in his black world.

There was a chill in the air. He reckoned that by sundown, the temperature would dip to at least fifty degrees, maybe even the high forties. As a Virginia man, Kings was accustomed to cold, having seen his share of frozen rivers and snow that fell on a slant, but there was something different about the cold that came with the howling winds of Texas, with no mountains to slow them down.

He dropped into a squat and reached back to slide his big knife from its sheath. Though he expected no trouble here, he always went about the ranch fully armed—except when in the parlor or dining room. His weapons had become as much a part of him as his arms and legs.

With this extra appendage he began slicing away at a stick, all the while listening to the girls chatter. They told him stories in a language he hardly understood—of wise old shamans and talking desert animals and a ghostly woman who wailed at riverside—but he smiled and listened with open ears, nodding every so often as if he knew exactly what they were talking about. Encouraged, they jabbered on.

Titus Jackson, John Bevans, and Fernando Elías rode by on cutting ponies to inspect the roaming herd. The major was expecting a detachment of cavalrymen from Fort Clark within a day or two. It was already understood that when the bluecoats came for their remounts, Kings and his men would roost up in the barn and stay there until the transaction was concluded. Not a sweating matter, not even a gun-packing matter. Many were the soldiers who had come within touching distance of Gabriel Kings and not known it.

When he had finished his carving, Kings presented little Sofía with the result—a hollow flute that chirped like a songbird and brought a smile to her face. Though her sickness from the night before had been attributed by her mother to a bit of under-cooked chicken, Kings hoped the rare gift would speed her recovery. It had the desired effect. Sofía whirled away from her sister, waving her gift like a baton, and Teresa skipped along after, halfheartedly clawing at the hem of the smaller girl's dress.

This was a good place. A damned good place.

He looked around at the large frame house, at the big barn. Across the way, windmill blades creaked. There was an overpowering smell of hay, manure, and honest work about the property, and it did a man good to breathe in those things every now and again. It had been years since Kings had done so.

It stirred within him old sentiments, but ones he'd considered with greater frequency over the last year. He ought to put his six-guns away, get a spread like this somewhere, raise a few head . . . It was one thing to dream, he told himself, and another to hope. A pardon from Governor Hubbard, let alone President Hayes, was as likely a reality as flying mule deer.

He turned his head at the sound of the major's approach—that slow, leisurely advance of a man delighting in a home built with his own hands. The two hounds came with him, slithering

147

under the bottom corral rung to lick Kings's fingers and press up against him. Jackson was jamming tobacco into a long-stemmed pipe, and when he spoke, it was as if they had been talking for hours.

"I've had these dogs a long time now," he said, "but I had one back home that was first-rate at tracking anything that walked or crawled. Finer even than these two. Had a nose on him for smells like a banker's got a nose for money. Name was Reliable, and he earned it. I expect I treated that ol' boy better'n some folks treat their own tads, sad to say. But, you know, as fine as you can treat a hound of this breed, they always seem to mope around with these terribly sad eyes."

He paused a moment to light his pipe. "You've got a hound's eyes on you, son," he said, after a few puffs, "and I can't say as I recall seein' any other kind on you. Ever."

Kings was in no hurry to respond. Still scratching dogs with either hand, he merely tipped his head up to meet his fellow Virginian's frank, open expression.

"You feel short on time?" Jackson asked.

"Shorter than I was last year."

"You ever study on bowin' out?"

The outlaw chuckled and finally pushed the dogs away. "More'n once, Major. But I've been playin' a rough game, and it's some easier to study on bowin' out than it is to do it."

Gone fishing, Jackson decided to add a few more inches to his line. "Ever study on gettin' hitched?" He sucked on his pipe, eyeing Kings to see if he registered any change. Unfortunately for him, the younger man had become adept at sidling his way out of condemning interrogations, and so parried the old soldier's thrust with little effort.

"I won't deny it's always been an ambition," Kings said slowly. "Then again, they say the married man gets buried sooner'n the wife. Makes a body think twice."

Seeing it would be pointless to pursue the question, Jackson chose to concede this skirmish. There would be another day.

"Looks like the weather's finally gonna break," he said, squinting skyward. "Old Man Winter's been holdin' the storm off longer'n usual this year."

Kings was struggling to stay in the present. His thoughts wanted to stray back to the night before—to the first truly restful night in some time. He and Belle had made brief but passionate love, out of the light of the moon on the dark side of the house, years of practice muting the action to near inaudibility. Afterward, when Belle had started to nod off against his chest, the night growing colder around them, he nudged her awake, kissed her forehead, and held the door open for her. She went back inside and he to the barn loft with a smile on his lips. But, like countless nights before, he went to his blankets alone.

"Skeery thing," Jackson was saying. "I've found the longer something takes to get here, worse it is when it finally starts."

The statement struck Kings as strangely prophetic.

CHAPTER 14

It hadn't been easy, giving that pack of lawdogs the slip, and it had taken time, but the fact was, he'd done it.

Going on a week ago Zeller lost sight of them through the glass of his telescope, having had little sleep and plenty of long, hard hours playing mental and geological chess with his pursuers. When he did close his eyes he only dozed, and when he did swing down it was to give his mare a breather and a drink from a hatful of tepid canteen water. That old girl deserved a month off on good *grama,* and she would get it.

Whoever they were, they knew the lay of the land as well as Zeller did, if not better. Still, however familiar they were with the terrain and however skilled at reading it, they had never used it the same way their quarry did. They were lawmen. He was an outlaw. They rode by the light of day and on the open prairie, he rode by the light of the moon and kept to the back trails and forgotten byways. There had been times when they had him sweating hard. But whereas the possemen, dogged though they were, stopped each night to rest their horses and replenish their energy, Zeller and his long-winded mare— veterans of innumerable chases like this one—pushed on.

It hadn't been easy, but he'd lost them. He could only hope the lawmen kept on the way they were going and didn't pick up his trail again.

He nearly fell on his face when he dismounted in the yard. No horses in the corral, no smoke or light from the cabins, but he was too run-down to care. He pulled his knife, cut the mare's cinch, and tore the saddle from her back. With the butt of his rifle, Zeller smashed the thin layer of ice that had formed over the water in the trough. He watched with satisfaction as his horse guzzled. After she'd had her fill and turned sluggishly away, it was his turn. Dropping to his knees, he blew on the water before drinking. As it was, he felt icicles stab his brain, but he had ridden through hell just to taste this water again, to feel this canyon's air again. It was a good pain.

He heated four pails' worth of water inside the main cabin, which he then poured into a tub. The water wasn't as hot as he would have liked, but he couldn't wait any longer and sank like a rock up to his ears. He soaked for hours, warming his chilled flesh, cauterizing and bathing his wound.

After he reckoned he'd soaked enough, Zeller stood to take a speculative look around the room, running fingers through his beard. He decided against a shave and got drunk instead.

The following morning he stumbled out of the cabin into the light of a bleak autumn afternoon. Not caring for it, he stepped back into the semi-darkness and got a fire crackling on the hearth. After that, he flicked a scattering of dead grass and debris from the threshold that had blown in when he opened the door.

It had struck him as a bit odd to have come back to such emptiness—where the hell were the others, and what motivated such a swift departure? There hadn't been any jobs scheduled, as far as he could recollect, and he hadn't found any note explaining where they'd gone. Then again, he hadn't exactly searched high and low for one.

He pushed those thoughts from his mind. Wherever they were, they'd be back. Besides, he could use the peace and quiet.

At the table, Zeller sat down with a weathered war bag full of hand tools to carry out a routine of his, a loving ceremony he performed after every ride. He cleaned the residue from the barrels of his disassembled Peacemakers, oiled the holsters, shaved away the rough edges from the sandalwood grips—anything that needed doing, he did, and any aspect that needed tidying, he tidied. He'd scarcely cheated death, but he would make sure that when his time finally came, by God, he would give his killers a show—whether they wanted it or not, and let them fight hard to bring him down.

When he finished with this business, he chopped wood through the rest of the daylight hours, during which a light snow powdered the landscape. So long as he had the time, he figured he might as well get reacquainted with the chores he'd left behind on the dairy farm of his youth, and those he'd largely neglected as a professional outlaw. He swept out both cabins, forked fresh hay into stalls, and brought his mare in before nightfall.

That evening, whittling by the fire, he picked up the sound of horses moving in the yard. He breathed a sigh of relief. That would be the boys. Zeller resumed his whittling, adding to the shavings between his feet, but after several minutes, he wondered why no one had come in yet. Then he heard the barn door clacking from across the yard. Strange . . .

He called out twice, trying Kings's name and Brownwell's, too, before he decided to go and see about it. There was something unnerving about the silence broken only by the sound of the door, so he set the knife down and tucked one of his guns under his belt. Taking up the lantern, he went out into the chill November night.

Zeller limped across the icy space, eyeing the ground for hoofprints and finding them. Shifting the lantern to his left hand, he gave the knotty planks a bump and entered the barn. Huffing streams of vapor, he hung the lantern on a nail and heard the firm, resolute footfall of a man stepping out of a stall and into the aisle. Zeller turned. The man was tall, wide, and unfamiliarly shaped.

"Kings?"

There was another sound to his left, a quick shuffle, and Zeller was moving with it when the gun butt made contact from above. It was dark in the barn, however, and the blow didn't land as precisely as his attacker would have liked. Gushing blood from just above the occipital bone, Zeller was still conscious when he hit his knees.

"How 'bout that?" he heard someone mutter, seemingly miles away. "Looks like we got us Dave Zeller."

He felt two pairs of rough hands heaving him to his feet, then going under each armpit to drag his limp body back to the cabin. Next thing he knew, they had bent him over the table, patting him down before relieving him of his weapon. One of the hands clamped down on his shoulder, forcing him into a chair at the head of the table.

Head throbbing, Zeller opened his eyes to find the world around him tilting this way and that. His vision was blurry, but he wouldn't have recognized any of his assailants anyway.

Somehow, he found the strength to be defiant. "I'll tell you sonsabitches what," he said, closing his eyes once more, "I been smacked harder for skimmin' the cream."

"Oh, I wish we coulda met under friendlier circumstances," Frank Wingate said, affecting a smile. He pulled out the chair to Zeller's left and sat down. Zeller recognized his voice as the one he'd heard in the barn, and thought that it must have been his pistol whose sting he'd felt. "But we are where we are. *Ain't* we, Yankee Dave?"

Across the room, Henry Coleman was leaning into the fireplace, tossing chunks of wood onto the flame. Jack Lightfoot stood at the far end, directly across from Zeller, watching him with great interest. There was something sick about this man,

Zeller decided, but he wasn't quite sure what.

He turned his attention back to Wingate but someone slapped a hand to the scruff of his neck and squeezed hard. Zeller winced as Dan Carver bent low, his voice oddly lilting as he spoke. "Lemme cut his throat right now, Frank. Lemme cut 'im ear to ear and see if that don't change his tune."

Wingate glanced up from emptying Zeller's guns. "All in good time, Dan, all in good time. For now, let the man go." He flipped the loading gate shut on one pistol, took up the other. "When d'you figure Kings'll be back, Yankee Dave?"

Zeller blinked as Carver unhappily released his grip. "It don't matter," he said. "You'll all be dead before he gets here."

He stared at Wingate calmly, but the smaller man had something to say about that. Quick as a viper, he backhanded Zeller across the face and he toppled over, landing hard with a streak of blood horizontal across his cheek. The adrenaline rush of being struck in the nose nearly freed him from the pounding between his ears, but Zeller took a moment, then slowly rose to his hands and knees.

"And who's gonna be doin' the killin', Yankee Dave?" Wingate sneered down at him. "You? I'd like to see you try."

"Aw, don't play with him, Frank," Lightfoot whined. "Let's just kill 'im and string his carcass up outside. Be a nice homecomin' gift for Mr. Kings, I'd say."

Zeller got to his feet, his features unreadable as he wiped the blood on his sleeve. He looked at Wingate, then away from him to Carver, whose grimace gave way to a brutish grin.

"I got me a better idea, Jack," Carver said and started toward Zeller. The deliberation of his approach and the way he held his left hand away from his side forced Yankee Dave to make a preemptive decision.

It wasn't hard.

"Well, fellas," he sighed, stopping Carver short, "if this is a get-to-know-ya, let's get to gettin'."

Zeller lunged at Carver. With one hand he ripped the man's gun free, then shoved him hard against the table's edge with the other. In his haste, Zeller fumbled with the hammer spur and shot lower than he meant to. Still, he managed to drill Carver in the stomach. He swung the pistol to the right, fluid this time, and fired again. The long barrel blossomed with a stab of hot light and Coleman twisted, blood spurting from his arm.

Zeller triggered a third shot at Wingate that missed and *thunked,* ripping a gash through the tabletop. Still clutching one of Zeller's emptied pistols, Wingate took his time. He half-turned, planting his feet, leveled his Smith & Wesson Schofield, and shot twice into Zeller's body from a distance of five yards.

Zeller was thrown back against the wall, then slumped down into a seated position. The lifeblood was seeping out of him, warming his middle and showing at the corner of his mouth, but there was a strange look on his face. He did not seem to be in pain—rather, it was as if a shadow of joy had come over him, joy at having killed one of the bastards and wounded another.

Then he did something.

He laughed deep in his chest, strong and loud, sounding healthier than he should have, but the laugh broke into a chuckle and died as quickly as it had arisen. He lifted his eyes and stared across the short distance at Wingate.

"You tell Kings," he said, smiling weakly, "not to keep me waitin' too long on you fellas." He coughed blood, and his voice failed to recover its strength. "Sure enough . . . he'll be sendin' you down after me."

Wingate broke open his weapon, spilling detonated shells across the puncheon. He came close and dropped to his haunches, saying into Zeller's face, "You'll wait a long while, you damn Yankee."

But Dave Zeller, knowing it wouldn't be long, had already

155

closed his eyes. He saw a haze, ember-red at first, that swirled and faded gold like summer hay.

CHAPTER 15

The twilight was deepening as the cavalcade entered Austin from the northwest. Streetlamps had been lit, and, while town proper was empty, there was plenty of light and sound coming upstreet from the playhouse, the gambling halls, and the bawdy houses. Somewhere, someone started a jangling tune on a piano, and a woman was laughing.

There was no mirth to be found among the horsemen, though. They had been on the trail for nearly two months—six weeks and four days was the exact count, but once a man got west of Austin, time really stopped mattering. From the watering hole where Tom Seward met his end, they'd pursued the second fugitive upcountry to the barren Staked Plains, the *Llano Estacado,* and it was in that desolation that they lost his tracks.

Outside Smith's Hotel, Stringer signaled for a halt. He dismounted and passed his reins to Leduc. "We'll head out again in a week," he said, looking up. "Need to reassemble, resupply, go over our next move. I know you don't have much stomach for politics, so Mincey and I'll report to the governor. Mind puttin' up the horses?"

"Not at all." Leduc braced both hands on the saddle horn and stretched. "Give him my regards."

Mincey climbed down and came up alongside Stringer—unshaven, rumpled, and a far cry from the spit-and-polish city detective from before. Delaney sat a crooked saddle nearby, and, unsurprisingly, the volunteers from Refuge seemed far worse for wear. As a whole, they appeared to have been drained of their zeal, exhausted to the point of falling out.

Stringer pulled his rifle from the scabbard, fitted it under one armpit, pocketed his hands, and ducked his head up the lane. "Come on, Walter. Let's go see Hubbard."

Leduc, Delaney, and the volunteers rode off for the livery. Stringer and Mincey trudged up the wheel-rutted road and soon came in sight of the dome and spire of the state capitol.

"We might hafta ride on the Big Bend after all, Walt," Stringer said.

Mincey looked at him. "I don't imagine the others will be too pleased to hear that."

"I ain't too tickled by the idea, neither, but it makes the most damn sense. Oughta strike soon, 'fore they start missin' home too much."

"Might have a point there."

"Damn shame we couldn't close the deal with Zeller, if that's who we was chasin'."

"Too early to go callin' this operation a bust or a jackpot, you ask me."

At the capitol, legislators were on their way out for the evening. Within, a clerk in gartered sleeves was flitting about the room, turning off lamps. As Stringer and Mincey endeavored to pass him, the clerk maneuvered into their path, informing the lawmen that the governor was preparing to head home.

Stringer extended the barrel of his rifle and brushed the clerk aside like a curtain. "Nothin' personal, son," he said. "I just ain't in the mood."

The governor's office was in disarray, with piles of books stacked like crooked chimneys on his disorganized desk and several boxes acting as giant paperweights on the floor. The door, when opened, clunked into an empty cigar box, the same one Hubbard had offered to Stringer and Leduc at their first meeting.

The man himself turned from the window with his sleeves rolled up and an amber-filled, square-bottomed glass in his hand. "Captain Stringer, Detective Mincey!" he said with genuine surprise. "Welcome back to civilization."

Mincey seated himself and said, "We may be back in civilization at the moment, Governor, but we won't be staying very long."

"Oh?"

Stringer nodded. "We plan to head back out in a week or so, after we resupply and have a good look at the way things are at the moment."

Hubbard drew closer, anticipation showing on his broad features. "And how *are* things at the moment?"

Stringer deferred to Mincey with a subtle gesture, and the Pinkerton straightened in his chair. "Well, two weeks ago," he began, "we were ambushed at a water hole by two members of the gang. We'd been trackin' 'em, and it was just a matter of time before they realized they were being followed. So they decided to do what a crook on the run does best. Luckily, we escaped without any wounds to speak of, and we managed a good fight. The outlaw Tom Seward was killed, but the man he was with—Dave Zeller, we think—got away."

The governor took a minute to digest the report, then spoke with his eyes on the floor. "Well, that's—that's somethin'. Mr. Pinkerton and I wouldn't have chosen you gents for this job if we didn't have the utmost confidence in your abilities. And we still do, boys, I can assure you. Only, don't let any of 'em get away next time."

Stringer gazed at the cigar box on the floor, more than slightly rankled at Hubbard's demeanor. Mincey, busy with the filling of his pipe, showed no outward signs of emotion, but his silence was telltale. For the first time in a long time, the governor sensed he might have said the wrong thing.

"You know, it's a damn shame," Hubbard remarked, moving back to his desk, "that I won't be here to see this righteous mission through to the end. My term's about up, boys."

Mincey dropped the match on the floor after lighting his pipe and seemed to change the subject. "Sir, we realize how late it is, but before you head home, the captain and I were wondering if you might have any input as to what our next step should be. You were an officer during the war, after all."

Hubbard sat down, expertly masking his slight embarrassment with a dignified descent and a ponderous frown. "That's a difficult nut to crack, gentlemen, and I fear that I've become less of a soldier and more of a politician over the years. But as I understand it, the Big Bend encompasses over a thousand square miles of arroyos and gullies them renegades know like I know my wife's purty face. I wouldn't think it wise to ride in there with anything less than a company of rangers. Even soldiers."

The metronome Stringer remembered so clearly stood on the edge of the governor's desk. He reached out a finger and set its beater in motion. "I had my way," he grumped, "I'd send him a damn telegram and have him meet me on open ground, though I doubt any telegrapher'd be willin' to deliver the message."

Minutes passed with nothing said, and the ticking of the metronome was loud in the stillness. Then Mincey looked up with a light in his blue eyes.

"Captain," he said, "you might just have somethin' there." He turned to the governor. "Have you made our employment and purpose known, sir? By word of mouth or by puttin' it in the papers?"

"I haven't. Mr. Pinkerton and I agreed this enterprise should be kept a secret so as not to inspire a legion of glory-hounds.

Most bounty hunters in the country have just about given up on trying to fetch the scalp of our Mr. Kings—and most lawmen, far as that goes—but if word of this got out . . . why, they might feel as if this was a . . . *competition*. We didn't fancy riskin' that."

"Let's risk it."

Hubbard blinked. "I beg your pardon, sir?"

"I suggest we print it in every paper this side of Chicago," Mincey said. "Kings has to leave his hideout sometime. He has to ride to the nearest town for provisions, or one of his men does, and where there's a town, there's newspapers, and if there are none, there's folks bound to be talking about what they've heard. Let the nation know, and in doing so, let Kings know about our cause, about our fight with two of his men. How that ended up. The news is sure to get him mad and when a man gets mad, he loses control of his faculties. He'll want blood for what we did to Zeller and Seward, and he won't rest till he avenges them. He's got a reputation to uphold."

"I might grant you that, but what is it you were saying about Captain Stringer's suggestion?"

"Well, in that same paper, why not run . . . an announcement? Something to bait him, to bring him out into the open, and let the chips fall where they may."

Hubbard persisted, "But what would draw him out, is what I'm asking. What kind of announcement? And how do we know he'd take the bait? I'd think the man's sharp enough to see through any such ruse."

Mincey puffed on his pipe. "Like I said, the news will enrage Kings, make him do things he normally wouldn't. He'd be blinded by his anger, prompting rash action. You said he hasn't been touched in twelve years, Governor. Well, that must've done something to the man's ego." He glanced at Stringer, whose eyes were suddenly cagey and alert, his posture straighter. "Put it out in the papers that, say, some kind of big hullabaloo—a celebration, an anniversary, anything—is to happen in this town, on this day. Somethin' to catch the eye, in the first place. And make it a town with a real fat bank. Why wouldn't Kings take the bait?"

"Have to contact the local authorities, clear it with them," Hubbard supposed. "But wait a minute, now. What kind of lawman would invite such a thing upon his people?"

Mincey did not hesitate. "The kind of lawman who wants to do the country a service—put a mad dog down for good. But leaving that aside one moment, sir, let's circle back to what you were saying—about him seeing through this. Our boy is *sure* to, of course. He wouldn't've survived more'n a decade on the run if he wasn't smart. He'll know it's a trap, but I've got a feeling he'll accept our challenge. He'll want to prove for good and all that he's above the law. That he's unstoppable, and any man crazy enough to try and tackle him is a dead man.

"He'll ride in to take the town bank, and we'll be waitin' for him. Him and his boys won't get any further than the dry-goods store."

Leduc held the pocket watch up to the light and stared at the hands that hadn't ticked in years. That the timepiece no longer worked didn't matter so much—it was the only heirloom in his family, having been handed down from his grandfather and finally coming to him when his father died five years ago. Moreover, there was the tintype on the inside, a likeness of his mother as a middle-aged woman, with a churchy shawl over her curly black hair and a blank expression on her very striking, very French, features. He ought to write her again soon, ease her worries once more . . . Leduc stroked the cold image with his thumb, then slipped the watch back down into his left vest pocket.

162

He and Delaney were stationed in the second room at the top of the stairs at Smith's. Two other rooms on the same floor were occupied by possemen, another at street-level, and already they could hear snoring through the walls.

Reclining comfortably on the springy bed, the Pinkerton was polishing his Model 3 Smith & Wesson. Leduc was in a chair by the window, his hat on the lamp stand at his elbow. Having secreted the watch, his attention was drawn to the street below. A well-dressed man was escorting his wife up the hotel steps.

"So how long, exactly," Delaney asked from the bed, "have you been a ranger?"

Leduc took a moment. "Eight years, this past August. How long you been with the Big Eye?"

"Seven. What'd you do before that, if you don't mind my asking?"

When Leduc threw him a quizzical look, Delaney explained, "Well, now, seein' as how it looks like we're gonna be in this thing for a while yet, we might as well get to know each other better. Won't have much time for these kinda questions on the trail, will we?"

Leduc wondered what to tell him. "Well, I was a shotgun guard for Wells Fargo for a spell. Before that I rode four years under Old Glory durin' the war."

Delaney nodded, not commenting on the curiosity of a Deep Southerner like Leduc serving in the Union army. "And were you conscripted into President Lincoln's service?"

"I was a volunteer," Leduc replied, and, suddenly, he felt like talking. "In them days leadin' up, you had rich plantation owners and bushy-bearded politicians condemning the Yankee invaders and their nerve to try and change our way of life. Way they figured it, we were fightin' our second war of independence, but myself, I couldn't see the sense in what the Confederacy said they was fightin' over. How could they claim to be fightin' for their natural-born rights while denyin' them to a whole race of people?"

"My thoughts exactly."

"So I caught a fast horse, rode like hell for Union Kentucky, and volunteered."

"See any action?"

Leduc turned away from the window to better face Delaney. "Three weeks after muster," he said, "we got bushwhacked on the road to Hopkinsville. Turns out it was Bedford Forrest and his cavalry, and, boy, did they have us outnumbered. We lost seven men, and I don't know how many more of our boys got shot up. We winged a few of theirs, killed four. Three troopers and an officer."

A loud popping noise came from up the street, but he had heard so much gunfire in his life that he scarcely paid it any mind. Outside a deputy's boots clouted the boardwalks as he ran to find out who had shot and why.

Leduc continued. "It was my ball that killed the officer, but at the time I wasn't thinkin' about his rank or if we could mebbe barter him. I wasn't but twenty. Hell, I was just fightin' to stay alive."

"You probably weren't alone."

"I served at Parryville, Franklin, and Wildcat Creek in Tennessee, where I almost got my head blown off by some kid younger, even, than me. I took his rifle, gave him a boot in the butt, and sent him back feelin' sorry for himself." He chuckled. "I rode through Atlanta with General Sherman all the way to the Atlantic, but I ain't exactly proud of everything that transpired on that march. Yes. I've seen some action."

Delaney spoke with eyebrows raised. "I'd say by the time you became a ranger, you were pretty used to gettin' shot at."

"Oh, yeah." Leduc got up and threw Delaney's coat at him. "Finish what you're doin', then take a walk with me." He held up a hand with his thumb and forefinger two inches apart. "I could tear into a good, thick steak."

At the front desk Delaney bent over the counter and asked the man where a fellow could come by some oysters and a hot meal. He already knew about the chili joint, he said, but was after a place with silverware and papered walls.

He joined Leduc on the porch a few minutes later, a brown cigar in his teeth, and stabbed a finger down the lane. "The Continental's where we're headed."

They found a vacant corner table and angled their chairs apart so they could both watch the goings-on. Delaney ordered a whiskey and a bowl of oysters on the half-shell, and Leduc requested a well-done steak with beans, spuds, and an iced beer. As the waiter moved off, both men considered their surroundings.

The air was murky with smoke, which blended with the warm glow of the globed wall lamps. A dark mahogany bar dominated the middle of the room, an oblong island adrift in a sea of thirsty men. Batwing doors in a narrow doorway to the rear separated the eatery from the noisy gaming parlor.

Delaney sat back with his hands knit over his belt and took the cigar from his lips to continue the conversation he'd started back in the hotel.

"I was seventeen the year the war ended," he began, "and, like a fool, I was sad to see the day 'cause I'd been wishing it'd last forever. Understand, my family has a long and proud history of living and dying in every Irish uprising going back to the time of Christ, so Dad wasn't about to let his only son run off and get killed fighting a war that didn't concern us. Lest I live up to my ancestral history here in the Land of the Free, he kept a closer watch on me than a mother hen."

"How'd you come to join the Pinkertons?"

"A few years after, Dad procured for me a job driving a milk wagon. One of the houses I stopped by every week, by the grace of God, belonged to Mr. Allan Pinkerton." He paused to sip his whiskey. "My days as a deliveryman didn't last long after that first meeting. That's what you call ironic, isn't it?"

"I bet your pa had a different word for it."

"You're not lyin'," he said, then glanced away, and for the first time Leduc noticed that the tip of the detective's left ear had been disfigured. Whether shot or cut, it was missing the lower third—the lobe and a good slice of cartilage along the outside. A surgeon's blade and needle had done the best they could, but Leduc wondered how he could have missed it before.

Their talk continued at a gradual pace, each man slowly feeling more at ease with the other, until the food arrived. At that point, the conversation ended, and they ate in silence. Delaney proved to be a fast and hearty eater, finding his portion too small. He ordered a second helping, as well as a beer and another whiskey. Leduc, as always, took his time. He looked up when the waiter had gone and said jokingly, "You *are* payin' for your own meal, you know that."

"I didn't think ranger pay would cover this," Delaney deadpanned.

As slowly as he chewed, Leduc had nevertheless finished his supper by the time the waiter reappeared with Delaney's order. He shoved his plate away and sat back, contentedly digging at a string of meat stuck between his teeth. It was only by sheer happenstance that his gaze at that moment landed on a seedy pair just now entering.

The one on the right was tall and stooped, wearing a blanket coat. The one on the left was shorter by half a foot, broadshouldered, with a shoestring mustache. He carried a pistol but his taller companion was apparently armed with nothing but the carbine in his hand.

Leduc recognized both almost immediately, mentally placing

their faces to names found in the leather-bound sheaf of warrants the rangers called their bible. He figured there wasn't enough rope in the whole territory to carry out every sentence, and he sometimes wondered if it would be so wrong to just kill these men wherever found. Captain Stringer was of the same mind, but stronger was his conviction that there had to be a dividing line between the lawless and the lawful. He'd also said there was nothing wrong, if forced, with a verdict issued by Judge Colt and a jury of five.

Leduc got to his feet. His right thumb, in a casual movement, flicked the thong from his gun hammer. "I'll be right back," he said to Delaney, then moved off.

By now the pair had reached the bar, belly-up with both hands visible. The tall one, Roy Harmon, spotted Leduc first. The ranger was careful in his approach—you never could tell what men of their stripe were apt to do. He noted that Harmon, the jumpy one, had carelessly placed his carbine down below the bar, out of sight. The muzzle was no doubt pointing upward, with the trigger guard facing out and an empty round under the hammer. Also, the bar was so swamped with patrons that there wouldn't have been enough room for Harmon to bring his piece to bear on Leduc without putting a hole in the roof first. That dealt him out as a possible combatant—that, and the fact that one of his hands already had a whiskey glass in it.

Jim Church's pistol lay in a cross-draw holster across his lower stomach, much more accessible than Harmon's carbine was, only he was bent so far over the bar that there was no way he could have beaten Leduc on the draw. When he finally took notice of the ranger, already standing within six feet, the outlaw could only stare.

Harmon made no effort to hide his contempt. "What in the hell d'you want?"

Leduc stood flat-footed, thumbs hooked behind his buckle,

ignoring the outlaw's question to ask one of his own. "You good Christian men stayin' out of trouble?"

"You bet we are," Church said with feigned bravado, but Leduc thought he heard apprehension somewhere in there.

Harmon persisted. "I said, what business you got with us? We just barely come into town a minute ago, and we're thirsty. Ain't no law against bein' thirsty, is there?"

"Wouldn't surprise me one bit, Roy," Church said, voice deep as a lowing bull's.

Of the two, Leduc figured Church was the one to watch. The man might look like just another down-at-heel cowpoke, lazy in his walk and in his talk, but he was dangerous. Leduc had known him as a horse thief, but it was said he'd killed two men down in Bexar several years back. As little as he trusted Harmon, the ranger's eyes never left Church.

Harmon was speaking again. "You got any papers on us? Legitimate or otherwise?"

"Got no papers on ya," Leduc admitted. "Not *on* me, least-ways. Reason bein', I've presently got bigger fish to fry than you two."

Harmon seemed to take offense to that. "What's that s'posed to mean?"

"Neither of ya would've happened to cross paths with Gabe Kings lately, wouldja?"

"Why?" Church asked. "You lookin' to bring him in?"

"Governor wants to have a sit-down with him, and he wants a few of us to make it happen."

Church snorted. "Don't figure that. You got sand, Leduc, you and Stringer both, but I think mebbe you bit off more'n you can chew this time. Nobody braces Gabe Kings and walks away—I don't care *how* many of ya Hubbard's payin'. I bet there's a hundred of your kind buried 'tween here and Juárez, and a couple dozen more just been left for the buzzards. For all the good you claim to be doin' for the state, I'd say it's fellas like Kings doin' the bigger service."

He paused to take up his glass but did not drink immediately. "But to answer your question, no, we ain't seen him lately. Tell you the truth, Roy and me never had any truck with his lot. We're in the horse business, not the bank and train business." He clicked his tongue and said apologetically, "So sorry we can't be of help."

Delaney was suddenly beside Leduc. "Any trouble here, Sergeant?"

"No trouble, Detective. Not tonight." He nodded in turn to the pair. "See you boys around."

He didn't wait for a parting word—wouldn't have received one anyway—but turned to Delaney and motioned for him to walk ahead. "Let's go," he said and gave Harmon's shoulder a good, hard squeeze as he edged by.

Outside in the lamplight, Delaney cupped his hands around a match and a second cigar. "Who were they?"

"Just a couple of two-bit stock thieves. Wasted my breath tryin' to get somethin' out of 'em."

Delaney waved the flame out and flicked the match into the street, nearly landing it in a pile of horse apples. "Somethin' on Kings."

"Yep."

"Another case of lockjaw."

Leduc heaved a deep breath in an effort to purge the frustration from his body. "Well, we best not let it get us down, Delaney," he said, trying for optimism. "We knew this was gonna be a high-stakes game goin' in, but there's one thing you can lay a safe bet on."

"What's that, now?"

"We got all the time in the world. Kings don't."

"He's had a good run so far. When d'you figure his time's

gonna run out?"

His father used to say that prophesying, like play-acting and play-writing, never paid for breakfast, but something compelled Leduc to speak on the corner of that Austin street.

"He's the last of a dyin' breed," he said. "If you recall, the Jameses and the Youngers got their hash cooked up in North-field not too long ago, and they ain't been seen or heard from since. You think about it, James and Kings are cut from the same cloth. Same as them Missouri boys, Kings is fightin' a war that ended more'n ten years back. He's just another holdout, waitin' to be brung in."

The detective tapped ash off his cigar and squinted out onto the thoroughfare. Under the boardwalk across the way, he could just make out the slinking silhouette of a stray cat that paused once to turn its unblinking yellow eyes on Delaney. He liked to imagine it was stalking a rat. He thought that they—Stringer, Mincey, Leduc, and himself—were playing a similar game, only their role, whether cat or rat, was less clear.

"What's takin' them so long?" he wondered aloud, looking upstreet.

Leduc looked, too, as if that would bring Stringer and Mincey down the hill from the capitol all the quicker. And for once in the history of looking, it did.

"Well, here's your chance to ask 'em," he said.

The men gathered in the street.

CHAPTER 16

Wingate went in search of extra ammunition through what he figured must have been Kings's quarters and found a Bible, of all things, instead.

The last time he'd picked one up was to say words over the grave he and his younger brother Charlie dug for their pap. He remembered he read from the Psalms.

Some days, if he sat still enough, Wingate could smell the stuffy dust and slogging rainfall of Clay County, Missouri; still feel the humidity and the pesky sting of mosquitoes along the back of his neck as he worked from five in the morning to well after sundown while his pap soaked up so much whiskey it eventually killed him. They discovered him facedown in six inches of ditchwater early one spring morning. Frank had just turned fifteen.

He'd been the oldest of three young ones, one of whom never survived infancy. Pap liked to attribute his drunkenness to that tragedy, but Frank had seen the time when his father couldn't even remember his own name, let alone the face of an unnamed infant who died so long before. Early on, it became bitterly apparent what kind of life Frank and Charlie seemed destined for—one as hard as the pallet they shared in the loft of the gloomy, two-room Wingate farmhouse.

Not long after Pap drowned, consumption robbed Frank of his mother, the same mother who spoke of God's unending love and tender mercies. It was around this time—specifically, about the time it came for him to again perform the reading at grave-side—that Frank lost whatever shred of faith that lingered in him.

His mother's will expressed her desire that he and Charlie be sent to their aunt and uncle in Springfield, and it had pained Frank to go against her plans for him, but the night before they were set to leave, he said good-bye to Charlie, crawled out the back window of the Widow Jones's boarding house, and left Clay County without so much as a backward glance. The first night out, he camped on the near bank of the Missouri River and used the entire book of Genesis and most of Exodus to get a nice blaze going.

Over the next few years Wingate spent time in Kansas and the Utah Territory. He moved into the Pike's Peak area to try his luck at prospecting in '57. Tin-panning for gold dust brought naught but disillusionment, and he was back in Missouri by season's end. He decided St. Lou was as good a place as any for him to kick his boots up, and, for a while, he made his living forking out stalls for the liveryman. He lived in a jerry-built shack out on the edge of town, and come sundown he would cover his head with a sugar sack and kidnap slaves at gunpoint, then return them to their owners the day after for a reward. On Independence Day of '59 he shot a Union man in the throat, then made tracks for the Cherokee Nation.

When Confederate forces fired on Fort Sumter, Wingate, who was at that time raising hell with a vicious former schoolteacher named Bill Quantrill, threw in with the troops led by General Ben McCulloch in time to serve at the Battle of Wilson's Creek. By the end of that day Frank discovered he had a knack for taking lives, so he decided to go along for the ride.

He rode with Quantrill through Independence, helped torch the Kansas town of Aubrey to the ground, and singlehandedly accounted for a half-dozen innocents at the Lawrence massacre.

He survived Quantrill and Bloody Bill Anderson both, escaped the threat of the gallows, and shunned all amnesty pardons offered by the government. He spent the next five years riding the steamboats up and down the Mississippi, and it was during this period of heavy gambling and whoring that he became acquainted with Dan Carver, who was a bouncer in those days. Not long afterwards, Jack Lightfoot joined their company.

Henry Coleman had been the last to throw in with them, vouched for by Lightfoot, and his relationship with Wingate had always been a strained one. Wingate generally held farm animals in higher esteem than darkies, but he never met the ox who could outshoot this particular darkie. That alone had been a good enough reason for him to tolerate Coleman's presence.

He sat down now on the edge of Kings's bed and let the book fall open where it wanted in his lap. Ecclesiastes, chapter three. "To everything there is a season," he read, "and a time to every purpose under the heavens. A time to be born, and a time to die . . . A time to kill . . . A time to laugh . . . A time to dance."

A time to kill. Well, there was one thing he and God could see eye to eye on, at least. As if that mattered.

He fanned onward into the book with a clumsy hand, heard the delicate onionskin pages tearing, and didn't care. A few chapters deeper into Ecclesiastes found Wingate pondering: "All things have I seen in the days of my vanity: there is a just man that perisheth in his righteousness, and there is a wicked man that prolongeth his life in his wickedness."

Taking up the bottle of good Tennessee sipping whiskey, he wet his finger with alcohol and ran it over his eyelids, one after the other—it was an Injun trick he'd learned from Lightfoot that supposedly gave a man his second drinking wind. Wingate had been swilling Kings's whiskey for the better half of the morning, and he didn't intend to stop until he'd killed this bottle off.

After a while, he shuffled down the hall and found Carver where he'd left him, but where the hell else could he go? The big man lay on his bedroll by the fireplace, stocking feet facing the door and a pillow beneath his head. He had awakened and was breathing raggedly, now that he was conscious of the agony that twisted his bullet-mangled guts. He rolled his head to the side when he heard footsteps.

"I'll say this fer ye, Carve," Wingate said, squatting beside him, "you may not be no nominee for sainthood, but you're one tough sonovabitch."

His attempt at humor was lost on Carver, who growled, "This ain't the first time I been shot."

"Even so, that Yankee bastard popped you good. A lesser man woulda kicked it on the spot."

"Yeah, well, I ain't headin' south till I see this job gets done." Carver licked his lips, clearly parched, and wiggled his fingers. "Gimme that bottle."

Wingate passed it over. "Where's Coleman run off to?"

Carver's laugh was cynical and ugly, but justified, Wingate supposed. "I been in and out all day, Frank. It look like I know or give a damn where he's at?"

While the slow-dying man drank, Wingate walked out to the porch in time to catch another grisly sight. Lightfoot, on horseback, had looped one end of a rope around his saddle horn and the other around the neck of Yankee Dave Zeller and was dragging the corpse across the yard to God knows where. The man had been dead three days and was starting to smell, and Wingate saw that a scrap of paper had been pinned to his bloodied shirtfront. He couldn't see it, but in clumsy scrawl it read, "Welcum home Kings."

"Jack!" he called out, stopping the half-breed before he made it too far. "Get on over here."

While he waited, Wingate leaned down close to make out a passage in the Epistle of James: "From whence come wars and fightings among you? Come they not hence, even of your lusts that war in your members? Ye lust, and have not . . . Ye kill, and desire to have, and cannot obtain . . . Know ye not that the friendship of the world is enmity with God? Whosoever therefore will be a friend of the world is the enemy of God."

Whoever James was, Wingate figured he'd had some experience on the other side of things. That was plumb insightful, what he just read—too insightful for a righteous man like this gent made himself out to be. But hell—who could call himself righteous with a gun to his head? If there was one thing Frank Wingate had learned, it was that sin found a man, no matter how deep a hole he dug or how many church house doors he closed behind him. Might as well accept it . . . and be a friend of the world.

"What is it?" Lightfoot asked, out of breath at the bottom of the steps.

"Where's Coleman?"

"I think he went off down the canyon a little while back."

"Good," Wingate said, raising his eyes. "Never know when Kings is gonna be back. When Coleman comes in, you take the next watch."

"When Kings *does* ride in, Frank, he's gonna be as unsuspectin' as a steer to the slaughterhouse."

"And just what in the hell're you fixin' to do with Yankee Dave?" Wingate stared hard at Lightfoot, not unlike a schoolteacher who'd caught a pupil doing something he shouldn't.

The breed smiled, showing crooked teeth. "Whaddaya think?" he said, turning to glance back at his horse holding the line taut. "I'm gonna hang it high somewheres on the way in."

"What fer?"

Lightfoot looked perturbed that he should have to explain his genius. "Well, I reckon it'll get Kings's blood boilin' right quick, maybe incite him to do somethin' foolish. Play right into our hands."

"Gabe Kings never played into *no*body's hands. He ain't survived this long for no reason, and he sure as hell ain't goin' quietly when we show him out. Now, I aim to do just what Spivey hired us to do, and that's irrigate Kings's liver with this Schofield. But by the Lord Harry, I'm doin' it humble."

Lightfoot was unconvinced. "You know what I found in that wooden box under his bed? The one from the Santa Fe Railway? I figgered there'd'a been piles of money inside—Kings's secret stash, judgin' by the size of the lock he had on there." He shook his head in disgust. "No such thing. Correspondences, buncha fargin' love letters from some woman named Belle. Bastard's gone soft."

Wingate shrugged in resignation. He figured Lightfoot would just have to wait and see for himself. "You want me to put that on your tombstone," he said, looking back down, "or would you prefer a scripture? I've stumbled across't a few interestin' ones, here."

Lightfoot showed his teeth again. "You're joshin' me, ain't ya?"

"Well, ya know, Jack, a wise man once said"—Wingate scraped the bottom of his memory's barrel—" 'Pride goeth before destruction, and a haughty spirit before a fall.' "

"Where's that wise man now?"

"Deader'n hell, I believe."

On the fifth morning of his stay at the Jackson ranch, the man for whom this reception was being prepared slinked about the property, going to and fro like a furtive barn cat, tipping doors wider and walking on eggshells in his cavalry boots. The last he had checked, the boys were up in the loft, playing cards and enjoying themselves. The major had ridden off with his son and foreman to see about a few animals that had missed the pen on the drive in from the pastures, and their Mexican mustanger was busy re-shoeing horses.

His wife was at work in the kitchen, and their daughters sat on plush stools in the drawing room while Mrs. Jackson patiently tutored them from the pages of an English primer.

That left Kings alone, for a short time, with the major's daughter.

Kings had been momentarily transfixed by her loveliness when she appeared at the head of the stairs. He knew she had done herself up for his benefit, almost as if she were trying to make an impression all over again. A flat-crowned Spanish hat sat upon her head, and her honey-blonde hair fell out from under it in a single, heavy braid. She wore a buckskin short jacket and full riding skirts, cinched at the middle by a woven rawhide belt, all of which accentuated her slim waist and curving hips.

The hour was early, and they rode stirrup-to-stirrup beneath a drab and murky sky. Whenever the trail narrowed, Belle would edge her mare closer to the flank of his stallion. Kings was acutely aware of the prod of her knee against his, and of the intention behind the supposedly accidental flick of her horsehair crop along the side of his neck.

Conversation was scarce, but they neither itched nor craved an end to the silence. The world, too, lay quiet around them, except for the wind that sang through the grass. It was enough.

They followed the Frio downcountry. Letting her take the lead, Kings trailed Belle to a bend in the river where a live oak had toppled over onto its side, affording either a hitch rail for horses or a bench for humans. This was their spot, a quiet place to reflect, to listen to each other breathe, and to give themselves over, briefly and rarely, to a shared passion.

He stepped down first, moving as he always did to help her down, though she was the last woman who needed help dismounting. She accepted his hands about her middle, as she always did, and hopped down.

She avoided his eyes when he took her reins, then gave him her back as he saw to the horses. Picking out a spot on the tree that was close to the water's edge, Belle sat with her hands in her lap, eyes down.

Kings sat beside her and reached for her hand, which she gave, but there was no response to his affectionate squeeze or gentle caress. Something was wrong. Her whole mood had changed from the outset of their ride to the moment of their arrival. She still hadn't looked at him.

He waited.

There had been times when Belle told herself she hated him, times she had sworn to God and Jesus and all the angels that she had no more love for him, only to plead forgiveness for her sudden anger and bitter outcry. There was a question that seared her heart but one she had never put to him directly, and she thought of it again now. Why had he not quit his ways a long time ago, before the infamy he now enjoyed made it impossible? Why hadn't he *ever* asked her to marry him?

She was trying to summon the courage to ask when she felt his hand on her knee.

"How'd you like to watch the sun go down in California?"

Belle looked around, stiffening when she saw that Kings was kneeling in the dirt. "There's not a sight on this earth like a California sunset," he said. "When the sun dips down behind them Sierra Nevadas, you'd swear you'd died and gone to heaven."

She heard one of the horses moving, turned her head to look, but his thumb and forefinger touched her chin and brought her gaze back.

"Few years ago, Sam, Dick, and me took a trip to California—not huntin' money, just desirin' a look at the Pacific. Well, third day past the Nevada border we come across this little valley. Got our horses from the depot and just rode right up into it, didn't even plan on it, just . . . happened into acres and acres of grassland. Trees so tall you could hardly see the tops and big around as a barn—forests of 'em; seemed to go on forever. Wide open skies and meadows for days, like the last unspoiled place on earth."

Her voice was small. "What are you talkin' about?"

"I'm about through with this business, Belle," he said. "Damn close. And damned if it's taken this long for me to come 'round, but I swear, the last few days—hell, the last few *months*—have given me half a mind to pull up stakes tomorrow."

For a moment, Belle's eyes came alive, but she caught herself. She had been on the cusp of plunging into his arms but settled back onto the creaking live oak. A sudden sense of irritation embittered her tone. "What about that other half, Gabriel?"

In truth, his plan was still in the rudimentary stages, but Kings knew he would never again come across a woman who commanded such honesty from him, or who could ever look at him with such fire that he had no choice but to regard her as an equal. There had to be another job, of course, to make up for Agave Seco's disappointing haul, and though he knew such vague talk might only incense her further, the outlaw king of Texas pressed on.

"I've got one more job in mind, one last bank. Where, I ain't certain; when, I ain't certain; but after we take it—and we *will* take it—I'm through, Belle."

"But why? *Why* d'you have to risk it all for one more blessed job? Can't you just—?"

"I need the money, sugar. Even the lion's share of all the jobs we pulled don't look the same after twelve years. 'Sides, I aim to build us a ranch to knock the shine off your daddy's in that little mountain valley, and stockin' it won't be cheap."

He'd moved closer, staring into her china-blues, and, to calm the storm, he put a hand on one cheek, then rose for a kiss. "I've no home to offer you but the one that's still in my head," he said when they parted, "and most every dollar I've ever had was come by dishonest. But if you'd be willin' to put them things aside, I'd like to show you California. Would you go with me?"

Belle's ire died with a sigh. "Am I supposed to take this for some kind of proposal, Gabriel Kings?"

"Your name wouldn't be Kings, where we're goin', but as soon as I can, I'll see to it you have a proper gold band to wear."

"You'll be comin' back for me, then? One last time?"

"With bells on."

CHAPTER 17

"What are your plans now, Gabriel?" asked the major, leaning an elbow into his bookshelf.

It was the day after Kings's proposal, and they were seated in Jackson's study, with only the hounds for company. Brownwell, Yeager, Osborn, and Woods waited below on the veranda, eager to be back in the saddle. The consensus among the outlaws was that, after six days of recovery in this comfortable safe haven, it was time to be heading home.

Kings's reply came around a lit cigar. It wasn't a question that demanded particulars, so he gave none. "Well, for the time bein', I reckon we'll make ourselves scarce, wait out the season."

He never discussed future movements with the major, not that he feared betrayal should their link be discovered. It was merely an unspoken agreement, and Jackson was glad to be kept in the dark.

The major's eyes went to the newspaper on his desk. "The lieutenant brought that with him when he came by for his remounts. There's something in it, I think, that should make you reconsider doing *any*thing for a while."

Quizzical, Kings stood and ambled over. He didn't bother to pick the newspaper up—he just let his fingers start from the top and work their way down the front page. They didn't have far to go before they came to rest on the words:

KINGS GANG TO BE BROUGHT TO JUSTICE, DECLARES GOVERNOR

Gang member killed, another wounded in gun battle
with lawmen;
"It is just a matter of time."—Gov. R. B. Hubbard

Without thinking to ask permission, Kings sat down in the major's desk chair and scanned the brief article.

The headline had done nothing but irritate him, and only mildly. There had been a number of headlines over the years, boldly declaring, as this one did, that the gang was living on borrowed time. And shortly afterward the headlines would declare—their publishers hanging heads, no doubt, from the warm safety of their offices—that the hunters had either returned empty-handed, or not at all. So why should Kings fret over an avowal from the lame duck governor of Texas that he and his men were, yet again, to be "brought to justice"?

The subheading was what gave him pause and momentarily took the breath from him.

Tom Seward was dead, reported the broadsheet, gunned down in a scrape with a posse commissioned by both Hubbard and President Hayes. Apparently, the Pinkertons were somehow mixed up in this as well.

At least Dave Zeller had managed to escape with his life, but how far he had gotten was another question entirely.

As Kings folded the paper, his eyes stumbled upon another announcement. Eight men out of ten would have passed it by to read about the Boston Red Stockings defeating the Chicago White Stockings in extra innings, but Kings passed over that report the way a hawk passes over a mouse for a rabbit.

The announcement was situated to the immediate right of the article. It spelled out in clear, fine print that on New Year's Day the town of Justicia would be holding a celebration "the likes of which the county has never beheld," with a band, dances from noontime to midnight, a buffet "catering to the tastes of our Anglo citizens and Spanish American friends alike," and fireworks. Justicia's doors, the paper said, were "open to one and all, and we invite our neighbors to the north, South, east, and west to join in our merriment."

There was something in that last sentence that rubbed him like sandpaper. Why should "South" have been capitalized when the others were not? Was it a misprint, a simple error? Could it have been intentional, a private joke on the part of a printer with lingering Confederate sympathies? His gut told him no. His gut also told him to wonder why a Texas editorial would be carrying an invitation to an event in Colfax County, which was somewhere in northeastern New Mexico Territory. His gut told him this wasn't a printing press bungle, but something else entirely.

"Gabriel?"

Kings rattled the paper as he folded it, then stood with it still in hand. There would be time to chew on the peculiarities of that announcement later. "Thank you for this news, Major," he said, making for the door, "dark as it is."

Jackson moved with him. "What are you gonna do?"

"Whatever I do, it'll get done. You can count on that."

Jackson was generally a temperate fellow, but today he was in no mood for subtlety, word games, or secrets. "I'm not a bettin' man, son. I don't believe in luck or chance, nor do I agree with goin' off on some reckless escapade at half-cock."

"Neither do I, Major." Kings put forth his hand to shake, a sign that he was through talking.

"I hope we have many more handshakes ahead of us," Jackson said. It was meant to be an order of sorts, but it came out sounding more like a question. A penny tossed into a wishing well.

Kings nodded and left the room but stopped halfway down

the stairs as Jackson addressed him, suddenly, by rank. It was the first time anyone had done so in a very long time, and it had the desired effect. "You take care of yourself, Captain. I wouldn't be the only one in this house to take it hard should some disaster befall you."

"Yes," Kings said, without turning, "I imagine them little ones would light a few candles for my soul."

Jackson's voice cut like a knife. "Belle would do more'n light candles. *You* may not bat an eye at the thought of a noose or goin' down in some haze of death and gore. I can't say what all kind of gloomy thoughts you entertain. You may even be lookin' forward to the day, but—"

"Sir, I have no intention of gettin' myself killed. Not today or tomorrow, not in Texas or anywhere. Fact is, I plan on disappearin', but first I've got a loose end or two needs tyin' up. After that, I mean to do just what you and I discussed the other day—change my name, put away my guns, and try to rebuild."

"Hell, you and I both know how long that'd last. You'd starve, Gabriel! You haven't known any other work but soldierin' and stealin', and one of those is out of the question for you. And even if you *could* keep your hands clean and your guns quiet, d'you think the government would just forget you and your men ever existed? That they'd give up the hunt, no matter where you go? I don't want my daughter worryin' herself sick over these things, but worry she does, and it makes me sick for her. Ah! You didn't think I knew, did you? Well, I've had my suspicions for some time now. Don't you worry, though—Martha ain't got the faintest idea. Be no end of racket in this house if she did, Lord knows."

He came down the steps. "Now, you listen to me, mister, and listen well. I love my daughter. I had to, I'd give my life for her, and I know you would, too. If there's anything left for me to want in this life, it's for Belle to find happiness. Her heart and soul are in this place, but she's not finding happiness here. There's a good chance she never will, not as another brush-country spinster.

"I think my daughter could and *would* find happiness with you, but for how long? Till her nerves are ruined, or until you get what you feel's been comin' all these years?" Jackson paused. "Dammit, man, don't you have *any*thing to say?"

Kings set his cigar, weakly smoldering, on the newel near his elbow with such precision one might have thought he was arranging some kind of exhibit. For a moment, it seemed as if he *was* about to speak. Instead, he put on his hat, tightened the strap, and went the rest of the way down, taking the newspaper with him.

Belle was waiting for him in the parlor, looking drained. She had overheard the last of their conversation and felt a horrible knot in her stomach at the revelation from her father's own mouth that they had been discovered. She did not fear him, only what he would say to her when Kings had gone . . . what that would mean. Was this the last time he was ever to be made welcome, their last good-bye?

"Miss Jackson," Kings said simply, taking her hand in his, "it's been a great pleasure."

She was aware of her father's presence at the head of the staircase. "Thank you, Mr. Kings," she managed, searching his face for some sign of encouragement—a crease, a crinkle, a glimmer that said everything would be fine. His features were somber, his mouth drawn in a tight line, completely unreadable.

He was silent for a moment, and then, bending down to kiss her hand, he said in a low whisper, "With bells on."

On the veranda, slouches straightened, coats were buttoned, and cigarettes went flying as Kings appeared and nodded all around. Apparently, their departure would be to little fanfare—the only well-wishers gathered were the Elías family, who stood in a cluster at the bottom of the steps to offer parting words of *"Vaya con Dios."* Little Sofía, clutching her flute, appeared to have tears in her eyes.

Seeing this, Kings approached the family, knelt, and opened his arms to beckon the tearful child. She came, sniffling, as did her older sister. He hugged them both tightly, then held the younger at arm's length to smear the wetness from her cheek with a gentle thumb. *"Adios, chiquita,"* he said, then turned and mounted. He waited while the others rode out of the yard, and with one last look at the woman standing in the doorway, he turned his horse and fell in at the rear of the column.

Belle watched him go for a precious moment more, then closed her eyes at the sound of her father's voice behind her: "Honey, let's talk."

The men rode westward, their tracks lost in the sleet that fell behind them. The first night out Kings told them of Seward's death but held off on voicing any designs of retaliation. The following days crept by in utter bleakness, though there was plenty of discussion by firelight. Kings himself sat apart, squinting and deliberating over the same margin of newspaper without volunteering a word or a thought. No man dared ask him to, as there were more than enough words and anger to go around.

One thing was clear—after twelve long years, a significant threat to the gang's security had finally arisen. Two gun-handy professionals like Dapper Tom and Yankee Dave had been put to flight, one of them killed, and, as Dick Osborn uttered just once before being hushed up by Leroy Brownwell, there now existed a possibility that the same could happen to every one of them.

Every one of them, of course, but Kings.

These men had spent a lot of time in the saddle with him, dodging bullets and the law's long arm. They had seen him sweat, seen him pray—however futile that may have been—and seen him go days without sleep. They knew that what flowed through his veins was just as red as theirs and just as easy to spill, and, Lord, had they seen him bleed, leaking till they'd thought he could leak no more. But always, he'd kept coming, charging into whatever fray they faced like a man bedeviled. Had he been any other, they might have thought him suicidal.

They were men who had survived and scratched a hard living out of hard times, who had earned some degree of respect in the world by taking it. They had not come by it easily, and neither did they dispense it liberally. In spite of their intimacy with his character, there was still something about Gabriel Kings that made each member of the gang look at him through the eyes of a child.

The entire panorama through which they rode was lightly dusted with a whiteness that clung to the catclaw and brush like bad luck. The sleet was a constant—not a downpour, but a continual, steady drizzle. They came in sight of the Chisos Mountains by noontime on the fifth day and the Rocking Chair by a weak-sunned one o'clock.

It was around then that Yeager urged his smoke-gray mare to the head of the column. He leaned into the gap to resume a private conversation initiated earlier that morning. "When you want me to leave for Acuña?" he asked Kings.

"Creasy ain't likely to have wandered too far, but on the off chance you have to do a little huntin' . . . sooner, the better."

"Day after tomorrow?"

"Well, they won't miss us for another two weeks," Kings said, "but you and your gal there feel up to it, go on."

Since leaving the Jackson ranch, Kings had had more than enough time to ponder the incongruity of that New Mexican proclamation, but it was no less confounding than when he'd first slapped eyes on it. The longer he stared at it, the more he reread the words, the more it resembled some kind of trap. It was anything but apparent, but if it *was* indeed a challenge, it just showed how truly desperate they had become, those bastards in Austin. He might have allowed himself to chuckle were he not still stewing over Seward's death.

After all these years of wasted time, manpower, and money, was *this* what they'd resorted to—a practical invitation to a necktie party, with himself as the guest of honor? Did President Hayes, Allan Pinkerton, Governor Hubbard, and whoever else hold him in so little regard as to even hope he might accept this invitation of theirs?

And yet . . .

The recklessness of his distant but not forgotten youth had only been watered down, not completely washed away. The game of life—and yes, death—wasn't just allegorical. And if his service under Stuart had taught Gabriel Kings anything, it was that life *is* a game, and it was imperative for those people whom circumstances cast as opponents to study the others' moves, as though actually sitting at either end of a chessboard. Feints, flanking maneuvers, bluffs, and all-out assaults were key elements in games like the one Kings was contemplating now.

Would he accept this invitation? *Should* he, was the thing. His thoughts raged against each other. On the one hand, it would be nothing short of insanity to knowingly ride into a setup. The best odds he had of getting out alive were three-to-one, because not only would he have to contend with this duly appointed pack of government manhunters, but with local law enforcement as well.

One was as bad as the other, for it was widely understood that Sheriff Tom Shepherd, the famous sovereign of Justicia jurisdiction, maintained a peaceful existence up there. And he wasn't one of those dime-a-dozen, big fish-little pond lawmen who could be cowed without much effort. No, he knew gun work. At one time, Shepherd had walked the other side of the street before being sentenced to a five-year stretch in the state prison at Huntsville. Now, having done his time and found religion within Huntsville's walls, he ruled Justicia with a Bible in one hand and a gun in the other. Or so Kings had heard.

It must have been quite a thing, the knowledge that an entire countryside of former friends and allies were now your sworn enemies. If there was one thing outlaws hated worse than a cut-and-dried lawdog, it was a turncoat. But to the extent of Kings's knowledge, Shepherd had yet to be sorted out by any of those former friends. Kings wasn't a friend, knowing Shepherd by word of mouth alone, and he felt no such obligation to count coup on the man, but if push came to shove—if he and his boys decided to see what Justicia had to offer—then he wouldn't hesitate.

Kings also knew that if they were to face up to a man like Shepherd, a few more hands would need to be brought in. He felt sure Yeager could convince Creasy and his crew to come along, back his play. That meant the proceeds would be divvied up into smaller portions than usual, but, in order to get those proceeds, they would first have to ride through a firestorm. So what was a few hundred lost or gained among friends if it improved their chances of riding away?

They had cheated the Devil before. They could do it again.

This omnipotent posse, overconfident in themselves and their authority, would turn around, lift their tails to scratch, and find the tables turned.

Eventually, the riders emerged from the narrow canyon corridor into the valley, their horses crunching snow and snapping brittle ocotillo.

From there, Kings pulled up twice, each time lifting his hand to close around one of his pistols. The first disturbance, a flicker of movement in the corner of his eye, was only a family of javelinas rooting through the brush.

The second time, the movement came from up ahead, some thirty or forty yards down the trail. Standing in the stirrups, Kings determined it was no animal, but a man. Whoever he was, he was either squatting on his haunches or on his knees under a cottonwood, and his back was to them. Whether he was packing iron, Kings could not be certain, but he had to assume so . . . *whoever* the fellow was. He drew his own iron but did not cock it. He made a kissing sound with his lips, urging John Reb into a lope.

The sound of hooves rattling on frozen stones brought the man's head around, and Kings was instantly on the alert. It was Henry Coleman, one of the three who rode with Frank Wingate.

What the hell?

The horsemen had closed to within twenty yards before Coleman found his feet. Slowed by the cold and by too long a period of immobility, the intruder knew if he went for one of his guns now he was a dead man. So he stood still, left arm held away from his side in a posture of surrender. His right—the shoulder still mending, heavily bandaged beneath his coat— hung straight down, hand and fingers stiff. His rifle was on the ground near the tree roots, out of reach. But maybe, if he could stall long enough . . .

At length, Kings said, "Your name's Coleman, if I remember correctly."

"Yeah," he replied, shifting from one foot to the other—testing, trying Kings to see how loose a rein he would give him. "Henry Coleman, that's my name."

"Where's your boss?"

The word had been chosen deliberately, and it elicited the expected reaction—Coleman gave a snort and ran his eyes over

Kings, head to foot, scarcely concealing his disdain. "I ain't called nobody 'boss' in my life."

"No offense meant. What brings you back to these parts?"

Coleman did not answer straightaway. "Why, curiosity, Mr. Kings."

Kings holstered his weapon and dismounted, his eyes never leaving the man. Only when he had both feet on the ground and both shoulders squared did he speak again. Some five or six paces separated him from Coleman.

"How can I be of help?"

"I just wanted to know, Mr. Kings, if you—"

Mid-sentence, Coleman went for his gun.

Kings had been waiting for the man's left arm to move and was not caught off guard as Coleman hoped. His mind had been at work from the moment he placed Coleman's face, and by the time he'd dismounted Kings decided that if things, for whatever reason, got ugly, and if it could be helped, he wouldn't fire a shot. He didn't want to make any more noise than he had to.

Kings slid the Bowie knife from its sheath and, stepping in hard and fast, struck Coleman across the face with the flat of the blade. The blow caught Coleman flush on the right cheekbone, stunning him, and that was all the opening Kings needed. He brought the blade around, slamming it upward into Coleman's belly and driving it to the hilt. The two men were suddenly face to face. Coleman's lips parted, but no words came out, only a gout of blood.

Kings said nothing, either—no gloating, no stark or poetic farewell. He withdrew the knife with a sharp twist, shoving his enemy away. Coleman fell to his knees, struggled to rise, couldn't, and gave it another try. He failed again, then rolled over onto his side. He thrashed once and went still in a stew of blood, viscera, and snow.

Brownwell spat tobacco juice. "Hellfire . . ."

Kings wiped the blade clean on Coleman's pant leg, then mounted up and took off at a fast clip. Minutes later, with the cabins in the distance, he halted before a lonely cottonwood to stare up at the welcome that had been left for them. The others spread out on either side, features uniformly grim.

Peering beyond the slowly twisting legs of what used to be Dave Zeller, Kings saw five horses in the corral, four of which hadn't been there prior to their departure. He saw Zeller's faithful dun mare and recognized the short-coupled bay with the white shoulder.

He also knew the man who rode it.

Kings calculated the odds and found them favorable. He kneed his horse to the right and addressed them all.

"I want y'all to fan out and make poor targets of yourselves," he said. "When you see that door fly open and the rats come crawlin' out, you scatter your shots. Bunch 'em up. Aim at *any*thing and *every*thing but them. Leave the rest to me."

The four dismounted, drawing their rifles on the way down. Brownwell scattered the animals, then led the advance. They assumed various positions about the place—Yeager and Osborn at separate intervals behind corral posts, Brownwell to the rear of the woodpile, and Woods to one side of a big rock—all with direct beads on the front door.

On the sprint, Kings was soon among the horses in the corral. The next moment, he was skimming through the cottonwoods to the rear of the cabins. As his men watched, trying to follow his movements, he disappeared briefly—it might have been a minute—then reappeared, crouching low in his stocking feet, on the roof whose chimney was leaking smoke.

Kings knelt, shucked his overcoat, and draped it over the lip of the chimney. Unholstering a Peacemaker, he peered over the edge of the rooftop and waited, as a fox before a rabbit hole.

Smoke began to seep from under the door. From within there was the sound of choking men, which soon turned to shouting. Kings heard the door bang open and rifles sounded from the yard. The lighter crack of pistols responded from the doorway, and bullets thudded into the cabin as Kings's men did as they'd been told. The air seemed to shake when someone from inside cut loose with a shotgun, spraying the sleety lawn with pellets that fell well short of the mark.

Kings waited until he heard hammers clicking on detonated cartridges before he moved, sliding on the seat of his trousers into the seven-foot drop to the ground. Cartridges continued to clink on the porch planks, cylinders buzzed as men hurried to fill them, and he rounded the corner of the cabin. Jack Lightfoot was on the porch, as was Frank Wingate, who was just closing his Schofield.

A fragment of time slipped by before the intruders became aware of his presence. Then Kings jerked his pistol, and the single gunshot echoed off the steep canyon walls. Lightfoot spun, falling into and bouncing off the cabin door with a hole in his heart.

On the heels of that shot, Wingate and Kings fired almost simultaneously. Wingate's bullet tore the fabric of Kings's left sleeve and Kings's shot sent woodchips flying as Wingate ducked around the opposite corner.

In no hurry, Kings pivoted through the smoke-clogged doorway, the muzzle of his pistol leading the way. Batting the air with his free arm, he stepped out of the light quickly and could just make out Dan Carver's bulky form.

The big man was on his feet, clutching the back of a chair for support with his left hand. In his right was a cocked pistol, though he seemed unsure as to where he should aim it. His face was a ghastly shade of gray, and large drops of sweat crowned his forehead.

"Frank, that you?" On the verge of firing, Carver shouted again, "Frank!"

Kings's third shot was well placed. The slug struck Carver below the left cheekbone and exited the back of his skull in a crimson bloom. Before the heavy body hit the floor, his killer was already sledging through the room, hooking a chair out of his way before opening the back door.

Two bullets perforated the wood, obliterating the latch. Then Wingate was running, and Kings stepped out onto the patch of ground at the bottom of the steps. It took him a moment to drag a sleeve across his watering eyes, and in that moment of blindness, Wingate could have made an end of him, but Kings continued, guns swinging low in either hand.

The land at the rear of the twin cabins was a half-mile wide for about two hundred yards. Then, the ground began to veer, starting at forty-degree angles, into chimney cliffs that tempted ninety sheer degrees. Both sides of the horse trail that led up into the higher elevations were choked with trees, and it was into those trees that Wingate's tracks took Kings.

There were two shots left in his right-hand Peacemaker, five in the other, and fresh rows of cartridges on both belts. Wingate had twelve loops left in his that still held cartridges, a spare belt over one shoulder, plus three rounds in his Schofield. It was an even game between men who had a bone-deep hatred for each other, only Wingate was running the other way.

Wingate leaned against an antler-scarred trunk to catch his breath. He wasted no more than half a minute, then went down the ridge to the right, bulling through the stand, and burst into a clearing. Head spinning, he was uncertain as to where he should go from there. After a moment, he elected to huddle behind a rampart of rock and reload.

Kings was calm and kept coming. One way or another, he was going to kill Wingate, just as he had killed Coleman and

Lightfoot and Carver. Nearing the same scarred tree that Wingate had stopped at minutes before, he heard the bark of a Schofield.

He dropped but held fire until he could discern from where Wingate's shot had come. One thing was certain—it hadn't been a direct shot from straight ahead, because the slug had torn a horizontal gash along the southeastern side of the tree.

Kings put an ear to the wind, searching for sound. He waited, then rose to one knee for a quick scan. No sign. Then he was up again and running, staying low. Here and there Kings paused to survey, always with something between himself and what lay ahead. The snow had soaked the thick wool of his socks, and where they showed through the slush, rocks hurt the soles of his feet. But he kept on, ignoring the pain.

If his guess was right, he and Wingate were cat-and-mousing closer and closer to a rainy-day-only, two-hundred-foot falls that had been dry and quiet for months now. He stopped again to reconnoiter at the mouth of a trench where snow, gravel, and boulders funneled down into a medium-wide depression in the earth. After a good rain, it would be murmuring with freshwater for the falls to spill into space. Kings had bathed under its shower more than once and hadn't been able to hear himself think for the force of the cascade.

He turned, looking back the way he had come, then crouched, holstering the left-hand Colt to reload the other. There was a fist-sized rock near his foot with dark-brown sod on the top and frost on the bottom, which let him know that Wingate had indeed come this way.

For a long time there was no sound, no crackle of snow under a shifting boot, no click of a gun barrel against stone . . . Not even the breath of a man being backed into a corner. Nothing.

Kings had no idea where Wingate was, whether he was close by or farther along, but was Wingate just as blind as he was?

Had he already pinpointed Kings's exact location, and if Kings moved again, would Wingate put one in him? There would be no easy way out of this, but Kings wanted none.

After a while, there was a commotion up ahead. Kings rose higher and caught sight of Wingate scrambling down the riverbed, turning an ankle here, nearly falling there. Stealthily, Kings got to his feet, winced, and started moving. He tailed Wingate swiftly, careful to stay well out of his periphery.

Things were coming to a head.

When he came to the shocking realization of the falls a hundred yards downriver, Wingate swore. He turned with his eyes on the ground. Then his gaze came up, and he stopped short because there was Kings with a black, long-barreled pistol in his fist.

Neither man spoke; neither man dared to move. Kings had his revolver out at shoulder-height, arm and gun barrel straight and still as though carved from a single piece of granite. His expression was calm, but Wingate, with his .44 hanging waist-high, wore an ugly snarl.

Finally, Kings said, "Hello, Frank."

"Hello, Kings."

"Come down to this, has it?"

"Been comin' down to this for a while. You just didn't know it."

"You forget what happened back on the Canadian?"

"I ain't forgotten. Our present situation don't make me no less thankful."

The call of a warbler sounded from down the canyon.

"Gotta say, you got me at a disadvantage here, Kings."

"Like you caught Dave Zeller at a disadvantage?"

"Got me there." Wingate forced a smile. "Your man—he went down fightin', I'll give 'im that."

"How you wanna play this, Frank? Even break with pistols?"

Wingate's smile stayed where it was, though Kings could see it was strained, even at this distance. "Well, I appreciate that, Kings—I surely do—though I don't know you'd call it even."

As one man, they holstered their weapons.

"Too bad things turned out like this," Kings said, keeping his hand on the pistol a moment longer.

"Way of our world, Kings. Sooner or later, we eat each other." Wingate turned slowly to show his enemy the right side of his body, his hand hovering near his buckle for the cross-draw.

"Who's payin' for your supper, and how much?"

"Two thousand dollars American. Ned Spivey says howdy."

"Didn't think I'd heard the last of him."

Stillness reigned for a time that seemed eternal. Then, from the corner of his eye, Kings saw snow crumble and crawl loose from a ledge. Wingate's hand slapped his left hip.

Kings was faster, firing just as his opponent cleared leather. The shot from Wingate's Schofield went wide as Kings's bullet entered his liver from a distance of thirty feet, the force of it bringing him to his knees at the lip of the falls. His side seeping blood, Wingate almost looked amazed.

Smoke curled from the barrel of Kings's Colt, the smell of it acrid in his nostrils. He looked into Wingate's eyes and thought of the hate he'd seen in those of Henry Coleman just before he died. It paled in comparison to the hate he saw now.

"Good-bye, Frank."

All emotion left Wingate's eyes as a second bullet punched through his forehead, and what remained of him toppled backward over the falls.

CHAPTER 18

Eight men awaited the arrival of the 12:30 train to El Paso, and, although the train was already a good forty-five minutes late, none of them said a word to the station agent.

They had come in ones and twos, ushered in by a north wind, to this squat frame building where trains stopped only briefly as they neared the end of the line. Once they had purchased their tickets, each group returned to whatever corner of the depot platform they'd claimed for themselves. They blew on their hands, stomped their feet, and huddled their shoulders against the cold, but there was little talk. The last to arrive was a tall man in a buffalo coat who came in from the southwest at a quarter to noon. He hitched his fine black horse with its tail to the wind and strode to the ticket window without looking left or right. He purchased his ticket and retreated to sit on the edge of the platform.

Kings was aware that he was being subjected to careful examination by the ticket seller, which was why he distanced himself so far apart from the others, and why he'd turned his back to them. To create the illusion that none of the men knew each other, they'd agreed to divide into groups and approach the depot from different directions at various times. Once there, they would avoid any visible form of communication. To further emphasize their disconnection, some—Kings, Brownwell, and Woods—dressed formally under their long coats, and only Kings had spurs on his boots. Woods had even toted a valise along.

Bob Creasy and Charley Davis wore the wide-brimmed hats, leather cuffs, and big-roweled spurs of working cowhands, while Yeager, Osborn, and Hardyman Foss were dressed neutrally.

With his left hand Kings reached inside his coat for the week-old telegram. The dateline read *Fort Sumner, New Mexico Territory.*

COME ON UP STOP WELL WORTH THE TRIP STOP
H. E.

Who could say if this excursion would indeed be well worth the trip, and who knew what the next few days would bring—glory and satisfaction, or death and defeat? Kings never had to worry about the steadiness of his hand before a job, and he'd never given much thought to the subject of his own death, never really feared it. But he feared it now.

Now, he had something to live for.

She would be waiting for him, as always. He finally recognized the pain his absences caused her, the nightmares that tortured her. He never wanted to bring her grief again, though he was well aware of the paradox of his present venture. A lot could happen in a week . . . a hell of a lot.

Geographically, their destination was approximately eighty miles downcountry from the Colorado border. It could well be called a town by now, no longer just another frontier mining camp scraping a chance at prosperity out of bare rock. The craggy, mesa-dotted terrain around Justicia had at least one stage line running through it and was littered with homesteads and ranches, though there were quite a few miles between neighbors out past the town limits. Indian attacks that had been so worrisome a few short years ago had become a rarity, as most of the hostiles had either been pushed to the south or interned on reservations.

From where Kings sat it was a two-hour ride west along the

tracks to El Paso, where they would await the four o'clock train that would take them on the second leg of their journey across the New Mexico line, and then north some two hundred and sixty miles to Fort Sumner, where they would make contact with this H. E.

From there, they could afford to catch their breath and sleep on feather beds for a day before horseback-riding another three, northwest to Justicia. At that rate, they would arrive no later than December 30, with plans to make their move the following morning, a day ahead of schedule. In doing so, Kings hoped to even the odds by catching the waiting lawmen somewhat off guard and in mid-preparation.

The unfortunate case of John Allen Blake was forgotten, and the more recent bad business with Frank Wingate had been cast aside like old coffee dregs. Kings could not let the same rage that had overwhelmed him upon discovering Zeller's body continue to infect him over the next week, though he supposed he might have a right to feel *some* anger. What was required of him on this mission, rights aside, was composure, a clear mind, efficiency. Anger, coupled with a hunger for vengeance, would only yield sloppiness, and that could lead to failure.

The train finally pulled in, but it would be another fifteen minutes before it got under way again. Each new passenger was required to fork over another five dollars to secure passage for their animals. Watching from the platform, the ticket seller took note of how even the cowhands, who otherwise looked to be down-at-heel, paid the fee without question.

Kings, the last to arrive, was last to board. Beneath him, the train was huffing steam into the wind. For a brief moment, his eyes caught and held with the ticket seller's, then he moved inside the coach.

The westbound jolted into motion while Kings was still on his feet. His men had scattered about the car, some even moving on to the next one down the line. He found Brownwell in the smoker. The 12:30 had now reached top speed, so Kings stationed himself in an empty window seat, lit a cigar, and watched the pale landscape sweep by.

The train had scarcely gone fifty yards before the ticket seller ducked back inside the depot and was dictating the most urgent of messages to the telegraph operator. He might have been a simple man who sold tickets at this small, next-to-last stop on the Sunset Route, but he was no fool. Knowing the faces and other distinguishing features of the state's many criminals was not a part of his job description, but he had always known the day would come when it proved useful. The face on one of the posters below his ticket window and the face he had seen beyond it might have differed slightly, but the description below the rough sketch matched. There was the sickle-shaped scar on the man's left cheekbone and the crooked little finger on his right hand. His black hair was graying, and the artist's rendering lacked the mustache and chin-beard, but there was no doubt in the ticket seller's mind that he had just come within arm's length of Gabriel Kings, the most famed outlaw west of the Pecos.

The telegraph operator in Austin was roused from his half-slumber when his machine chattered to life. Once he transcribed the message, he was out the door and into the chilly afternoon air, dashing pell-mell for the capitol building. The message in his hand read:

G. KINGS AND 7 MEN ON TRAIN TO E. P. STOP
CONTACT OFFICE THERE POSTHASTE STOP
REQUEST INFO ON REWARD STOP

★ ★ ★ ★ ★

The governor's men found Stringer checking his horse's hooves in the livery. He was in his shirtsleeves, hatless, and his gunbelt hung from a shovel hook on the barn wall. Gray hair tousled, eyes squinting, he looked anything but an officer of the Texas Rangers.

"Captain Stringer," the taller one said, "the governor just received a telegram. Kings was spotted on a westbound train a little less than an hour ago. Seven men boarded with him, but it wasn't clear if they were all in his company. We've made contact with the depot in El Paso, told them to notify us as soon as his train pulls in, and let us know where he's headed."

"Governor told us to tell you he thinks Kings has taken the bait," added the second.

The captain straightened, seemingly unaffected by their report. The governor's men traded confused looks as he guided his horse rump-first into the stall, collected his hat, and reached for his gunbelt. His footsteps were shuffles. They'd anticipated a different reaction, but they didn't know this was how it was with Stringer.

He slung the long-barreled pistol about his waist, adjusted it so that it rested just to the front of his hipbone, and finally acknowledged his visitors with a raised chin and resolute voice. "Well, gents, we best get a move on."

Stringer, Leduc, and the Pinkertons had to sit and wait at the telegraph office for another three hours before they got confirmation that Kings was indeed headed north. *Now* was the time to move quickly. The Refuge possemen were on standby, and as soon as the awaited telegram was received, Delaney sprinted for Smith's Hotel to rally them.

It was late in the afternoon by the time they all assembled at the railhead. Their window of opportunity forbade the slow, overland horseback route across peaks and canyons to Justicia.

It was absolutely essential that the lawmen board a fast train for the initial lap.

Because of the positive impact their task would have on business, a wire from Atchison, Topeka & Santa Fe Railway president Thomas Nickerson declared that he had personally arranged for the lawmen to be given right-of-way over all other traffic. He had also secured a special unit of passenger and stock cars for them, asking only that they repay his kindness with success.

Leduc supervised the loading of horses, pack mules, and the necessary equipment. When he finished, he joined Stringer under the depot porch, where he faced their volunteers.

The faces of the men, seven in all after Jensen bowed out, were singularly etched with dour anticipation. Uncertain of what lay ahead, these civilians had made it plain their safety was expendable if it meant a safer frontier for their families and any who came after them.

Stringer opened by saying, "You all know why we're here, and what we have to do. Our job hasn't changed. We're to apprehend Gabr'el Kings and bring him before a judge for his crimes. Lookin' around, I'd say we have a slight advantage in numbers, and we'll have a sheriff and a few deputies on our side when the time comes. Now, I know it felt good to do what we did to Tom Seward and Dave Zeller, but for all that's holy, boys, don't you for a minute underestimate *this* man. He's spent most of the last twenty years on the run and should've died more deaths than any of us by now, so whatever you think he's capable of . . . expect more. If any of you are havin' second thoughts, I wish you'd leave now."

When no one moved, Stringer continued. "I guess I don't have to tell you, then, that we ain't headed to no church social. That's why I do appreciate you showin' up. I've never been a married man or a father like some of you are, but I know the courage it took for you to come here this mornin'. Therefore, I won't do you the dishonor of sugarcoatin' things. I do *not* know what's in store for us. I do *not* know if this is just another wild goose chase; if it's glory awaitin' us at the end of this trip or failure. I don't know how many of you are gonna come back to your wives and kids. What I *do* know is that I'm right honored to have you men ridin' with me."

He scanned the rows of eyes and saw the same sentiment reflected back. "Now let's go and make them wives and kids proud, by God."

They boarded and were under way within thirty minutes.

The four o'clock train departed relatively on time and was now chugging steadily under a black night sky. Ageless New Mexico was beginning to take shape as this loud portent of industrialization passed through it. A coyote paused at the peak of a snowy outcrop to watch the iron horse pass, curious and unafraid as any good scavenger, before continuing on its way through the brush.

Inside the dining car, the sound of rattling dinner plates and mealtime chatter could be heard, fair if not first-rate cooking smelt, and eight or nine passengers seen. Kings and Brownwell were among them, dressed like lawyers but eating like Southern farmers—chicken breasts with grits and coffee. No one, not even the conductor who had strolled by earlier, was suspicious of the way their talk quickly died whenever someone strayed too close.

When he finished eating, Kings sat back to stare out the window into the nothingness beyond and so, into his own reflection. He absently tugged at his beard as Brownwell wiped his mouth.

"I think we oughta go over it one more time," Brownwell suggested, as he had countless times before, "how we're gonna tackle this 'un . . ."

Kings nodded, still locked in a staring competition with himself. If he concentrated hard enough, he could see his father in the pane.

Brownwell proceeded, ticking the participants' names off on his fingers as he went. "All right, then—you, me, and Andy head into the bank on New Year's Eve, day ahead of time, in the hopes that we catch these boys off guard. There'll be some of ours close by outside, makin' sure we're the only ones inside at the time, keepin' watch for this—" He chuckled then. "Say, what did the papers call 'em, Gabe? Gabe?"

Kings seemed to awaken, blinking as he turned his face toward Brownwell.

"Off somewheres else, was ya?"

" 'Super posse,' " Kings replied, as though he had been exorcised of some spirit of diversion and was now free to carry on. "Papers called it a 'super posse.' Makes you wonder if this country is starved for heroes."

Brownwell tried for a joke. "I thought that's what we were— Robin Hoods of our time, you, me, and the James boys."

"Robin Hoods, huh? Tell me, Leroy—when was the last time any one of us gave our money to the poor? Someone other'n a whore or faro dealer? Only a damn fool would set stock by them lies. See where that guff got young Johnny Blake."

Brownwell frowned. "You all right?"

Kings hailed the waiter for a refill. When he looked again at Brownwell, stirring a sugar cube into the coffee, it was as if a shade had been drawn over his face. His eyes were clear and focused, his features stiff and robbed of any emotion other than what the moment demanded.

"If you recall, General Lee was outmanned and outgunned at Fredericksburg, but he routed the federals in a way that hadn't been seen since Bull Run. This posse's gonna be lookin' to run the tables on us, but you watch—it's gonna be Fredericksburg all over again, and I'll tell you why."

"I'm all ears, pard."

"A fella might get the notion that the reason we're goin' to this place is to account for what they done to our boys. I'll not deny that's part of it, but it ain't all. Tell you the truth, it's got somethin' to do with their nerve. Their sonovabitchin' nerve. They bit off more'n they could chew this time, the damn government, and we're gonna prove it. For us to ride in and take this bank, which we *will* do, will be to ride into the pages of history."

Brownwell knew he was facing a different man from the one with whom he had sat down to supper. He was, in spite of himself, awed by the coldness in his friend's eyes. "Oh, make no mistake," he said slowly, "you've earned your place, Kings."

The Virginian lifted his cup for another swig. "And even if this ain't the party we expect, if I'm wrong about this 'super posse' bein' there . . . Well, so much the better."

They sat talking for a few minutes more, putting all thoughts of the job aside. When they finished their last cup, Kings declined Brownwell's offer of a nightcap back in his compartment, and they parted with backslaps. Kings left a few dollars on the table for the waiter and roamed for a while, moving from one coach to the next. He tipped his hat to a well-dressed older man who lingered in one of the cars, reading a book under a lamp.

He found Hardyman Foss alone in the smoker. With his chair angled to face one of the windows, he had the makings in his lap but didn't look up until Kings dragged a chair over and sat down.

"How you doin'?" Foss asked.

Kings seemed not to have heard. He crossed his legs and watched Foss roll the paper between his fingers, lick the open edge, seal the cigarette, and light up. Foss took a drag, exhaled slowly, then squinted with one eye through the smoke.

"You find somethin' interesting?"

"I just never got the hang of rollin' my own. Myself, I always enjoyed cigars." He searched inside his coat, found a dark leather case, and removed a maduro. He chewed off the end and asked Foss, "I don't suppose I could bother you for a light?"

Foss produced one and held it under Kings's cigar until it caught flame. The Virginian blew smoke and settled back in his chair, re-crossing his legs the other way. It was nearly one o'clock in the morning.

"I'm doin' fine," Kings said. "How 'bout you?"

"Never better. Thinkin' 'bout turnin' in."

"Just thought you'd have one more smoke afore you went?"

"Yeah. You?"

"I don't sleep too well these days. Most the time I only get around five, mebbe six hours' rest. I do a good deal of thinkin'."

"What about?"

Kings exhaled twin jets of smoke through his nose. "Lots of things."

The car fell silent for a moment, then Foss said, "In all your travels, Kings, did you ever make it up to Idaho Springs?"

"No, never did. Have you?"

"I give it some thought. Matter of fact, I'd like to head up there after this is all over and get a good soak in them hot springs. Kicker, ain't it? A man can stay warm in the winter and be nekkid as a jaybird at the same time. That's quite a picture."

Kings allowed himself to smile as he imagined it. "It is."

"Yeah, way I got it planned out, I'll just skip on up to Colorado when this is done and work my way north, one mile at a time."

"Well, you won't be able to do that right away."

"How's that?"

"Considerin' the law's gonna be hot to catch or kill us, we won't have time to divide the loot then and there. You'll all meet someplace safe about a month from now and Brownwell or Yeager will give each of ya what's due."

"Brownwell or Yeager? Where you gonna be?"

"I'll be a married man by then, Mr. Foss, and on my way west."

"So you'll have already got your cut by then."

"That's right."

"Well, I don't much care for that."

Kings turned his head a fraction of an inch. "To be honest, it don't much matter to me if you don't care for it, Mr. Foss. Rest assured, you'll be paid accordingly. I've never cheated a man out of what he's owed."

"Hell if I know that for the truth," Foss grumbled. "You could be gallivantin' off to Canada with a bigger cut than you're due, for all I know! Hell, if I had the chance, *I* would!"

"You and I are different men."

"Now you're callin' me a cheat?"

"No, sir, and you know it." With that, Kings stood up. The luxurious feeling he had been enjoying was disrupted. "Have a good night, Mr. Foss."

Foss was stone-faced. He told himself he would keep his peace for the time being. He managed a chuckle and said, "You're not an easy man to get along with, you know that, Kings?"

Kings appeared to consider that. "It's been said of me."

He left Foss there, and the train pushed on into the night.

CHAPTER 19

The lawmen spent the two days of Christmas within the high adobe walls of Fort Union, thanks to the hospitality of the commanding officer, Captain Edward Whittemore. Soldiers and possemen alike were in high spirits, and liquor was allowed to flow—in moderation, of course—on the parade ground. Stringer and the others joined Whittemore in his private quarters, where the military man filled five glasses from his private stash of Monongahela. They solemnly toasted the imminent New Year and drank another to the success of their endeavor. When the hour to retire came, Whittemore detained Stringer for a few private minutes and asked him whether he could be of any assistance.

Stringer declined, saying he felt confident in himself and his men. He also said he did not think it would be in Justicia's best interests if a portion of the 15th Cavalry rode off to help them arrest or shoot eight outlaws.

Whittemore replied that he felt the same, and that he was not offering a detail of his soldiers. What he *would* be willing to loan Stringer was the pride of the fort, a Gatling gun that stood on a tripod on the western watchtower. Stringer was welcome to secure it to a wagon bed and take it up to Justicia if it would make his job any easier.

In that case, Stringer accepted, and gladly.

The lawmen gathered their horses for the second, less comfortable leg of the journey on the dreary morning of the twenty-sixth. Three pack mules were laden with bedding and an optimistic amount of food for the return. Kullander the freighter handled the two-mule team that carried the dismantled Gatling. Delaney sat beside him as a sort of shotgun guard.

With a handshake from Whittemore, Stringer assumed position at the head of the group, Mincey to his left, Leduc to his right, and gave the word to move out. Justicia was within eighty miles to the northwest, and they had three days to make the hill country.

Old Testament justice would be meted out, and, one way or another, the rampaging of Gabriel Kings would be at an end. Whether the final verdict was rendered by some earthly judge or the Creator himself, that wasn't Caleb Stringer's department, and neither was it Paul Leduc's or Walt Mincey's or Pat Delaney's.

They just had to arrange the meeting.

Kings was seated at a table on the ground floor of a Fort Sumner saloon, his back to the stove that warmed the insides of the adobe structure. The floor was hard-packed dirt, the coffee, boiled water poured over old grounds, and the whiskey, corn. It was by no means a lavish establishment, but it suited his purpose.

Brownwell sat to Kings's left, scooping pinto beans from a plate, while Yeager, to his right, nursed a coffee. Seated directly across from Kings was a small, shifty man wearing a beat-up derby hat.

It was just past the mid-morning hour, the day after Christmas, and there were echoes of civilization coming in from the two-wagon street beyond the doors. A sharp whistle preceded the crack of a whip as a muleskinner got his team into motion. Townsfolk pleasantly greeted one another as they bustled past, full of holiday conviviality. From next door there came the honest, pleasurable sounds of a hammer and saw.

The man in the derby was H. E. Simmons, the same H. E. who had telegrammed Kings two weeks prior. He was Kings's informant in the New Mexico Territory, a man who made a living any way available to him—none of them legal. He was neither intelligent nor brave enough to rob banks or trains on his own, but he had been run out of numerous towns for various underhanded dealings, once for trying to sell a buckboard full of freshly painted gold bricks for $200 apiece.

His acquaintance with Kings originated several years before, when the outlaw posted Simmons's bail—what had landed Simmons in jail that particular time, neither remembered. They met at the local bar afterward, where Kings made an offer of occasional partnership and a cut of the proceeds of any operation in which Simmons might be called upon to assist. That day had finally arrived, and at just the right time. Pickings were slim in Fort Sumner, and so was H. E.'s billfold. He'd been only too eager to scout out the settlement of Justicia for Kings.

Simmons ground out his cigarette on the underside of the table and leaned forward, speaking in a voice heavily accented with the inflection of a native of the upper East Coast, somewhere far, far away from Fort Sumner.

"There's a big eastern mining company diggin' around up there. Magnate's got it in mind that all the silver ain't quite played out. Ain't struck the mother lode yet, but, even so, the paymaster heads out once a month, carrying ten thousand to pay the miners."

"Deposited where?" Kings asked.

"Savings bank on the corner of Third and Chivington. North end of town, between the dry-goods store and some old empty building."

"Doors open for business at what time?"

"Not likely to on New Year's Day, Mr. Kings."

"Why I plan on strikin' the bank New Year's Eve."

"In that case, nine o'clock," he said. "Employees start arrivin' a half hour before."

"That's when we'll arrive, then. Describe the place."

"It was built by a fella from St. Louis. Got pretty red-brick walls, two teller's cages, and the vault's in the rear of the building. I got a look at the box when I went in. Sizable, but it shouldn't be anything your man can't take care of. Seward, was it?"

Yeager glanced at Kings. "Tom . . . uh, Tom ain't with us any longer, Sim."

"Dave Zeller, neither," Brownwell said.

They had spoken, but Simmons looked to Kings when he asked, "They the ones I read about in the paper a little while back? I'll be damned. Never have put too much stock in what the papers say—especially 'bout you boys—and I didn't then. I'd'a sworn the paper said one of 'em was only injured, though."

Brownwell glanced uneasily at a very quiet Kings. "Fact of the matter is, Zeller and Seward won't be joinin' us in Justicia."

Simmons seemed to have trouble accepting this, and looked to Kings as a drowning man would a branch just out of reach. There was more than a hint of apprehension in his voice. "You mean to say that just the, what, *five* of you plan on takin' this bank? Six, including me?"

Yeager answered for Kings. "No, no, we brung three capable fellas along with us. They'll do their part, and that makes nine."

Simmons's relief was still registering when Kings posed another question. "How big's the opposition?"

Kings had already explained, briefly, the resistance they would face in the lawmen to whom all this could be accredited, but he needed a firm idea as to the kind that awaited them in Justicia.

"You mean Shepherd? Well, I expect you heard of him, but what most folks don't hear is that he's got quite the entourage to back him. One of 'em's this big colored fella who won't go to the outhouse without a rifle in hand. Scary thing, givin' guns to coloreds."

He cackled at his own joke, thinking surely that would garner a similar reaction from former Confederate soldiers, but to no avail.

Simmons cleared his throat and continued. "From what I saw, there was two deputies in town and then there was Shepherd himself, but it turns out there were three more that weren't in town—rounding up horse thieves, it seems. So that makes six men in all. Somethin' caught my eye was that the ones in town was wearing their sheriff's badges but more or less acting as city marshals, making their nightly rounds. They take an interest in town business and regulate it, which makes me think they're the only law in town. Sort of all-encompassing, if you take my meaning."

"Well, ain't that interestin'," Brownwell said, folding his arms on the table before him. "Sounds to me like Tom Shepherd's got the town in a stranglehold. Treed 'em with a weapon more powerful'n his gun—reputation." He glanced at Kings. "Could be we ought to've pinned on a badge a long time ago."

"Easier pay," Yeager said dryly.

Simmons was almost vehement. "Oh, there's nothing crooked about Shepherd's operation, no, sir! He's runnin' a tight ship up there, but he's a God-fearin' man now."

Kings traded looks with his lieutenants. Curiosity aside, the information only confirmed what they had suspected. On top of the expected posse, they would have to contend with an efficient and seasoned group of lawmen. Well, that was just fine. It wasn't like they hadn't come prepared.

Kings stood and paused with a hand on the back of his chair. Brownwell and Yeager, as though run by the same motor, did likewise, but Yeager, still holding his cup in both hands, seemed reluctant to leave the saloon's relative warmth. Kings looked down at Simmons, who was still in his seat.

"Sim," he said, "take us by the gunsmith's."

Outside, the sun was beating down hard, steadily melting some of the snow that hadn't been cleared from the streets. Kings, Brownwell, and Yeager walked down the middle of the thoroughfare like they owned it, scarcely making way, even for the occasional man on horseback. Simmons, as though embarrassed to be seen in their company, slinked along the boardwalk. They turned the corner onto Second and, a few doors down, entered Rose's Armory.

Once inside, the men fanned out to avoid exposing their backs to the door. Simmons, hesitant, moved out of the open doorway when Kings waved him forward and motioned to stand beside him at the counter. The sight was not unlike a father beckoning his anxious boy, though a son might have been more eager to watch his father buy a gun.

A man who could have only been Mr. Rose greeted them with a ready smile. He was wiping his oil-streaked hands with a cloth. "Yes, sirs? How can I help you?"

Kings spread his palms on the countertop. "My friends and I are goin' shootin' in the Rockies. Like to take a look at your wares."

The eyes of the proprietor, who was obviously a huntsman himself, brightened. "Shootin', you say."

Kings nodded. "What would you suggest in the way of rifles for a fella"—he clapped Simmons on the shoulder—"who's never been on a hunt before?"

"Well, now, that depends on what sort of game y'all expect to hunt."

"Elk, mostly, though I expect to run into smaller game up there," Kings replied. "This buffalo coat I've got on is a bit on the aged side. I'd like to bring down a bull if I can." He nodded at the mounted deer's head on the wall. "Impressive."

"Is, ain't it? Look at the tines on him. Not my kill, though. I ain't hunted a day, seems like, since we come out here."

"I already got a damn rifle," grumbled Simmons.

"What model?" Rose asked.

"It's a . . . Colt's revolvin'."

The gunsmith was visibly amused. "That relic will bring down a pronghorn, sure enough, but that'll do nothin' to a buff'ler but make him mad. 'Sides that, as I'm sure you've found, the real problem with the Colt's revolving is the gunpowder: what it'll do is, it sometimes gets out of the cartridges and lodges in the cylinder. Gas leaks, you pull the trigger, and next thing ya know, you're tryin' to put out the fire on your sleeve."

"A Sharps, then?" Kings suggested.

"Fresh out o' them, dang the luck. A Spencer wouldn't be a bad idea, though. Just keep away from the buff'ler. Be like twistin' his ear."

Rose went to the rack that dominated the right wall. He found one of the rifles in question, and hefted it with care. He cranked the lever forward, opening the breech, and presented it to Simmons.

"It's a fine weapon," Simmons allowed, eyeing it at arm's length after dry-firing it. "And, by God, you're right about the Colt's revolving—I rarely use it for fear of gettin' my hand blown off." He glanced at Kings, then at the gun in his hands. "I suppose I'll take it."

"You'll be needin' cartridge tubes," Rose said. "You load 'em in there, through the butt. Seven rounds a tube, .56-caliber."

Kings waited until he had returned from the storeroom with the right amount of tubes Simmons would need for a hunting expedition.

"You got a pistol to speak of, Sim?" Kings asked.

The conman, perturbed that Kings had used his name, drew

his weapon in a manner that said he used it about as often as his old rifle. That was the trouble with most Westerners—nearly everyone wore a gun. Men who knew how to use a gun *well* were an entirely different matter.

At the sight of the pistol, Kings nearly smiled. It was a pocket gun, a hammerless Smith & Wesson. Likely a .32, good for over- or under-the-table gunplay but inadequate in every way for what awaited them. He was right to bring Simmons by here.

Rose opened the display case and arranged a Colt Peacemaker, a .44-caliber Merwin & Hulbert, and a '75 Remington for Simmons to inspect.

As the grifter did so, the gunsmith looked again to Kings. "You fellers not from around here?"

"Sacramento," Kings replied.

Simmons raised the Merwin & Hulbert, aimed at the deer's head, and pulled.

"Sacramento, huh? Long ways from home to be huntin', ain'tcha? I'd'a thought you'd get a lotta game out there."

"Well, the valley's gettin' civilized, Mr. Rose, at a rate you wouldn't believe. What with the mining corporations and all the houses and churches going up, a lot of the game's moved on to wilder parts or higher elevations."

"Shame."

One would have thought that Kings and Rose were old friends by the way they each leaned into the conversation, elbows on the counter, speech as slow and nowhere-bound as a Sunday afternoon.

"Tarnation," Rose grumped, "I'd do anything just to be able ta pack up and do what you fellers are doin', but I got a business to run and—well, Zoe, she'd just raise holy hell the minute I started cleanin' my old Sharps." He rubbed the back of his neck and chuckled. "You know how it is with wives."

Kings chuckled in kind. "I do, indeed. You have any children, Mr. Rose?"

"Yessir." The gunsmith beamed. "We got three. One of 'em's married and workin' on a family of his own. Decided to try his hand at the ranchin' business a few years back and got married to a foreman's daughter instead. I don't blame the boy, but I'd think raisin' beeves is easier'n raisin' children. Don't you?"

Rose's laugh was infectious, and Kings was sorry he had to lie to him. "I'd have to agree with you, sir."

Simmons signaled Rose. "Hey, partner. I'll pay for these now."

Kings offered his hand, and Rose clasped it with enthusiasm. "You have a pleasant New Year, Mr. Rose."

"You do the same, Mister . . . ?"

"Kings."

"You do the same, Mr. King. Good huntin' to ya."

Kings led the way out the door. Simmons seemed buoyed, not dragged down, by the added heft of his newly acquired firearms and followed more closely behind the professionals as they made for the boarding house. No one spoke until they rounded a corner, out of sight of the armory.

"Helluva gamble there, Kings," Brownwell remarked, "givin' that gunsmith your uncommon family name."

"Leroy, there's certain folks you can lie to and some you can't. You can lie to politicians and John Law, but not to family men."

It came quickly to the office of Sheriff Tom Shepherd that a large body of lawmen had hitched their horses just up the street in front of the High Grade Hotel. Of course, he had eagerly been expecting them.

For his part, Stringer had intended to take a quick nap in his room before meeting with Shepherd. But because this town was no different than all the others, word spread like wildfire, which is why he found himself calling things to order within thirty minutes of arrival in Justicia.

Besides himself and Shepherd, also present were Leduc, Mincey, and two deputies—a short, red-haired white man and a tall, shaven-headed Negro cradling a Winchester. The sheriff himself was of medium height, rugged, with slate-colored eyes and a walrus mustache. His voice was soft, his manner rigid, perhaps overly courteous, and he was not at all what Stringer had expected.

Shepherd's weapon of choice was as much a surprise as his demeanor. Stringer hadn't seen the LeMat grapeshot revolver in some time. Confederate-made, it was a relatively unpopular nine-shot 1855 model chambered for .36 caliber. The real advantage to it was that its cylinder rotated around a smooth-bore, sixteen-gauge shotgun barrel, which could be fired by flicking a switch on the hammer. Reputation and manpower be damned—with a sidearm like that, Shepherd could afford to speak softly.

After a brief introduction, Shepherd and his deputies waited for Stringer to fill them in.

He gave them a quick version of all that had transpired since October. He related again how they answered only to President Hayes, Allan Pinkerton, and the governor of Texas, and how he had in his possession a federal commission to prove it.

Stringer hated to, but he couldn't help but scowl as he concluded, "Up to this point, though, for all our . . . omnipotence, we've had pretty poor luck."

Shepherd's Anglo deputy spoke up. "Didn't I just read about you fellas in the paper not too long ago? Seems to me like you ain't exactly hurtin'."

"Neither of the men we tangled with was Kings," Leduc said. "And we only accounted for one of 'em. The other made off."

The sheriff regarded Stringer with a sober countenance. "And you're certain Kings is comin' this way? That this all hasn't been in vain?"

Stringer nodded. "Matter of fact, we expect him to be no more'n two days behind us. Three at the most."

Exchanging looks with his deputies, Shepherd crossed to the door and opened it. "Then it seems like we've got quite the welcome to plan for Mr. Kings. Once you've settled in, come by my office, Captain. We oughta devise somethin' along the lines of a strategy." As an afterthought, he added, "On second thought, be best if all of you was present."

"While you're at it, maybe you oughta convene a town meeting tonight, Sheriff."

Startled, Shepherd glanced around to find Pat Delaney standing in the hall. The Pinkerton moved into the room, introduced himself, then informed Stringer, "We stowed the big gun down at the livery, and the others are sortin' out their sleeping arrangements with the fella downstairs. Half of them'll probably have to hole up at the boarding house down the street, way things are lookin'."

Shepherd turned to his Negro deputy. "Dobie, get the word out. Anybody has an interest in their share of this town, you tell 'em to congregate at the church house tonight at seven o'clock sharp."

Dobie nodded, all business. "Yassuh, Sheriff," he said and hurried down the stairs. Shepherd and the red-haired deputy left shortly after.

Leduc splashed water from a pitcher into the porcelain wash basin on the dresser. "Been meanin' to ask you, Cap—why this town, in particular? Couldn't have picked a more out-of-the-way place."

Stringer sat down on the edge of the bed, unknotted the kerchief at his throat, and eased onto his back. He suddenly felt ancient, and in more need of a shave and a bath than he ever had in his life. "Exactly why I picked it, Paul," he replied. "Its location puts it a far piece out of Kings's regular circuit of operation. It's unfamiliar to him, both the town and the surrounding countryside. On top of that, I'd heard what kinda man this Tom Shepherd was, what kind of hand he is with a gun, and I knew he'd be runnin' a tight ship. We sent the word out, and, as dicey as this whole shindy might appear, the good sheriff sounded willin' and able to lend a hand."

The captain made a croaky noise in the back of his throat, which Leduc recognized as the signal that he was through talking and ready for his *siesta*.

Delaney sat down to pull off his boots, and Mincey took the Queen Anne chair by the window, pipe in his mouth and rattling a matchbox. Downstairs in the lobby, the grandfather clock rang out twelve times, reaching the ears of the men as clearly as if it had been in the room with them.

It was December 28.

CHAPTER 20

Kings lay still in his blankets a few minutes longer before removing the hat from his face. Above him was a deep magenta sky, smudged with eastern morning yellow. Flinging his bedding aside, he shook out his boots and pulled them on before standing slowly, stiff with cold. Still in that limbo-world between slumber and coherence, he moved like a machine, his hands working as if with a mind of their own. He girded his waist with the gunbelts, just so, then hugged his buffalo coat tight and meandered out of the ring of bodies to answer nature's call.

The air was wintry, and the tops of the bull pines swayed under a high wind. He took his time heading back into camp, taking pleasure in the almost nonexistent sounds of a waking world before inevitably stumbling back into the harsh, rude sphere of clattering cups and pans, of men making less than harmonious morning sounds.

The one exception he allowed was the bubbling of coffee over a fire, which Charley Davis had going by the time he returned. Kings got in line behind Woods and accepted a cup but waved off a dollop of whiskey. "Go on, man," Davis encouraged, sticking his flask out farther. "Really warm up your insides."

Kings covered his cup with a hand and walked away so abruptly Davis thought he might have offended him. Yeager stepped up and waited until Davis had tipped the pitcher forward and put a little coffee in his cup before putting the

221

man's mind at ease. "Don't concern yourself about him. He's always like 'at before a job."

Simmons had moved up by then and was blowing on his coffee. "How do you mean?"

"Uncommon quiet, face like the wrath of God. Don't be surprised you don't hear a peep from him till a minute before we go into the bank."

Davis nodded his understanding and stepped away from the fire, eyes searching for Kings and finally finding him among the horses. He was tickling the nose of his big stallion, a smile threatening. "He don't speak all that much to begin with," Davis remarked.

They broke camp around eight o'clock, with the sun's rays still leaking through the trees on their right, and headed due north at an easy lope. They had left Fort Sumner two days before, on the twenty-seventh, nine in number with the addition of Simmons. The new terrain obliged them to move at a slower pace than Kings might have preferred—they averaged about twenty miles a day. He estimated them to be at least another day out from Justicia.

Reaching a strip of river near noontime, they pushed through the trees another mile upstream until they came to a sandbar. It was occupied by two sizable wolves ravenously tugging at the remains of a bull elk. One of them glanced up at the horsemen before delving back into the open ribcage. When Kings nudged John Reb a step forward onto the sandbar, the same wolf swung fully around, flattened its ears, and bared its teeth. Kings fired two rounds into the air, and the wolves were forced to abandon the carcass until the men passed by.

A little over twenty-four hours later they came in sight of rooftops. The horsemen reined up at a high enough vantage point at the edge of the tree line so they could take in the panorama. The snow was a foot deep on the outskirts, but the main road leading into and through town had been cleared. Two miles long and one wide, the settlement in the middle of this long and narrow valley was cosmopolitan in comparison to the rough camp it had been six years ago. Where once it had boasted only one double row of buildings, there were now five rows—four streets and six cross streets—with structures of weathered false-front, brick, and stone.

No one spoke, but Kings felt their collective gazes from both sides. He sat his saddle a moment longer, inhaling a lungful of cold, high desert air before opening his mouth.

"Here's how it'll be. Os, you and Simmons ride in ahead of us and do what it is y'all two do best. We know what kind of reception to expect, but keep your eyes open for any fortifications that might have been made, any escape routes that might be blocked off. I don't think it'd be wise to linger for more'n an hour, so when you've seen enough, head for them boulders to the east yonder. We'll be there, awaitin' your report."

"When are the rest of us headin' in, Kings?" Creasy asked.

"Not till tonight."

"Say what?"

"Well, now, Crease, if we was to go ridin' in nine strong in broad daylight, you expect whoever's down there to just let us spend a peaceful night in one of their hotels? Expect they'd wait for us to strike their bank afore openin' the ball?"

While Creasy, and every other man who had anticipated heading into town for the night, considered that, Kings continued.

"Now, I expect each of you boys to make use of your time. Get to know the layout of the town from the heights here, so that when we *do* walk the streets, it'll be as familiar to you as your hometown. Believe me, our comin' out of this alive will depend on it. We're gonna ride in, three at a time, at half hour intervals, startin' at ten o'clock. We'll scrounge out someplace to hole up for the night, and tomorrow mornin', we'll do what we come here to do."

"Catch 'em unawares," Woods said, "hittin' that bank a day early?"

"That's the idea. Most all places of business are apt to be open only half the day, and, as it is, folks' minds will likely be on other things, anticipatin' the . . . big celebration and all. If there's one to begin with. Any luck, we'll catch them john laws with one leg in their pants and be able to breeze out of this town in better shape than we'd planned on."

If the men's confidence in the infallibility of this operation had been unstable before, the confidence that seemed to have taken root in Kings touched the general morale in a godlike way. It was visible in their faces and their saddle postures. The chatter of a woodpecker's beak seemed louder than it should have in the stillness, and, in the midst of that chattering, Kings nodded at Osborn.

He and Simmons moved out, and the horsemen remaining on the knoll receded into the trees. Osborn, seeing that he was ahead, slowed his mount until H. E. had no other choice but to come abreast of him. Side by side, they entered Justicia.

The settlement proved to be more alive than it appeared from the trees, with townspeople on the boardwalks, horses standing three-legged at hitch rails along the street, and a farmer securing water barrels to a buckboard. Halfway through town, the newcomers passed under a canvas banner that had been stretched between second-floor verandas, with the words "Happy New Year" painted on. Thirty-eight-star American flags hung in windows, although New Mexico had yet to obtain statehood.

A man emerged from a corner café, and, by chance, his and Osborn's gazes met. He was a bear of an old-timer in a bulky coat, the color of his eyes startlingly green under a gray Stetson with a hole in the crown. Even as his horse carried him farther away, Osborn felt he was being watched. Instinctively, he knew that old-timer must have been, if not the leader, a member of the posse awaiting their arrival. No, a man like that didn't play second fiddle to anybody. He was the boss, all right. Probably sizing Osborn up for a coffin, eyeing his neck for a noose.

Dick hooked his horse into the rails under a sign that showed a dove on a branch. When he glanced back the way he came, the jefe wasn't where he had been. Simmons was on the other side of the street, strolling across the boards with his mackinaw wrapped around him. For his own reassurance, Osborn felt the bulges of his twin sidearms, hidden between body and long coat, then shoved through the doors of the White Dove Saloon.

By this time some of the others were stringing a rope corral along the ridge overlooking the eastern side of town. The ground up there was flat enough to lay out a small, temporary campsite. Brownwell spread his blankets and sat down to inventory, clean, and assemble the two spare revolvers he had brought along. Woods dealt cards to Creasy and Foss while Yeager and Davis carefully went down-slope about a dozen feet to an outcropping and settled in to survey.

Kings slapped snow from a sizable rock with one of his gauntlets, sat down, and took a long look around at the buttes, the ageless crags crowned by spires of black pines. He had hoped to sit a while, appreciating the peacefulness in his surroundings, to contemplate something other than what was coming, but Brownwell spoiled that hope.

"Kings?"

"Yep."

Brownwell dabbed oil on an old shaving brush and began to lightly coat a pistol cylinder. "Might be a little late to be askin' this," he said, "but be square with me. D'you, honest to God, think we can fight our way outta this one without losin' half our men in the doin'?"

"I wouldn't be riskin' their lives if I didn't."

Brownwell wasn't satisfied. "You 'member what happened to the James boys? They got shot all to hell up in Northfield, and them squareheads never so much as *looked* at a gun 'fore that day. Here we are, goin' to meet hard men, professionals. They're gonna be settin' up in their windows and on their rooftops, takin' potshots at us like so many fish in a barrel, I'm thinkin'."

Kings shook his head. "Don't you go believin' this is gonna be an uneven fight. All but one of our men are professionals, too, and we never stopped fightin'. There's a big difference, Leroy, as you know good and well, between livin' outside the law and livin' within it, and how that makes a man.

" 'Sides that, we got somethin' the James boys didn't—we ain't ridin' down there blind to the knowledge of what's in store for us. The reason the toll was so heavy on your fellow Missourians was 'cause Jesse underestimated the folks in that Yankee town, which is a bad habit he should've dispensed with back in the war."

"I dunno. Closer the hour gets, this starts to look more an' more like suicide."

"Fine damn time to say so."

Brownwell shrugged, rolling the cylinder into place and thumbing the ejector rod down into its slot with a click. "Like I said. Figure you know what you're doin'."

Kings bristled for a time, not wanting to entertain the likelihood of defeat. "You're damn right, I do."

After enough time had passed for his sudden ire to die a natural death, Kings asked in a calmer voice, "You ever consider what we've been doin' all these years *is* suicide?"

"Never did think of it that way."

"How *did* ya think of it?"

"I don't know precisely," Brownwell admitted. "Just sort of

took things one day at a time."

Kings didn't comment.

"I never asked you this before," Brownwell said, "but you been actin' kinda peculiar as of late and I gotta know . . . do you regret it?"

"Regret what?"

"Anything. What you done."

Kings's smile was wry. "What bothers me ain't the *doin'* so much as havin' to do any of it at all; fact that I was dealt so rotten a hand with no other option left to me. I coulda hauled Clive Parker into court and gone about it legally, sure, but him bein' a lawyer—" He shook his head. "I own about as much land today as I would've back then, had I done that. No, sir, old Sam Colt's way seemed the only choice to see that justice was done."

"Sam Colt's the best friend men like you an' me ever had, boy."

Kings fanned a slow hand down his face and, with his next words, confirmed the suspicion that had nagged at Brownwell since early spring. "I'll square with you on somethin' else. Put plainly, regrets or no, I'm tired and I want outta all this . . . mess. Mind's made up, Leroy. After this job, I'm through. You want 'em, you can have the reins to this outfit and welcome, but me—I'm about played out."

Brownwell stopped what he was doing and looked up. "Hell, we're *all* about played out, Kings," he said quietly, but with a tone that hinted at bewildered impatience. "That don't mean we have the option to get off the horse. They won't *let* us."

"I ain't asked for another man's by-your-leave since '65."

"They'll chase your ass to the four winds."

"Let 'em. They was to mount bloodhounds, it wouldn't mean spit. Come a week from now, it'll be as if I never existed."

★ ★ ★ ★ ★

"I don't like it."

Red-haired Eli Cutting crossed to the window for what must have been the twelfth time. "I don't like it one bit," he echoed. "They're prob'ly up in them hills right now, back in them trees, watchin' us like buzzards."

"Why don't we just ride up there and surround 'em? You don't wait for a snake to strike atcha before you smash it with a shovel."

The speaker was another of Shepherd's deputies, a bulldoggish Wisconsin native named Bauer. He was seated on the edge of the sheriff's desk, facing the door, with a scattergun across his lap and throwing restless glances. It was as if he expected Kings to come barging into the office at any moment.

Dobie Bell, cracking peanut shells between his teeth, glanced at the clock on the wall. "You boys don't settle yo'selves down," he said, "you gonna be blastin' at shadows all night. Those gentlemen ain't due till January fust."

"Oh, yeah," Cutting said without moving away from the window. "They ain't *supposed* to be here till January first, but there's no tellin' what a man like Kings is apt to do or not do. He's no run-of-the-mill criminal, now. He was a sojer, so you can bet he's got him a plan."

"We never gone up against any like these," Bauer seconded. "None of us."

"Well, now, we showed the Drury boys a pretty rough time, as I recall."

Cutting snorted. "Hell, Dobie, Ed Drury's a snot-nose kid next to Gabriel Kings, and none of them other Drurys was old enough to've fought in the war. Kings, now, he's seen action. Rode with ol' Jeb Stuart."

"Bedford Forrest, I heard it was," Bauer said.

Dobie was characteristically optimistic. "Shep ain't frettin' about these boys too much. And we up to our ears in reinforcements now. That Stringer, he sure seem capable."

"I worry about how quick he is on the trigger. He seemed plumb wore-out when we went to see him."

The door clattered in the frame as Deputy Whitehead stepped in from the midday cold, and with him, their heavy-shouldered Mexican colleague, Arballo. Each man, fresh from the café, held a steaming plate of pork and beans.

Whitehead seemed to have heard Cutting's last statement because he said, "Speakin' of being quick on the trigger . . ."

All heads turned in his direction as Whitehead limped closer. "We just took a stroll down by the livery barn and saw a most intriguing sight."

"What's that, Fred?" Bauer asked.

Whitehead nodded at Dobie. "Hit the nail on the head, what he said 'bout reinforcements."

Cutting chewed his lip. "Yeah, there's eleven of 'em, ain't there?"

"*Y unos cientos más,*" Arballo mumbled.

Cutting frowned. "Say again?"

"He said, 'and a few hundred more,' " Whitehead translated.

"What's he mean by that?"

Whitehead took a bite of ham. "They brought a Gatling gun with 'em. Got it tucked away in a stall, wrapped up in a tarp like a big Christmas present. These boys mean to bury Kings, if they can find all the pieces."

Dobie looked at the floor and muttered, "I'll be dog."

"Mister, you just bought yourself a sanctuary."

Kings thought it was an ironic choice of words on the part of the upstairs girl.

A roll of greenbacks slipped on the underhand and an odd request whispered into her ear had persuaded two of them to give Brownwell, the asker, and the others shelter for the night. They were led up to the second floor of a combination saloon and cathouse on the outskirts of town, four or five men and two women to a room. Abstinence an essentiality, a good night's rest a must, this place of ill repute would be their coop until dawn.

In the room closest to the stairs, Creasy was leaning back on the two rear legs of a chair with his boots on the windowsill, burning a cigarette down and contemplating. His ears were filled with a clamor of whooping and a tin-panny piano from the bar below, muffled by the locked door. He could also hear the snoring of three men—Davis, Osborn, Simmons—in the room around him, as well as the soft moaning of a painted lady. And then there was the rustling of clothes and scraping boot heels of a man getting to his feet. Hardyman Foss knelt beside him.

Creasy offered his cigarette. After carefully eyeing it to see whether the smoking end was lipped beyond acceptability, Foss tendered it into his fingers and took a drag.

"You know Kings said no diddlin'," Creasy said.

"I heard His Majesty. I's just pettin' her a little bit."

"You got a beef with Kings, Hardy?"

Foss evaded that and raised the cigarette a second time. "Speakin' of amorous affairs," he said, "I guess His Majesty's got plans to be married."

"Where'd ya hear that?"

"Man told me so hisself."

"Finally gonna call the preacher, is he?"

"You mean you heard about these plans of his already?"

"He's mentioned it."

Behind them, the girl moved from the throw pillows on the floor where Foss had engaged her to the bed beside Osborn. Foss didn't open his mouth again until the creaking of the bedsprings had died.

"Speakin' only on the hopelessness of us all," he said, "and not His Majesty in particular, but what kinda woman'd be desperate enough to marry a man like him?"

"Finer woman'n any of us could ever hope to latch onto, to hear him tell it. Name of Miss . . . Belle . . . Jackson." Creasy said her name as if each syllable tasted of honey.

"Back in Virginia, I suppose."

"Not so—she's out on the Frio River."

"That a fact?"

"Uh-huh. I guess her papa's got himself some land out there."

"You ever been there?"

Creasy shook his head and took back his smoke.

"Be a good place to hole up."

"*Fine* place to hole up," Creasy agreed. "Just about the only door in this world left open to him—save a jailhouse door—and his own personal lady to drop in on. No charge for her services. Helluva place."

There was a group of miners in the street below—two of them in the middle, liquored-up and circling like roosters, a fistfight in the making, with their rowdy co-workers egging them on. This spectacle presently diverted Creasy's attention from the subject of Belle Jackson. *Where the hell are these iron-fisted lawmen Simmons went on about?* he wondered.

"Well, I reckon I'm gonna be turnin' in," Foss said. "Got us a big day tomorrow. You comin'?"

"In a minute. Think I'll wait to see the winner."

"What time is it?"

Creasy held his watch up to the moonlight. " 'Bout a quarter to the big day."

"Well, soon as one of them fools kills the other, you best bed down. We got orders from His Majesty."

They congregated in that very room five hours later, before the sun was up—some standing, some sitting, some coiled over chairs, pushed into one corner while the working girls still slumbered in the other. The men who had not been informed of their role in the robbery eagerly anticipated the coming layout of the plan.

Kings leaned on the sill, fully armed and dressed save for his coat, and made it clear to them that, although they were indeed the challenged party in this affair, he had no intentions of meeting their adversaries on the defensive. He specifically asked Brownwell, Yeager, and Woods if their former commanding officer, General Stuart, had ever turned down the opportunity to draw first blood.

"Hell, no," Brownwell said firmly, and Kings repeated, "Hell, no."

Squatting by the door, Osborn half-raised a hand. "What d'you have in mind, Kings?"

"Leroy, Andy, and I will be takin' our morning coffee on Fourth Street, eight o'clock. At a quarter past, we'll pay our bill, get on our horses, and ride down to the bank. Simmons, you said there's a back door to this place."

"Yep."

"Where?"

Simmons squinched one eye and took a moment to recollect. "Right corner of the building, I believe. There's enough room in the back alleyway for you boys to hide your horses. No fence or posts to tie 'em to, so one of you is gonna have to stay back there and hold 'em."

"Andy, that'll be you, seein' as how it only takes one to cover a teller, and Leroy's got a street howitzer in his saddle boot. I'll deal with the cashier and be go-to-hell if I'm fooled by stories of time locks."

He turned to the next three. "Sam, you, Dick, and Simmons are to squat in front of the sheriff's office where you can't be seen. Soon as a few of 'em get up and movin', follow 'em around for a bit, see what they're about, but don't let 'em feel you breathin' down their necks. Shootin' starts, you head 'em off where they are and cut 'em down."

"That case," Brownwell said, looking at Simmons, "lemme exchange weapons with you for today. My shotgun'll do ya better for street shootin' than that Spencer."

Simmons, clearly edgy, shrugged to show his indifference. "All right, then. I 'preciate it."

Kings faced Creasy. "You ever been to a magic show, Crease?"

Creasy looked puzzled. "Yeah, when I was a kid."

"And what was the secret to the magic man's success? A diversion. While you're lookin' over here, somethin' else is happenin' over *here*. That's you and your boys' job. You fellas kick up a big enough fuss on one end of town, that'll divide the attention of these john laws and better our chances."

"What'd you have in mind?"

Kings threw a glance at Brownwell, a bare trace of a smile on his face. "Well, hell, what's New Year's without fireworks?"

"I may have a few poppers in my saddlebags to he'p with that."

"Makin' our job easy, then," Creasy said.

"Now, how about afterwards?" Davis asked. "When and where are we s'posed to meet up to get our due and proper?"

Yeager looked up from the floor. "In two months, we'll rendezvous at the Mission. You'll all get your cut there." He glanced at Kings for approval and received a nod.

The lull returned as the men waited for him to continue, but he was apparently through talking. Bedsprings creaked as one of the women shifted, then resettled with a sigh.

"All right, boys," Kings said, as much to himself as to them. "Let's be about our business."

Chapter 21

Tom Shepherd stepped out of his office. He drew the LeMat from its holster, rechecked every load, and secreted the heavy-barreled pistol in the deep pocket of his overcoat. It was an uncommon habit that had stuck with him from his days as an outlaw, always keeping a hand on his weapon and his weapon inside his coat whilst out on the street. Indoors, it stayed in the holster on his belt, but even as he and his deputies made their morning rounds, the touch of the LeMat, for no special reason, was comforting.

He lingered on the front step until the last man out closed the door behind him. They talked for a bit—Shepherd, Dobie, Bauer, and Arballo—until the lazy morning conversation played out. Then, one by one, the deputies separated, meandering down certain paths until Shepherd was left alone outside the office. He decided to take a stroll up First, to the High Grade Hotel, where Stringer was. He meant to talk to him some more about the plans they had gone over yesterday.

The air was brisk, and it did more to wake Shepherd up than the two cups of coffee he'd just drunk. As gusts of warmth streamed from his lungs and licked up before his face, he felt strangely alive, his thoughts far from the impending firestorm. Even stranger, he thanked the Lord, as he did every morning, for his time inside Huntsville Unit, for the preacher who brought him to the beginning of wisdom, and, finally, for leading Shepherd to this place and this job.

On the opposite side of the street a black-bearded man trailed Shepherd by half a block, mingling with passersby on the boards. When Shepherd stopped to share pleasantries with a grocer, the man hid behind a signpost and waited until he continued on.

A few minutes later Shepherd approached the butcher shop, which was located beside the stage station. Directly across the street was the High Grade.

The sheriff paused to let a wagon roll by, his head turning to watch the wheels run southward. Instinct, perhaps guided by the hand of God, prodded him to keep turning.

The black-bearded man stopped suddenly on the boardwalk behind him. Their eyes met, held. Then the stranger tried to swing the double barrels of a sawed-off shotgun from under his long coat.

Shepherd pulled the LeMat.

Having covered the length of Fourth Street three abreast, the horsemen funneled single file down an alleyway between buildings, emerging unseen midway between Chivington and Martin Streets, with the rear of the bank directly across. Kings and Brownwell dismounted to approach on foot while Yeager, still in the saddle, stationed the animals within fifteen feet of the bank's back door.

He turned their heads back toward Fourth, with himself positioned in the middle. When the last hoof had shifted, Yeager twisted in his seat and watched as Brownwell and Kings closed on the rear steps.

"Make one noise and I'll blow your stalkin' guts out your back."

Shepherd had Osborn up against the doors of the butcher shop and was holding him in place with a forearm under the chin and the barrel of the LeMat against his belly. Osborn's sawed-off was on the ground with both hammers uncocked and the muzzles still cold.

"I'm backin' you into Mr. Henderson's shop here," Shepherd said. He released Osborn's chin for a second to wrench the left-hand door open, then continued, "You're gonna stay real quiet 'til I get you into the back room, and then you're gonna tell me what your boss's next move is. Do that and I might recommend you just get a stretch in the pen. Move!"

Osborn shuffled backward into the butcher's, deliberately moving his heels at a snail's pace. "You can take that offer with ya to hell, Sheriff," he said, still backpedaling, then spat in Shepherd's eye.

Shepherd flinched, and Osborn attempted to break loose, but the lawman was quick to recover. With an advantage in height and strength, he managed to wrestle the outlaw to the ground, left hand firmly gripping the collars of Osborn's coat and shirt.

Shepherd addressed the proprietor, gaping down from behind his counter: "Mr. Henderson, open up your meat locker."

The scene might have struck Henderson as comical if he'd had time to look at it that way—Tom Shepherd bodily dragging a strange man through his store—but the butcher, still holding his cleaver, leapt at the sheriff's command.

Once inside the locker, Shepherd holstered his pistol and squatted to get both hands under Osborn's armpits. He grunted as he hauled the prisoner to his feet, then grunted again as he ducked to evade a backhanded swing. Bobbing back up, Shepherd smashed a right at Osborn's face and watched him fold to his knees. He moved quickly, clamping Osborn's wrists in irons, then looped the chain securely around a meat hook hanging from the ceiling. "Now, then! Will you cooperate?"

Osborn leered through the blood streaming from his nose. "Again, I must respectfully tell you to go to hell," he said, then lunged to catch a heel around Shepherd's leg. The lawman stepped away quickly and closed the door behind him, ordering Henderson to keep it locked until he returned.

Then, pistol once again in hand, Shepherd was out the door and sprinting across the street to the High Grade.

Brownwell's boot thundered into the back door. As soon as it flew open, Kings surged into the bank and raised a gun on the cashier, who half-turned, then froze with fear. The metal deposit box in his hand slipped, clanked heavily against the walnut counter, and spilled a mess of coins all over the floor.

"Everything okay back here, Loyal?"

The teller appeared, unknowingly walking his chest into the hard, unyielding barrel of a Spencer rifle. His face went from a healthy winter pink to shirt-collar white.

Kings glanced briefly at the teller, saw that Brownwell had him covered, then returned his attention to the petrified cashier. "In spite of what you both may think," he said, "neither of us wanna use these guns. And we won't, so long as you help us do what we come here to do and refrain from foolishness. Sound fair?"

Before either could reply yea or nay, Kings asked his man, "You the cashier?"

The cashier's eyes slid toward the teller, but Kings's short bark retrieved his focus. "Do *not* look at him, Loyal! If you ain't the cashier, I'll ask him, but for now, I wanna know . . . are *you* the one can open *that* safe for me?"

"Best thing you can do for yourself at this moment is answer him, friend," Brownwell said. The cashier nodded.

"That's all I wanted to know, Loyal."

Kings guided him by the shoulder into the vault. They came to the safe, and Kings dropped a cotton sack with shoulder straps at the cashier's feet. He commanded, "Open her up."

Behind them, Brownwell's eyes snapped at the teller when

the man asked, "Could you lower that gun, please? I am not armed and—"

"Shut up."

"—I don't mean to fight you."

"You're fightin' me now, mister. Just shut up, and you won't have to worry. We ain't in the murderin' business."

The arrow point of the smaller hand had come to rest on the *VIII* on the watch face belonging to Bob Creasy, but the larger was stubbornly positioned three ticks away from the *VI*. Davis's timepiece, on the other hand, had it at one minute to the appointed time.

Creasy shrugged. "Fireworks are goin' off a little earlier'n expected," he said and slipped a match from behind his ear. He struck a flame off the back wall and put it to the end of the fuse. It spat as the flame caught and began to hiss as the spark inched toward three red sticks bunched beneath the floorboards of the sheriff's office.

Then they ran like hell.

Deputy Whitehead went stiff, trying to identify the noise. He was just fitting the key into the lock on the weapons cabinet, holding a broke-open shotgun between his body and left elbow and carrying a spare pistol in his belt in addition to the one on his hip. When the shooting started, he wanted to be ready.

The sound was faint, and Whitehead followed it as best he could, treading softly. It led him to the rear of the office, past the holding cell that Cutting was anxiously sweeping out.

Whitehead's movement caught Cutting's eye, so he paused in his diversion and leaned out of the cell to watch. Something unseen appeared to be leading Whitehead like a dog on a leash, and Cutting knew something was afoot when he saw the deputy set down the shotgun, go to one knee, and then to his elbows.

All he could see of Whitehead were the soles of his boots and his rear in the air.

Dropping his broom, Cutting stepped out and asked what the hell was going on, but Whitehead waved him silent. Whitehead drew his hip gun and, with his left hand, fitted the head of his knife into the crack between the floorboards. He had located the source and found the noise to be a mysterious hissing, which didn't make a whole lot of sense. It was far too cold for a snake to be . . .

The hissing faltered. A white light pushed its way up from beneath the floorboards, and Deputy Whitehead heard no more.

At the sound of the explosion, Deputy Arballo turned and started running, drawing his pistol as he hurled dumbfounded citizens out of the way. From behind a buggy parked across the street, H. E. Simmons tracked him, waiting until the Mexican was in the open. From thirty feet away he threw Brownwell's shotgun to his shoulder and fired, the blast muffling the screams of a woman standing close by. The deputy staggered, his right side peppered and his upper thigh perforated. He collapsed in the middle of the road but managed to keep a hold on his six-shooter.

Simmons broke open the shotgun, fumbling a few shells from his pocket that fell through the spokes of the front buggy wheel. He knelt to retrieve them and heard the air above his head pop as a bullet from Arballo's pistol just missed. The deputy was sitting up, yelling through the pain and steadily returning fire.

Rattled, Simmons finally succeeded in securing one shell. He jammed it in, snapped the breech, and edged out from behind the buggy. Arballo, finally given a clear shot, raised his gun again.

The two men fired at nearly the exact same moment. Though none of the eyewitnesses would ever agree on who the honor went to, it was Arballo who fired first, but he himself couldn't know it because the bullet had scarcely left his gun when Simmons's double-ought spray knocked him back.

An instant later, Simmons lurched into the open, limply dragging his double barrels along the ground. The severity of Arballo's last shot was still uncertain to the dazed and huddled townsfolk, who continued to watch as Simmons tottered four more eerie steps. Finally, he pitched onto his face, never to move again. When the coroner finally turned Simmons's body over, he and every citizen that dared to gather around found a neat blue hole, dead center between the eyes.

A cloud of gun smoke hung in the air, then dissolved against a sudden breeze. The street was still only for a moment before one man stood up and took a look around, then another. But the day seemed reserved for gunfire, for only a few seconds went by before another volley sounded from uptown.

Too late, Dobie came around the corner, breathing hard, his face twisted in exertion. He paused, ignoring the questions of the crowd, checked on Arballo, then started running again, swearing aloud to himself that he wouldn't be late a second time.

"Ain't gon' be late, ain't gon' be late, ain't gon' be late . . ."

A voice from outside clapped like thunder: "Gabr'el Kings!"

Brownwell, who was nearest the entrance, approached the bank's narrow, windowed doors with caution. Flattening himself against the wall, he peered through the glass, searched, and finally pinpointed a figure behind a stack of crates. Slid across the top of one was the barrel of a rifle. Behind the figure, a thick column of gray smoke roiled above the rooftops, staining the clear morning sky. There was shouting from upstreet, and, here and there, clots of people were forming, their collective attention drawn to the site. Men spilling water over the edges of buckets and pails hurried to the burning wreckage.

Brownwell heard footsteps, and then his periphery was muddled by Kings's black form crouching on the other side of the entryway, both pistols in his hands, a white strap of the cotton sack over his shoulder. He rose up on his toes to examine the shape the entire situation seemed to be taking.

Caleb Stringer stayed where he was—not letting them see him, waiting for backup. How many men were there likely to be inside? Two or three at the most, with perhaps one more in the alleyway, holding the horses. He scanned the windows of the dry-goods store to the right, then the vacant structure to the left.

He called out again, "Gabr'el Kings, I'm a captain in the Texas Rangers, appointed to bring you before a justice of the peace to answer for your crimes, and I have the men to back me! Will you come peaceably?"

Nothing from the bank. A flicker of side movement caught Stringer's eye. He looked and, to his relief, saw that it was Shepherd, who had appeared out of nowhere and was crouched behind a similar form of cover to Stringer's immediate left, the big LeMat pistol extended in both hands. Several yards behind the sheriff, that colored deputy of his was standing flat against a false-fronted building, rifle raised. Whether there were any more close by, Stringer did not know, but he felt the very human clutch in his stomach loosen a degree.

Shepherd risked a peek. "Kings! I've already got one of your men in custody. He put up a scuffle and got clobbered. No reason for you to do the same. Now for the last time"—he raised his voice then, grating over the words—"will you come along peaceably?"

★ ★ ★ ★ ★

Within the bank, Kings's mind was swimming. He could feel the steady rhythm of his pulse accelerate. Under ideal circumstances, two-on-two, Kings would have met these men in the street, but now there appeared to be another piece in position, tipping the odds, however slightly, against him. His option, and there was only one, was clear—get out and get to the horses.

"Hell with 'em," he spat. "Let's ease outta here."

Brownwell crept away from the window, staying out of the light. When he felt he had withdrawn a safe enough distance to be out of eyeshot, he swung around—too fast, and the barrel of Simmons's brand-new Spencer shattered the globe of a lamp he didn't know was there.

The front of the bank disintegrated under the sudden fusillade. Windows imploded, doors were blown to flinders, red dust kicked up in puffs as lead thudded into brick. Blinded by muzzle flashes but otherwise unharmed, Brownwell threw himself down and scrambled for the back door.

Yeager had his hands full, trying to maintain control of the animals. He was only too eager to throw the reins in Kings's and Brownwell's faces, shouting, "Reckon it's time to go!"

Kings hugged the cotton sack close to his chest. Fingers flying, he managed to button the top half of his buffalo coat around it, adding a good eight inches to his girth and sufficient padding should he find himself on the wrong end of a stray bullet. "Time to go!" he echoed.

Brownwell reached a hand into his pack and came out with a stick of dynamite. Putting the reins between his teeth, he lit the fuse, and, as they booted their horses into motion, he chucked the explosive over the bank roof. If Brownwell had gauged the distance correctly, he imagined it would land right about where those lawmen would be organizing . . .

★ ★ ★ ★ ★

As it happened, Brownwell's aim was off by only a few feet, though it was considerably closer than Stringer might have felt comfortable with. He, Shepherd, Dobie, and another man had rushed the bank after the initial volley, only to find the two employees crouched under counters with their hands over their heads. Back in the street, confusion was being shouted down as other gun-wielding townsfolk joined them. When the dynamite landed, its hissing was scarcely audible over the warring voices.

When the sound finally reached Stringer's hearing, the spark was too close to stamp out, and the only measure left—to run, push against the crowd of bodies, and hit the dirt—seemed futile.

Stringer was knocked off his feet by the blast, and it was only by pure luck that he wasn't killed. Brownwell had grabbed the one stick whose fuse had been ruinously cracked by the day's cold, which greatly diminished the force of the explosion. It did little damage other than raise pulses and set ears to ringing.

Tom Shepherd thought the ranger had been killed, or at least severely maimed. Wispy smoke was licking up from his boots and trousers, but when the sheriff opened Stringer's shirt, Shepherd was surprised to find only bruising.

"My Lord, but if that ain't a miracle," he muttered. Stringer sat up, forcing out tubercular coughs, but Shepherd told him to stay down a minute.

The older man waved him away, gasping, "I never had a fight I didn't finish standin' up."

"Captain—"

"Sheriff, I once fought two days with a Quahada arrow in my hip on the Brazos River. Jesus ain't callin' my name over no kiddy's firecracker."

★　★　★　★　★

Creasy and Davis reached the horses, held by Foss in an alley a block away. In the cramped space Creasy mounted first, then kneed his horse into the clear, allowing Davis enough room to swing a leg up. Reassembling then, the three drew their pistols and spurred back toward the chaos, firing overhead.

Their appearance galvanized the townsfolk who had rushed to put out the flames. The outlaws screamed and whooped, jostling pedestrians, spurring their horses after any that broke off, and shouting things like, "Bring that stray back here!" and "Don't that fire look pretty!"

In all this confusion, they had blinded themselves to the fact that civilians directed by Walt Mincey were pushing wagons into the street, cutting off their nearest exit, and possemen rallied from the boarding house had skirted the buildings to their rear. Patrick Delaney, who led the charge, stepped out with a borrowed .50-caliber Sharps rifle. He centered on the meaty part between the closest robber's shoulders and squeezed.

His precision had devastating results for Charley Davis. The buffalo gun was designed specifically for long-distance shooting, and at a distance of forty yards, it may as well have been a cannon, because it blew a hole in Davis as wide as a fist. He dropped from the saddle and landed on his back.

Creasy fired wildly at Delaney, missed, then leaned down and eyed the gaping exit wound in his friend's chest. He knew the answer but asked nonetheless, "Charley, can you ride?"

"I'm through, Bob," were Davis's last words. He coughed blood, and his eyes rolled back, as though watching his soul escape and ascend to be judged.

Creasy twisted his rearing paint horse away, shouting at Foss, "Let's get outta here!" He felt a sudden pain in his thigh, and about that same time a bullet punched through Foss's right shoulder. Hearing a clatter and turning his head south, Creasy saw the fortifications and a half-dozen rifles gleaming hotly in the early morning light.

Knowing there was no other option—knowing there were trees on the other side of those rifles—Creasy aimed his horse directly at the barricade. Gritting his teeth against the imminent barrage, he rammed hard with his spurs. He heard a voice that sounded miles away yell, "Fire!" just as the paint went airborne. Bullets struck Creasy, threatened to knock his body out of the saddle, but somehow he kept his seat. The paint came back down to earth, stumbled, and managed to resume its gallop. Shots sounded after them, but the gap had widened, and for the moment Creasy had avoided the inevitable.

Foss had been on his heels from the moment of his wounding to the moment of flight, but on the cusp of jumping himself, Foss's last nerve dissolved. Too late, he heaved back on the reins with a roar, meaning to wheel around and try another route, but his roan screamed and went to ground ten yards shy of the barricade. It scrambled to its feet and walked toward Davis's horse, dragging its unconscious rider through the dirt by his left foot.

Walt Mincey ordered a ceasefire, stepped over a wagon tongue, and jogged toward the animal with his rifle trained on the slackened body of Hardyman Foss. He slapped the man's boot free of the stirrup and stooped to check the wound. "He'll live," he said to no one in particular, then straightened to watch the wall of a frame building next door to the wreckage cave in.

Sam Woods stumbled out of the hardware store on legs that felt as sturdy as water. He looked like a man half out of his mind, wild-eyed and breathing hard, his ruined left arm swinging with every turn of his body as he searched for an enemy, an ally—*anyone* that might be moving toward him and not ducking away from the swinging barrel of his gun.

Standing in the middle of Second Street, blood coursing down his arm and off his fingertips, he bellowed, "Kings!", but the echo faded without a response. He tried again, going on to the next name that leapt to his mind, "Brownwell! Somebody! Dammit, I'm shot up . . ."

And then . . . salvation.

Bob Creasy was riding hard in his direction, torso reddened with blood. Grunting as more pain swept down his arm, Woods stepped farther into the road to wave him down. Creasy reached out to pull the wounded man up behind him.

Deputy Bauer burst out of the very store Woods had emerged from only seconds before, his side aflame with a breathless cramp. He'd cut across two blocks at a sprinter's pace in the hopes of running down the man who had ambushed him all the way over on the south end. They had traded lead for two whole minutes back there before a townsman stepped out of his home to put a rifle slug in Woods's elbow. Bauer himself suffered only a scratch, but Woods, wrecked wing and all, had managed to outdistance the deputy.

Suddenly, Bauer heard the heavy sounds of a horse being slowed from a run to a stop, and then he spotted Creasy picking Woods up. Bauer levered a fresh round into the chamber and took careful aim. His shot smacked into Woods's lower back. Creasy returned fire, but Bauer dove for cover.

"Go!" Woods gasped, and they were off, having been flushed east on Independence Street. Hot blood coursed down the animal's withers and flanks from the six wounds Creasy and Woods had between them.

The three-man group of Gabriel Kings, Leroy Brownwell, and Andy Yeager moved south on Fourth at a trot, holding their horses for the race that surely lay ahead. So far, they had fared much better than their fellows, two of whom were in custody, two dead, and two more gravely wounded.

The street was quiet, almost as if they were riding through a dreamscape, another world. The west end had been alive with gunfire for the last nine minutes, but that was not the case from this side of the scene. Faces turned away from windows as they passed, but it wasn't an easy feeling that rode with the men— the contrasting calm only wound them tighter, made them expect a shot in the back at any second.

Out of nowhere, Kings heard his name on the wind. Slowing to a walk so he could better place the location of whoever had done the calling, he thought it might have been Woods. He hadn't sounded too far off, maybe a few blocks, but Kings didn't raise his voice in reply for fear of marking their position.

"Sounded hurt," Yeager whispered. "Think we oughta ride to him?"

Again they heard a shout for help.

"I wouldn't," Brownwell advised. "Look, there's trees yonder! Not two hundred yards. Sad to say, but it's ever' man for himself now."

At that moment a rifle cracked, and all three flinched at the sound. Like the call for help, it hadn't been far away, but it wasn't aimed at them. There was a reply from a pistol, and then, on its heels, a second-story window went up, and the snout of a shotgun angled down at them. Yeager fired across his body, the round shattering glass above the shooter's head, then shouted over his shoulder, "That's it, then!"

They kicked their horses into a gallop, but the getaway was stalled at the intersection of Fourth and Independence when Creasy's horse, laboring under its double load, nearly collided with Brownwell's. Woods, slumped to one side behind Creasy like a sack of potatoes, smiled with delirium and said, "Hot damn, it's the boys!"

"You all that's left?" Kings asked but went unheard above the commotion. When the teetering Creasy came alongside, Brownwell leaned over and snatched the frantic animal's bridle.

A shot rang out, whining nastily as it ricocheted off a metal street sign, and then another, this one of a higher caliber. That shot missed, too, but came significantly closer as Brownwell jerked, deaf in his right ear. Boardwalks rumbled as marksmen scrambled for position, spilling into the street from half a block away. It was Caleb Stringer, standing in the middle of the road, who fired the shot that nearly downed Brownwell.

One man moved away from the pack and to the right to try for a clearer shot. Kings caught sight of the buffalo gun in his hands, with its unmistakable length, and a thought turned his stomach. If that fellow could fire and reload quickly enough, he could plink away at their backsides at his leisure . . .

As the remnant of his shattered gang hurried away, the Virginian held his stallion steady, squeezing with his knees, and threw out his gun arm. Sighting down the barrel, he did not hear the report of a dozen rifles, nor did he flinch as a dozen bullets *whapped* wide, high or low. His mind shut down, and, in that moment, nothing else mattered but his pistol and the target.

He feathered the trigger. The gun kicked, and the man with the Sharps jerked and fell into the man behind him. Kings waited long enough to see the results of his marksmanship, then turned John Reb and rammed with his spurs.

The others were two lengths ahead. The stallion surged, closing the distance impossibly fast. At the head of the charge was Yeager on his smoke-gray mare, swinging his quirt and yowling like a banshee. Brownwell on his stocky chestnut was stirrup-to-stirrup with Creasy and Woods, stiffening an arm against Woods's shoulder to keep him from slipping.

John Reb's neck stretched, and his powerful haunches carried his rider past them with ease. Had Kings been of a mind to slow up and send Brownwell on, he wouldn't have been able to.

The black was soon gaining on the smoke-gray, and Kings felt the horrible sensation of riding down a giant funnel, as though the buildings on either side were closing in like double doors. The space through which their exit must be made was getting tighter and tighter.

It was an all-out run for freedom, and, as the horsemen exceeded rifle range, with the edge of town and outlying wilderness well in sight and welcoming, it seemed apparent that the Avenging Angels—or what was left of them—had made it through. They had only to pass the livery barn, maybe pause to open the corral gate and scatter horses, effectively covering their tracks and eliminating almost all hope of a lawman's chase . . .

And then, from the semi-darkness of the livery, streaks of flame shot from the muzzle of a Gatling gun, sweeping across the street in a staccato roar. A heretofore inactive Paul Leduc cranked the lever with unrushed calm and watched the carnage, the effects of his accuracy, with a flinty look of satisfaction.

Brownwell's horse screamed and went down as .45-70-caliber rounds pocked its side and flanks in a red spray. Brownwell landed on his knees and came up clawing for his pistols, but he never cleared leather for the volley that riddled his groin, chest, shoulders, and neck. When the barrel of the Gatling slid away, the damage done, Leroy lunged at the carcass of his horse, wanting the rifle he had sheathed to help Woods. He toppled face-forward onto the bulk only to realize that the scabbard was trapped underneath. Life left him with a grunt of frustration.

In all of Creasy's years as a fugitive, he had never known such resistance, such mayhem. Always their robberies had been fast, hit-and-run operations. There had been some shooting from time to time, but never like this. He had never known *this*. Desperately, he wheeled his horse around, and, in the process, Sam Woods lost his seat.

As he fell, Sam knew he was finished. He landed in agony on

his wounded arm and rolled in the dirt, as if to outdistance the gunfire. All around him slugs *whacked* into the walls of buildings and exploded a trough in a shower of splinters and water. Woods got up, reeled blindly for some shred of cover, and then went down as he was jolted from behind, again and again, by fire.

Creasy didn't get much farther. Swinging the Gatling hard to his right, Leduc turned the lever and the barrels barked one last time. Spent and smoking brass dropped in the livery dirt, and Bob Creasy threw his hands into the air, falling headlong into the street.

A haze of gun smoke blanketed fifty feet of road, and stillness descended like a giant bird as the Texas Ranger stepped out to survey his handiwork. He was sorry about the horse but felt nothing for the men who lay where they had fallen.

A few brave townspeople emerged from cover. While there was still plenty of fear and shock to go around, more than one raised their voices to shout their thanks and admiration for the ranger who had finished the fight. But as he went from man to man, boot-rolling them onto their backs, Leduc's grim and somewhat sickened expression hinted that it wasn't finished after all.

Gabriel Kings had gotten away.

CHAPTER 22

Kings and Yeager did not slow their horses until they were two miles outside of town. Drawing up at the crest of a steep hill, they knew they couldn't linger very long.

Snaking around the foot of the slope was the eastern road stagecoaches followed into Justicia. It would be unadvisable for them to take it—tracks would be easier to follow on a manmade path than through the trees. There was no other route left to the outlaws other than what they could blaze for themselves. It would be rough going, because the trees were thick, and their getaway must be made as quickly as possible. Furthermore, separation was the order of the day—as undesirable as that might have looked to them, the tactic would improve their individual chances of escape, and a man could make his escape better if it was possible to do so at his own pace.

"Where'll you head?" Kings asked, eyeing the terrain below.

"Eastward," Yeager said, "homeward. I don't think them boys'll chase me clear over to Clinch Mountain. You?"

"Jacksons', if I can. Either of us makes it out the Territory, I'll leave your cut below cabin number two."

Yeager shook his head. "Don't know that I'll be back that way anytime soon. Far as I'm concerned, I never heard of Texas. You might as well take it all with ya."

"I'll set it aside then," Kings assured him, then holstered his pistol to reach over his horse's neck for one last handshake. Yeager stared at the proffered hand for a moment before edging close enough to squeeze it. They had been through a lot, these two, and were saying good-bye the only way they knew—with stony faces and firm grips.

"I'll send for ya sometime," Kings said. "Ain't gonna be right off, but I'll send for ya."

"You don't hear back from me, I'll be restin' with my fathers."

"That ain't gonna happen." Kings paused, then realized there was no more time. "So long, Andreas. Stay off the roads."

Yeager started to move off, then tugged on the reins and turned in the saddle. He had taken a bullet in the left shoulder, but he couldn't afford to stop and treat it immediately. There was a thought in the back of his mind that he dared not entertain. How much longer could he ride? How much farther could he get? He was a quiet man by nature, one who rarely opened his mouth to speak, who never offered his opinion unless asked. It wasn't in his nature to blame Kings for what had happened—wasn't even in his mind, because Kings was his captain and a captain worth following—but his parting words seemed to blame another.

"We ought to've been there for General Lee," he said, then clucked to his mare and let her pick a way down the trickier side of the slope.

Kings did not wait to watch his friend go. He turned John Reb's head south, down the face of the slope that took a more gradual path to leveling out, so Kings reached the bottom before Yeager did.

Miraculously, he had been the only one to make it out of Justicia unscathed, and that fact, coupled with his survival instincts and the strength and endurance of his mount, gave him great confidence that he could reach Texas—and after that, California—alive.

They would assume he was wounded, and when all was said and done, he was the one they wanted. Would they even bother following Yeager? If they did, his trail would be hard to miss. Yeager's shoulder had been leaking a good amount of blood . . .

Kings couldn't decide which course of action he preferred they take.

Back on the streets of Justicia, Caleb Stringer sat his horse, staring painfully to the south as his volunteers scuttled about, taking far too long to collect themselves and get mounted. Every minute wasted meant another mile lost. That Kings and Yeager had made it out alive was a devilment of the worst sort. Leduc was practically in fits about it, and Stringer couldn't blame him. No one should have made it through that ungodly stream of fire he'd unleashed, much less anyone at the front of the stampede. Though the sergeant had accounted for three of the five, he counted his part in the ambush a failure.

The fact that Pat Delaney lay dying from a high chest wound, with Kings himself responsible, gave the lawmen all the more reason to burn with anger.

One of Shepherd's two remaining deputies, Bauer, pulled his horse in beside Stringer and waved his Winchester like a battle standard. "Sheriff said to tell you he's stayin' behind to tend to the mess here," he said. "Dobie and I are comin' with you, and we'll follow whatever orders you give us."

Stringer gave them their first when they reached the summit where Kings and Yeager had separated not long before. "At least one of these snakes is bleedin'," he announced, noting the spots of blood from Yeager's wound, then hooked his mount to the side so that he could better examine the faces of the men. After dividing them up in his mind's eye, he pointed at Bauer. "You know the terrain?"

The deputy nodded.

"Then you'll ride with Detective Mincey. You men to the left of me will go with 'em and follow this blood trail leadin' off to the east. The rest of ya, with me and the sergeant. We ride south." He found Dobie's face. "Deputy?"

"Yassuh, Captain?"

"You think you know the land the way your partner does?"

"Yassuh, Captain."

"Then take point."

Dobie was a freedman from Kansas, the first in a long line of slaves, but he hesitated now at the prospect of leading white men anywhere. It showed in his face as he moved his horse alongside Stringer's, but the flinty resolve in the captain's eyes encouraged him to ease forward another step. And then another, and then on down the slope.

Finally, the hunt was on.

Kings knew he couldn't ride without stopping. Sooner or later, he would *have* to. He knew the limits to which he could push his horse, and he would not—*could* not—test those limits. If anything, he would ride John Reb slightly below his daily limit, then recover the distance lost in the morning. More than once he leaned forward and gave the stallion's neck a good strong clap of reassurance, willing his life into the power of his animal.

He had cheated the Devil before. He could do it again.

There was no sound but the jangling of saddle gear and the steady thudding of hooves beneath him. The air was cool on his sweat-beaded face, which he mopped clean with a hairy sleeve. Beneath the buffalo coat, the cotton sack bulged outward from his chest and extended over the saddle horn like a fat man's paunch. Kings hadn't yet had time to count it, but he could tell by the weight that he wasn't carrying the haul he'd expected to find. Not beer money but not a fortune, either. Coupled with the losses suffered, it was a discordant swan song for a man and a gang whose entire career had been a blaring rebel anthem. The sting of Agave Seco waned in comparison.

At midday he dismounted on the top of a bald ridge for a drink, and to look over his shoulder for what must have been the dozenth time. He raised his field glasses. From such an unobstructed elevation he could see for miles, and what he saw was nothing . . . no posse, no gleam of sunlight off a rifle barrel, nothing but a myriad of black trees studding the rolling, gray-and-white-patched hills.

Kings estimated he had roughly five more hours before dusk, which would leave him a few minutes more of sufficient light by which he could navigate. As much as he hated to stop, the threat of the oncoming darkness wouldn't bode well for that posse, either. They too would have no choice but to encamp till morning, or risk losing sight of his tracks. In their haste to catch up, they weren't likely to have brought along lanterns for night-riding. But even as he reasoned this, Kings's mind was plagued by the possibility of being crept up on in the dead of night and shot while he dreamed. Would the need for sleep, for himself and his animal, result in his death?

If he had Yeager with him, he might have been willing to turn and make a stand. But the way things stood right now, that was out of the question. A man didn't need to be a military tactician to know that.

Though he had greatly admired General Stuart's fighting spirit, Kings never sympathized with the general's firm belief that to retreat was to shame oneself. Right now, Kings had to run like hell and, somehow, make it back to the Frio River.

To Belle.

He remembered the flecks of brown in her blue eyes, and the soft, salty taste of her skin under his lips before he left her at the foot of her father's stairs. He remembered her body against his, and then he mounted up and wheeled the stallion, starting again at a brisker pace.

John Reb trusted his rider's touch, and over the next few

hours, with dusk pressing down on them and the sun quickly losing itself behind the treetops. Kings kept him on a south-bound course until it became too dark to see clearly. He reckoned they could chance a few more miles, provided he came up with a sufficient means of lighting the way.

He paused to break off a dead and brittle branch hanging low, just longer than his forearm. Deciding that his neck could stand to be a little colder, Kings unwound his woolen scarf, tied it securely around the broken end of the branch and used it to catch up a good amount of gooey tree sap. That done, he struck a match, the sap caught fire, and the darkness retreated—but not far.

Holding his crude torch out over John Reb's shoulder, Kings saw that to their left was a deep gulley. Opposite, a snowy plateau loomed and dead ahead, horizontal across the trail, was an uprooted pine, torn loose by a tumbling boulder that still rested beside it, embedded in scree.

Quickly assessing the geography and the choices it left him, Kings tried the obvious option—to move across the ledge between the tree and the declivity just beyond. But the stallion, generally nimble-footed and unafraid of heights, fussed under his rein, pawing at the disturbed ground before backing up. Kings tried again, but, living up to his name, the black refused once more.

The alternative route looked damnably precarious but no more than forcing a skittish, half-ton animal down a path he didn't want to go. It was a massive tree, as tall now as it had once been wide, so jumping it didn't seem tenable. With enough coaxing, Kings got the stallion up and over the pile of scree, but just as man and beast descended onto even ground, there came a queer squeaking sound from overhead. No noise was too insignificant to dismiss, so Kings paused, listening intently. Gradually the squeaking became a low crumbling, and then climaxed as a rolling crash.

With a scream, John Reb buck-jumped and bolted. Kings, caught off guard, was thrown from the saddle. Landing on his side, he rolled over and was temporarily blinded by the glare of the torch that had fallen near his head. Snow and debris tumbled down, over and all around him, and just as he was getting up a rock struck him in the center of his back. His wind gone, Kings crumpled and fell forward onto his belly, the loot sack only semi-cushioning the landing. He threw up his arms, interlocking his fingers over the back of his skull, just in time to absorb another stone as it clouted and bloodied his knuckles. Swooning, he tried to scramble free of the avalanche but did not get far.

The world went black, black and cold.

Stringer's party pitched camp before sundown. The tracking made for slow going and had a poor effect on morale. Huddled about the fire, someone wondered if the others were faring much better. Had they caught up with their quarry and spilt more of his blood on the snow? Another volunteer raised the question whether Kings—if this was indeed Kings they were following—would dare to ride through the night, but no one felt like entertaining that thought.

Their chatter was suddenly interrupted by Stringer, who assigned hourly shifts before going on to say they would be back in the saddle by sunup.

When he came to, it was still night. He lay still for several minutes, gathering his wits, trying to recall how he had wound up under half a hillside. The weight of it had him pinned like giant, frigid hands, rendering him nearly immobile from the waist down. Anchoring his front end by digging two holes with his elbows, Kings began to wriggle. His head pulsed with pain, his teeth chattered uncontrollably, and, as he wriggled, his breath went out in ragged streams. It took nearly half an hour of constant straining to slide free of his icy cocoon.

Slowly, he got to his knees, then rocked back on his heels to compose himself. His entire body shivered in spite of his coat and the extra padding of the loot sack. Thanks to this double binding, his guns and knife were all secure, but as merciful as that was, his heart sank when he took a slow look around and saw that John Reb was nowhere to be found.

This realization alone might have caused a weaker man to despair and resign himself to a slow death, but Kings wouldn't allow his thoughts to venture down that road. Experience was what would save him now, as it had done so many times in the past.

Even so, it was an act of will just to stand, and an even greater act to take that first lurching step. As disoriented as he was, he knew he had to get off the trail he had been following, considering that while he had lain under that mass of snow, his pursuers must have closed the gap and might even be on this same path. He deviated by only a few dozen yards, immersing himself in the pines.

Fire. Before he went any further, he must have a fire. It didn't take much strength to snap off a few branches, even in his cold and woozy state. Dropping them in a cluster, he fumbled the Bowie free and with it peeled a large, single strip of bark away from one. Laying this strip flat with the yellowish underside facing up, he knelt over it and, using it as a table, sawed the lead caps off two bullets. He emptied the casings of their gunpowder, distributing the black grain evenly onto the strip. On one end he placed some branch fragments and pine needles, and on the other, one of the empty cartridges.

Tipping the Bowie at a low angle, with the point of its blade touching the cartridge rim, he felt around, sifting through snow to uncover a stone. With this he struck the pommel of the knife—once, twice, and a third time before he ignited the powder.

His fingers were stiff and bloody from where the second rock had cut him, so he rubbed them vigorously over the weak flames. Liquid coaxed from a handful of crushed snow cleaned the small wounds over his knuckles and joints, and he tried to bury himself within his coat, rubbing warmth back into his chest. The sack he dropped beside the growing fire.

He had no idea how long he had been out, but there was just enough sky showing through the treetops for some speculation. Shifting around so that he faced north, he lay back and searched for the Big Dipper. He found it, held there for a moment, then let his eyes wander toward the Little Dipper. Finding the crucial light of the North Star at the end of the little handle and using both of his hands as markers, he envisioned the North Star as the center of a clock face. An imaginary hour hand went out from it on a line with the outer two stars in the bowl of the Big Dipper, and after a short time on his back, Kings guessed it was somewhere between eleven o'clock and midnight.

Four hours. He'd lost four hours.

After a time, he got up to fashion himself another torch before stamping out the fire. He went back to the trail and swept away his tracks. When he reached the tree line again, he paused to look back, reviewing his handiwork and approving it. He also saw that the avalanche had, in actuality, done more good than harm. The pine tree, which had stood so tall even on its side, was almost completely submerged in snow, with only a few black tufts of needles poking through here and there. The trail was no longer immediately traversable to anything larger than a badger.

It had been roughly fifteen hours—over half the day—since his breakfast of two biscuits and a cup of coffee at the Long

Branch Café, and his ears were just now becoming attuned to the grumbling in his stomach. There was nothing to be done about that, though—not if he wanted to conserve what few bullets he had, and keep his whereabouts in this wilderness yet unknown.

On foot in unfamiliar territory, the rate of travel he might have accomplished on horseback would now be reduced to a fraction of a fraction, and it was a long way back to Texas. All he could hope for was to come across a river or creek that would inevitably—eventually—bring him into contact with human life. He needed shelter, but, more importantly, he needed a horse.

In the meantime, he paced himself by taking short rests every so often. Keeping his blood circulating and his legs warm was essential, which he endeavored to do by performing basic calisthenics—pumping his arms, taking high steps through the snow. He kept alert for any movement, any sound, with a Colt in his right hand and the torch in his left. The loot sack, which he now carried on his back with both arms through the loops like an infantryman, was only a minor burden. It might even come in handy if the weather got worse and he managed to find a small cave or cranny to hole up in. Its bulk could be used as a stopper of sorts.

A reprieve from his gnawing hunger came at about the third hour of tramping, in the form of a whitetail deer carcass. Upon closer examination, it turned out to be a doe, which, judging by its size, was more than a few fat summers and lean winters old. It did not appear to have been brought down by a pack of wolves, as it was not savagely torn asunder and unrecognizable. The two puncture wounds below the jaw identified the killer as a cougar. After emptying the now gaping cavern of the doe's torso, the big cat made off with the right hind leg as well. That didn't leave much meat for Kings, but with a little barbaric intuition he could scrounge some nutrition from this animal yet.

Using his knife as a surgical instrument, he made an incision in the skin and, pressing his full weight onto the blade, was able to saw through sinewy muscle and bone and tear a thin foreleg free. Baring it down, he found the right groove and with little effort split the shank down the middle. He cleaned the inner groove of its pasty marrow as if it were honey.

He scoured the inside of another of the unfortunate deer's limbs, washed it down with crushed snow, and walked on, having spent no more than twenty minutes at the carcass.

Not an hour from there he heard the sound of rushing water.

If Caleb Stringer had previously attributed the longevity of Gabriel Kings's career to wartime skills, he was now beginning to think that luck had as much to do with it as anything. Having recently arrived at the site of last evening's avalanche, Stringer felt that, short of the Lord striking the man down on the highway as He had Saul of Tarsus, the increasingly cold tracks they were following would prove about as useful as teats on a boar hog.

With the avalanche blockading the road ahead, they had no other option but to descend an unforgiving incline and follow the gulley until they found a gradual enough slope to lead them back up onto Kings's trail. Once they came to a place where they could make the ascension and not risk another avalanche, the lawmen strung out again along the path.

After about a half hour of tracking, it became distressingly apparent that they were following a meandering, riderless horse.

Led by the stream, Kings emerged from the trees into a moonlit glade. Along the banks was a cabin, a lean-to and a rail corral that, from a distance, appeared to contain a horse and a mule. Dousing the flame of the torch in the snow, he entered the clearing with caution, keeping an eye on the dark-windowed structure.

Kings hadn't gone very far before he saw footprints. They all appeared to have been made by the same man. Drawing closer, Kings found a multitude of animal skins cobwebbing one side of the cabin . . . A hard-working man, and likely a light sleeper, to live in this solitary and defenseless place.

Whatever luck that had so cruelly eluded Kings in Justicia seemed to have found him at exactly the right moment. It soon became clear that, while the mule was inside the corral, the horse was no more inside it than Kings was. Rather, it stood free, dabbing at the snow in the hope of finding some browse, and appeared to be saddled.

Then Kings noticed the three white stockings and could have shouted for joy.

John Reb turned his ears toward movement, and caught Kings's familiar scent. The man froze, hoping the stallion wouldn't betray his presence, but John Reb stood stock-still and stared. Slowly, Kings raised a hand and beckoned, and with a foal-like eagerness, John Reb came to him.

"I thought I'd lost you, brother," Kings said to the horse, looking with great affection into the big brown eyes. He guided him into the corral, then slid his rifle from its scabbard. With it in hand, he moved to the front door, shoved it open, and stepped in.

Whoever lived here was content to do so simply, with little of the comforts of civilization. The room was nearly bare, save for a chair and table that looked to have been assembled as hastily as the cabin itself. Everything appeared to have been here for quite some time. There was wood stacked beside the low-burning fireplace, and a broom stood in a corner. Kings found pots, pans, and coffee tins in a cupboard.

Stepping lightly, he crossed the floor and moved into the hall, holding the Winchester in both hands. At the door of the back room he stopped to press his ear against it, straining to pick up any sound. The room on the other side was silent as the grave, and, when he entered, Kings saw nothing but a wooden pallet on the floor and some hides that had been used as blankets.

Suddenly, there was a thud, and Kings felt a brush of air as the door was kicked closed behind him. He stiffened at the unmistakable touch of a double-barreled shotgun against his spine, and the silence was shattered by a hoarse voice.

"I got you dead to rights, mister. You wanna take another breath, you set that Winchester aside, nice an' easy. Good. Now get them hands up. Turn real slow."

The man was craggy-faced and completely bald but with a long unruly beard. The weapon in his hands carried an oily gleam and, unlike the rest of his belongings, appeared to be in fine working condition. He stood wide-legged in his long johns and trousers, eyeing Kings with hostility.

"You got a belt-gun under that coat?" he asked.

Never one to argue with a shotgun, Kings nodded.

"I'll ask you to drop that, too. Left hand. And that sack you got there."

The sound of the belts falling to the floor was magnified in the stillness. The trapper seemed to loosen with the knowledge that the man before him had been disarmed, and he straightened as much as age would allow. "Now, then," he said, breathing heavily, "would you mind tellin' me what the hell you're doin' in my place? Mean to murder me in my sleep, do ya? Steal my hides?"

Kings shook his head. "Lost my horse and my way. Luck led me to the stream, and I followed it here."

"You come outta them hills on foot? Generally, a man without a horse in these parts is a *dead* man."

"Didn't come very far."

The trapper was unconvinced, and it showed in his expression. The story, while plausible, was not without its curiosities. The fellow before him was tall and, apart from the bulk of his coat, seemed well-made. The lines in his face spoke of a harsh past. Even so, a long-legged man with good wind and a strong will would be hard-pressed to last very long out there if he was unfamiliar with the land. For twenty years the trapper himself had scratched a difficult living out of these mountains, reaping what he could from creation, but he had learned the hard way, and over time.

Maybe this stranger was telling the truth. Then again, maybe he did, in fact, have murder and thievery on his mind. If the former, he could move on. If the latter . . . well, it was the trapper's hands that held a gun.

"You don't see a lot of cotton this high up, friend," he said, gesturing to the sack at Kings's feet.

"That's true enough," Kings conceded, "but I never said I was carryin' any."

"What if I was to ask you to set it down and slide it over to me?"

"I'd say what's in this sack is no concern of yours."

"Is that so, now?"

"Only bring you trouble you don't need."

"Trouble with the law, I guess you mean. That case, I don't suppose you *would* be of a mind to steal my hides, would ya? Money in there, I expect. Somebody's hard-earned savin's?"

Kings did not deny it, but neither did he admit it. Valuable time was slipping away, as he needed to be, so he affected an unassuming tone and said, "If you could spare some coffee and mebbe some food, I'd be obliged. If not, I'll be on my way."

He had gradually lowered his arms to waist-level, palms out.

While interrogating him, the trapper had failed to notice this, but he noticed when Kings started to bend over to retrieve his pistols.

"Hold it there!"

Kings moved fast, imperceptibly so, and before the trapper's finger could tighten against the trigger, Kings swatted the double barrels aside. The force of the blow swung the trapper half-around. Snatching up one of his belts and gripping it by the pistol, Kings swung hard at the back of the man's skull and felt the holstered iron connect with bone. The trapper collapsed without a sound, as did the shotgun.

It was a hell of a way to begin the new year.

There was a rear door, and, exiting through that, Kings went to the lean-to. In it he found, among other tools, a length of thick rope that he used to truss the old man up, hand and foot. A sizable lump had begun to form on the fellow's head, but he was still breathing, and Kings bound him in a way that would not hopelessly ensnare the man like the animals he trapped. He should be able to free himself within an hour or two, though Kings would be long gone by then.

Before he left, he sat down, briefly, to his first meal in nearly twenty-four hours. From one of his reclaimed saddlebags he brought out some food he had packed for the trail—jerked venison and a few biscuits, which had gone as hard as the jerky. It wasn't a feast, but it would tide him over for now, and the trapper's coffee was good and strong. He boiled one tin and stowed another couple in his bag.

As he chewed and drank, giving his sore-footed body a chance to recuperate, he realized how physically exhausted he truly was. He filled and finished off one last cup, wondering whether he should chance a quick and much-needed catnap. Heavy though his eyes were, Kings decided he couldn't risk it if he hoped to stay ahead of his trackers, who would no doubt be getting an early start this morning, if they weren't already on the move. Though he hadn't kept diligent track of time over the last few miles, he estimated it was about four in the morning.

Outside, he took down one of the hides, shaking as much of the stiffness out of it as he could before rolling it up like a bedroll. At the corral, he allowed John Reb to eat from a feeder bag he filled with some grain.

When a sufficient amount had been consumed, Kings nudged the big head away, refilled the bag, and hung it over one of the corral posts for the mule. He mounted up, and, with the Winchester again in its scabbard, gunbelts on his hips, and the loot sack on his back, he eased through the open gate. Closing it behind him, he rode out.

The sun would be rising soon. He tied himself to the saddle with more of the trapper's rope, in case his fatigue got the best of him. As he steered his horse toward the pines at the edge of the clearing, Kings allowed himself to reflect on what he'd barely ridden away from. And on the men who hadn't.

Sam Woods, Dick Osborn . . . Bob Creasy, Davis, and Foss . . . Simmons. Leroy Brownwell. Why should he, the worst of them all, be so lucky as to be breathing free air now, to be as confident as he was now? The fear he had felt as he crawled loose from that avalanche only a few hours ago was diminishing with every step, even more so now that he had recovered the stallion. Given a good enough lead, a desperate man could vanish forever. He had before and was about to again.

John Reb walked on toward the Texas line.

CHAPTER 23

On the morning of January 8, 1879, John Bevans and Fernando Elías loaded a pair of wire-cutters and a half-dozen spools of barbed wire into the back of a wagon and drove out to the low hills west of the big house. Both were experienced rangemen, adept at working all manner of four-footed livestock, be it horses, cattle, or sheep, and didn't care much for work that couldn't be done from horseback. Still, this needed doing.

With after-breakfast cigarettes dangling from their lips, they took turns condemning fence-mending as old ladies' work, then shared a chuckle at the thought of Mrs. Jackson in a sweat-stained shirt and rough jeans, stringing wire.

Eventually they reached the section of fence that required their attention. Bevans wheeled the horses so he could ease in parallel to it.

This was the sight that greeted Kings as he moved into the open from a stand of live oaks. Leading John Reb and a bay gelding stolen from a homestead just outside San Angelo, he was mounted on a buckskin whose previous owner, a lone Comanche boy of no more than sixteen, had attempted to count coup on Kings five days before on the desolate *Llano*. The boy had failed. Apart from that encounter, it had been an uneventful journey, though a grueling one—a hungry journey, a cold journey, and, more importantly, a posse-less journey. He was glad to see it come to an end.

He had made it.

Fernando was the one to spot him, but he could only squint and was unable to identify who it was. Touching Bevans's arm, he ducked his chin in the direction of the blurry shape moving toward them. *"Mira."*

"Whaddayou reckon?" Bevans asked.

Fernando claimed his Winchester from the footboard. He straightened and balanced the rifle muzzle-up on his thigh to let the incoming horseman take note and beware. *"No sé,"* he replied, curling his thumb around the hammer. "He has two horses?"

"Three."

They sat until the horseman came within sixty yards. Bevans caught a glimpse of the white-stockinged black stallion, and only then did he think to examine the rider's posture, which enlightened him, as it had on his last visit. He told Fernando to lower the Winchester. "It's Kings."

"Pero ¿dónde 'stán sus hombres?"

"English, 'Nando, English."

"His men, where are his men?"

"That's a good question, *amigo.* Go-oo-od question."

Kings reined to a halt with only a few yards separating them. The San Angelo bay had been walking sluggishly with its head down and jostled into the Comanche horse from behind. Snorting in surprise, the bay tossed its head, making Kings's arm rise and fall almost in a salute, but he still hadn't acknowledged the rangemen. They looked him over and knew he had come a long way.

A moment passed as Kings examined them in turn, frowning as if struggling to place them. Then he nodded, glancing from one to the other. "Fence-mendin'," he croaked. He sounded as if he hadn't spoken in some time.

"Sí, señor."

Kings nodded again, as though giving approval to the work.

"Surprised to see you back so soon, Kings," Bevans said.

He gestured in a vague direction meant to encompass the big house. Clearing his throat, the man declared, "I'm headin' in."

"Sure," Bevans said, watching him closely. "Go right ahead. There might be some breakfast left over."

The Virginian kneed the buckskin, but the ranch foreman detained him with a hesitant question: "We'll be out here most of the mornin', Kings. Should we, ah . . . we need to be watchin' for anyone else to come along?"

Briefly, there was no sound except stamping horses. Eventually Kings shook his head, his grimy features bleak. Then he spurred off at a twelve-legged lope.

Bevans and Elías watched him go. When the receding shapes shrank to gnat-size, Bevans glanced at his Mexican friend and tossed his head as a signal that they should get to work. He stood, buttoned his coat all the way to his chin, and got down.

Titus Jackson balanced one-legged with his right foot on the bottom step of the veranda. He was buckling his spurs and did not notice when Kings seemed to materialize out of thin air behind him. Taken off guard by the clatter of a gate latch being lifted, Titus spun and watched as the strange man turned three strange animals into the main corral. Squaring his shoulders, Titus walked out to meet him, purpose in every step, and loudly—perhaps *too* loudly—asked the man his business.

Kings closed the gate and stepped out into the open, hefting his saddle against his right thigh. His rifle hung at his back, dangling muzzle-down from his left shoulder by its sling, as did the cotton sack. He did not identify himself immediately, figuring that the Jackson boy should have no trouble recognizing him.

He figured wrong. Titus's walk had slowed, and he was no longer as bold as he had been just a second ago, with the obstruction of the corral to divide them. He stopped with twenty paces between them, squinting.

Kings knew what the kid saw, what he looked like. A thought struck him then, and a smile tweaked one corner of his mouth. As disheveled and fatigued as he was, he could still make young bucks like this one, full of juice, stop in their tracks and wish for a Bible.

He was the first to speak, waving his free hand. "Take 'er easy, Titus. Shape I'm in, you could order a Colt by post and still beat me to the punch."

Titus looked incredulous for a moment, then laughed uneasily. "Hellfire, is that you, Mr. Kings?" He glanced around. "You come in by yourself?"

"Uh-huh."

"We need to expect anybody else?"

"Nope."

Beyond, the front door opened, and a pair of hounds surged inelegantly onto the veranda, woofing as they went out to investigate. Their master appeared in the doorway with his hands curled around a cup. As the hounds began to bark, Arthur Jackson turned and ambled back into the dining room, where Belle was handing dirty plates to Oralia.

His daughter looked up, catching sight of him from the tail of her eye. A small smile dimpled her face, and, for a bright, brief moment, Jackson was taken back to a time when he could still hold her on his lap as they rode two-to-a-saddle. His memories shot forward to the night of Kings's last departure, recalling all that had been said between them as a lamp, trimmed low, flickered into the wee hours.

Since then, Jackson had told himself—more than once—that no matter what had been said, no matter what promises had been made, nothing was set in stone. Nothing, save that Belle was in love with a man whose better qualities were outweighed by his status as one of the nation's most elusive and notorious criminals. It seemed a cruel joke to be played on a father who had chased away every reputable suitor between here and Austin.

In sixty-one years of living, he had been brave in the face of many challenges—execution at the hands of a foreign army, drought, disease, near bankruptcy, and stock theft. Against all these he had come out on top, but he'd been powerless to prevent the deaths of three of his five children, those things most precious to him. As a result, he had loved and cherished the two that remained like no father, to his mind, ever had—grown closer to his children than any father ever had. And he had defended them, over the years, like a lion, but now, as he returned to the door to meet the man who had sworn to take his daughter away, Jackson looked within and found himself unprepared, once more unable to defend.

Kings had set his rifle and gear down on the porch, unaware of Jackson's presence on the other side of the cloth-screened door, and was swatting the dust from his clothes.

Jackson said, "Gabriel," and edged the door open to let him in. He extended his hand, which Kings accepted. "You're back."

News of what happened at Justicia had not yet been made public—at least not via the state legislature—but a vague overview of what transpired on New Year's Eve had circulated by word of mouth. Its reach only extended to a few counties outlying Justicia, however, and so Jackson was in a position of complete ignorance when he said, "You look like hell. What's happened?"

Kings was about to reply when Mrs. Jackson appeared beside her husband. She covered her mouth and touched his arm. "My Lord, son," she breathed, "are you all right? You look exhausted!"

"That's an accurate assessment, ma'am."

The major coughed, his hand coming to rest at the small of

her back. "My dear, if you could fill Gabriel a hot bath . . . ?"

With a perceptive glance at her husband, Mrs. Jackson left them, calling for Oralia's assistance. The Mexican woman came out into the parlor, wiping her wet hands on her apron. She swept past the men, hurrying to catch up to *la Señora*, but paused briefly to look back at Kings.

Ya regresó el Señor Reyes, she thought, then wondered with a quiet smile as to who would be happier to see him . . . *la Señorita* Belle, or the girls.

Kings waited until he and Jackson were alone again, but the major waved a hand. "We'll talk later," he said, then ducked his head toward the kitchen, where clattering dishes sounded. "She'll wanna see you first."

Belle was at the sink with her sleeves up to the elbows, scraping plates clean and dousing them in a sudsy washbasin. As she paused to tuck a loose strand of hair behind an ear, Kings stomped his boot three times, making the jinglebobs of his spurs chime like bells. She turned and her eyes went round. The plate in her hand slipped from her fingers with a splash.

"You are a welcome sight," he said, with a tired smile.

"Gabriel!" He stepped into the kitchen, and she threw her arms around his neck, squeezing tightly. "I couldn't stop worrying," she said in a rush. "You—you said there weren't gonna be but one last job and that after that we could be together, but it all seemed too good to hope for, and I knew . . . I *knew* you'd be killed—".

"It's like I said, darlin' "—he kissed her on the mouth—"I always turn up."

"Is it over?"

"It is, for both of us."

Belle collected herself then, remembering propriety, and stepped back. She cleared her throat and wiped away the beginnings of moisture from the corner of one eye. "You look done-in. Would you like me to fix you a bath?"

"Your ma's already on that." He crossed the floor to a small table in the corner, one arm held out and feeling for the nearest chair as though he were blind. Gripping the backrest, he sagged onto the seat with a mighty sigh. "I could use a drink."

"Oh. Oh, of course!" She glanced around, then gestured toward the pot on the stove. "Coffee? Something stronger?"

"Water."

He sat there and listened to her quick step and the swishing of her skirts as she took a glass from the cupboard and went out the back door to the pump. There she would find Oralia and her mother, and avert her eyes to keep her excitement secret.

It was very quiet in the kitchen, and, with an elbow on the table and his cheek resting in his open palm, Gabriel Kings allowed his eyelids to droop. Just for a few seconds, just until she came back.

Such a quiet kitchen . . . He could get used to a quiet kitchen with coffee on the stove and patterned paper on the walls. The thought faded, and so did he.

After five days and four nights on the trail, the Stringer-Leduc party rode back into Justicia.

Upon realizing they had aimlessly tracked an empty-saddled horse for five miles, three men doubled back in a northerly direction until they returned to the avalanche site while the others continued on, clinging to the direction Kings had apparently been heading. Using their bare hands and rifle butts, two of the backtrackers had dug desperately, hoping to find Kings's stiff and lifeless body. The other had milled about, searching the snowy ground for footprints on the off chance that Kings had somehow avoided such a death and struck out on foot. If there had been any to begin with, it seemed the hunted man had swept them out, at least until he reached the tree line. Any hope there might have been of locating his sign amongst the pines was lost when another snowfall broke.

The others had pressed on, finding the stream and following it onward. Eventually they reached the clearing, where they found the trapper, who had since freed himself and grumpily informed the lawmen that he hadn't the foggiest as to where their prey had gone.

Gabriel Kings, it seemed, had vanished again. Still . . . it was a long and hard way back, and winter could be cruel. God willing, it would be.

The men didn't know it, but the Mincey party was also despairing of ever catching up to Yeager, though they were still a half day away from turning back.

Despite these developments, the operation could very well be considered a success. The gang had been broken, and the leader was still running, which made Paul Leduc, who had predicted such a fate to a skeptical Patrick Delaney back in Austin, a prophet of sorts—Louisiana's first.

The structural damage inflicted by the outlaws on the town was nothing that could not be repaired. The population had lessened by four. A merchant had been trampled to death by one of the horsemen responsible for the jailhouse explosion, and another had caught a stray bullet fired from an outlaw gun. The other two casualties were deputies, Eli Cutting and Fred Whitehead. Somehow, Diego Arballo had survived his peppering at the hands of H. E. Simmons, though the severity of his wounds made it unlikely he would continue as a deputy.

And, of course, there was Delaney himself, who'd expired on a boardwalk not long after Stringer and the others pulled out.

The townsmen and deputies had all been bachelors, which made their deaths, while tragic, a little less so in the knowledge that they left no wives or young ones behind. Stringer recalled that Delaney had a wife named Jane, and he was appreciative, when told, that Sheriff Tom Shepherd had eulogized the detective at the previous day's shared service.

Stringer decided he would leave the duty of writing Delaney's widow to Mincey.

The possemen dropped their horses off and went their ways, some to the boarding house and others to the saloon. Dobie went to find Shepherd, while Stringer and Leduc walked to the High Grade Hotel, where a whole floor had been cleared and a room sectioned off as a holding cell for the two surviving outlaws.

On the street, people stopped to stare as the rangers marched past, but the lawmen didn't stop to give the opportunity or encouragement for questions. As they passed the funeral parlor, Stringer stopped short, then drew closer with Leduc to look upon a photograph that had been posted in the front window of the establishment. It was clear that the subjects of the photo were none other than the five outlaws killed in the raid, seated side by side on a bench as though awaiting a train.

Leroy Brownwell, Bob Creasy, and Charley Davis had their shirts unbuttoned to show their riddled torsos, but Sam Woods and H. E. Simmons, who had suffered arm, back, and head wounds, were fully clothed. Wrists were folded in laps and boots were crossed at the ankles. Their features were almost relaxed, all but Simmons's, whose eyes were open and whose death mask made him look dazed and exhausted. Two rifles bookended the line of dead men, and five pistols, presumably having belonged to each, were laid at their feet, muzzles pointed out toward the viewer.

The photographer who had arranged them certainly was a theatrical fellow.

The rangers continued on to the High Grade, where a deputized citizen directed them to the second floor, last room on the right. They encountered more recently appointed deputies along the way, who clutched their rifles and paced as though they expected another attack at any time.

A fair-haired man wearing round spectacles and a handlebar mustache sat beside the door to the last room on the right. He held a Winchester across his knees and the last bit of a homemade sandwich in one hand. Pulled from his reverie by the approach of the two men, he suddenly straightened and popped the morsel in his mouth.

"You got 'em in there?" Stringer asked.

The man nodded. "Yes, sir, we've had 'em sequestered here last couple days, since our jail's, ah . . . bein' rebuilt."

"You got a man outside, watchin' the winder?"

"Two men."

"Where's Shepherd?"

"Down at the jail, last I heard, overseein' the repairs."

"Our two prisoners . . . either of 'em wounded?"

"One."

"How bad?"

"He'll live to swing, Captain."

"What's your name, friend?"

"Rodd, sir. Henry Rodd."

"Well, Mr. Rodd, these boys owe the state of Texas a mighty big debt. They'll be standin' trial in Austin."

"It don't matter where they swing, Captain, so long as they swing."

Leduc spoke up. "Tomorrow mornin', we'll be takin' the prisoners to the railhead just east of here. We'd be obliged if you men could stand one last watch through the night."

"Sure thing."

They started to turn away, but Rodd stopped them. "There's one more thing, Captain."

Stringer rubbed the coarse bristle on his chin. "What's that?" he asked, hiding his impatience.

The townsman seemed uncertain, almost embarrassed to have brought it up. "One of the prisoners has been askin' for you specifically. Says he's got something to discuss with you. Something you'd be interested in hearing."

Stringer exchanged a sideways glance with Leduc, who appeared only mildly interested. They had dealt aplenty with prisoners seeking a pardon but had only rarely come across the wretch with any information that was actually worth one. What could this fellow possibly have to say or offer? This *was* a man who might have information concerning Gabriel Kings, however, and seeing as how their efforts hadn't yet produced Kings's corpse . . .

"Open the door, friend."

There were two beds inside, with a knit rug on the floor between them. In the beds were the two prisoners, manacled hand and foot to the brass head- and footboards. In the early days of his service, Stringer had come across the bodies of men tied down by Comanches in the same manner, to be roasted under the hot sun—or worse. By comparison, these boys had it much easier, though there was nothing easy about the thought of a gallows in one's near future.

The outlaw on the far bed was staring out the window as Stringer and Leduc were let in. He was short and dark, with a pointed black beard below a nose purpled and swollen. Leduc would later discover that Shepherd had given him a good pop at the butcher shop, and that since his capture he had clammed right up. Stringer recognized him as the man he saw riding into town the day before the shooting started, but he couldn't put a name to the face.

Neither could he do so for the second man, who only had one shackled arm raised behind his head. The other rested across his chest in a sling. He wore a patchy growth of beard and was considerably taller than his roommate, his feet nearly touching the footboard, and, while the other made a point of ignoring the lawmen, this one regarded them openly. Not with hostility, but interest, looking each of them up and down, as if taking their measure and making up his mind.

At length, Stringer addressed the wounded man. "They said you wanted to talk. What about?"

He seemed amused by Stringer's direct manner. "So you're the boss, eh? I recognized you from the way my pal here described ya." He tilted his head to look beyond Stringer, at Leduc. "Who's 'at there?"

"This ain't a social call, mister. Now, unless you got somethin' worthwhile to say, we'll see you tomorrow, bright and early, when we take you down to the railhead."

"Oh, I got somethin' worthwhile for ya, awright," the man said, shifting in an attempt to sit up straighter. He glanced at the other outlaw, who may as well have been deaf. "And I want a full pardon in exchange."

Paul Leduc wagged his head. "That ain't our department, fella. It's the court's, but so long as we're here, you might as well tell us whatcha got."

"Awright, I getcha," the man said, smiling shrewdly. "Not about go all in, callin' me instead. I'd hate to play cards with either of you boys."

The lawmen stared at him. Metal clinked against metal as the other outlaw stretched an arm, still feigning indifference to the dialogue.

"I don't know how it ain't yet occurred to Dickie there," Foss was saying, "but in exchange for a pardon, I'll give you Gabriel Kings's neck."

That got Dick Osborn's attention. "You button your damn lip, Foss!" he snapped.

"How you gonna give us Gabriel Kings," Leduc demanded,

"when no one—not even us—has been able to get a whiff of him?"

"None of ya knew where he was gonna be a week after this job."

"You backstabbin' sonovabitch!"

"I'm lookin' out for my own neck, boy," Foss said calmly. "You was smart, you'd'a beat me to it." His attention shifted back to the rangers. "Y'all didn't come back with his body over a horse, didja? You gimme back my freedom, and I'll tell you how to get there."

"No, no," Leduc said, leaning forward and clutching the footboard with both hands. His eyes bored into the outlaw. "First, you're gonna tell us how to get there, an' only if this don't turn out to be a wild goose chase, we can start talkin' about your freedom. Savvy?"

"I savvy."

"Where is he?"

"I want somethin' in writin'."

"You'll have it. Where is he?"

Foss hesitated, for two reasons. First, because it hadn't been a recent practice of his to do business with lawmen, let alone trust them. Second, because he felt Osborn staring at him with the intensity of fire, but what loyalty did he owe Kings, and why the hell should he step off into the air for him?

Finally, he shrugged and said, "He'll be holed up someplace down south on the Frio River—at the Jackson homestead or ranch, one of the two. He's got a woman there, said he planned to marry her after the job was done."

"I will beat the life outta you, Foss."

"Jackson's a common name," Leduc pressed. "Might be more'n one Jackson family in that area."

"Look for the one's got the most land."

Leduc turned, wrenched the door open, and confirmed with

Henry Rodd that the nearest available telegraph station was in Springer, a mining town situated along the A.T. & S.F. railway. This meant that Leduc, fresh from the saddle, would have to mount up again and ride thirty hard miles to the southeast and wire Ranger Company D headquarters in San Antonio. For the moment, that hot bath he had been looking forward to would have to wait.

As the thunder of his boots going down the stairs faded, Stringer focused on the more loyal of the two prisoners, who, if looks could kill a man, would have presently had the murder of Hardyman Foss added to his list of offenses.

"How come you didn't come to us with this?" Stringer asked. "What do you think you owe Kings? Or what do you think he owes you? You think he's gonna come blazin' into Austin and bust you out? He's forgot all about you, boy."

Osborn glowered at him, as though the question scarcely deserved an answer, but the answer he gave was firm. It was also barbed for the man in the other bed. "I owe him a damn good livin'. I may be a lousy thief and I may have killed a guy or two in cold blood in my time, but I'm no Judas."

Stringer left the room, and, as he went down the steps, he wondered at the truth behind the old adage. On the one hand, Foss's betrayal confirmed it. On the other, Osborn's fierce allegiance seemed to have contradicted it.

But Osborn was no saint. He was just one of many cut from the same cloth, and, on a different day, he too might have offered Kings up as a sacrificial lamb.

Caleb Stringer was still convinced that there was no honor among thieves.

Ranger Sergeant Mike Donovan was widely held to be a capable man. A native Texan, he had spent the first few years of manhood as an eight-dollar-a-day cowboy, but the life proved too dull for a fellow of his tastes, and so, on a whim, he joined the forty-a-month Texas Rangers in 1875. Since then, he had risen fast in the estimation of his superiors. A survivor of four frontier skirmishes, two apiece with the Kiowa and Comanche, he had also taken part in the quelling of the Mason County War. His career had certainly taken the turn he'd hoped for, but when he was called into company headquarters in the late afternoon of January 14, Donovan received an assignment that dwarfed all the others in scope.

"You mind if I ask why, sir?" he'd inquired of his commanding officer. Donovan indicated what was written on the paper he'd been handed. "Says here this Arthur Jackson's a respectable businessman, that the army gets some of its best horseflesh from him. Says he was an officer in the Mexican War . . . family man. What sorta charges we lookin' at?"

By way of answering, Captain D. W. Roberts had produced another paper, this one a telegram. "Read that there, Sarge, and you'll find that Major Jackson might not be as respectable as we might think."

The dateline made Donovan frown—town of Springer, New Mexico Territory?

POSSIBLE GK AT JACKSON RCH STOP SEARCH FRIO R AREA STOP ARREST ON SIGHT STOP KILL IF NECESSARY STOP

LEDUC

"We received that just minutes ago. Leduc's a sergeant in our own Company D. 'GK' is Gabriel Kings."

"Gabriel Kings? Wasn't Cap'n Stringer on that case?"

"Was and still is, and now you are, too. Grab as many men as you think you'll need and get movin'. With this kind, you never know how long you'll have to act."

That conversation took place yesterday, and it had been nearly an hour since Sergeant Donovan and his two corporals entered the southern gate onto Jackson land, crossing under a sign that declared it as such and glimpsing a sizable group of horses from afar. The property sprawled out on every side, stretching from horizon to horizon, making visibility of the western and eastern fence lines impossible.

Aside from the animals that eyeballed them as they rode past, their arrival had gone unchecked. After another quarter of an hour and still no sign of the main house, the rangers began to lope their horses. Eventually they reached the yard, and as they slowed down to approach at a walk, a man who could only be Arthur Jackson stepped onto the veranda. He walked to the edge, stood with his thumbs hooked in his vest holes, and waited.

They came on. The corporals' eyes roamed the perimeter while Donovan focused on the man, saying nothing until the rangers halted just short of the steps. "Major Arthur Jackson?"

"I am, sir. Who might you be?"

Donovan edged back his coat to reveal the star-in-a-circle. "Sergeant Donovan, Company D out of San Antone. Corporals Hume and Gossage, there."

"What can I do for you?"

"Sir, does the name Gabriel Kings mean anything to you?"

Jackson's expression did not change. "Yes, as a matter of fact, it does."

"Is he here?"

"No, he's not."

There was a beat of hesitation, then Donovan shrugged. "No offense meant," he said, "but we have reason to believe otherwise, Major. I hope you don't mind if my men take a look around."

"I suppose you've got a warrant, Sergeant?"

Donovan patted his breast pocket.

Jackson waved his arm in a broad motion. "Then, by all means, take a look. I have nothing to hide."

The rangers dismounted, and Jackson waited while Donovan directed his men to search the grounds, with one starting at the seemingly empty quarters to the right of the house—where the Elías family slept—and the other at the barn directly across. Gossage had his rifle in his hands, and Hume had his pistol out, cocked and ready.

After hitching his horse, Donovan mounted the steps, unfolding both the warrant and telegram. He stopped just below the major, who regarded him with no hostility and took what was held out to him with a genuine look of confusion. For a moment Donovan considered that he might have been sent to the wrong Jacksons.

After the major finished reading, a hint of a smile altered his features. "Well, now, what would make your commanding officer—or this Leduc fellow, whoever he is—think that Kings'd be *here*?"

Donovan was watching him closely. "I wouldn't know that, sir," he replied. "I just go where I'm sent and do what I'm s'posed to."

Jackson raised his eyes. "Well, that's exactly what I wanna know, Sergeant. *Why* you were sent here. The specificity of this telegram is damned curious, I don't mind tellin' you, and a little offensive."

The ranger's gaze swept the yard and found Gossage emerging from the Elías family compound. Gossage paused in his search to look back and shake his head. At the barn, there was no sign of Hume. Donovan shifted his attention back to Jackson and lowered his voice.

"If it turns out he *is* here, sir, then my men'll find out soon enough. If he ain't, that don't mean he's never been." He paused. "So I'm afraid I'm gonna have to ask you straight out—do you admit to knowing the man?"

"No, sir, I do not."

"You said his name meant somethin' to you."

"Of course," Jackson said softly, but with a hint of frustration, "as it does to every law-abiding man in Texas. You'd have to ride a thousand miles before you came across someone didn't know his name."

Donovan's brow furrowed. Jackson came down one step so he could look the young man in the eye.

"Let me tell you something, Sergeant," he went on. "I came into this country when it was little more'n raw wilderness, and for the last twenty-four, damn near twenty-five years, I've broke my back to make it a suitable place to raise horses and a family. And besides lookin' after my own, I have the responsibility of providing for the family of my hired hand. I do that by livin' honest, furnishing remounts for a lot of the boys out of Fort Clark. Now, you tell me . . . why the hell would I risk the welfare of my people to give a man like Kings so much as a cup of coffee?"

Donovan looked uncertain. "Would you mind if I stepped inside?"

"Not at all."

The ranger suggested a perusal of the upper floor. Jackson waved him on, directing him toward the staircase, then followed at a respectable and trustworthy distance as Donovan climbed with one hand on the railing. The other hand, Jackson noticed, lifted his pistol halfway out of its holster, then let it slip back, thus loosened for quick action.

Donovan's pistol would stay where it was, because all the search amounted to was the disturbance of two rangy hounds that had been napping in the major's study. One by one, each door was nudged open, every room explored, and, to Donovan's thinly veiled surprise, the wanted man was nowhere to be found. Still, he was troubled by a gut feeling that Jackson's hands weren't as clean in the story of Gabriel Kings as they had been made out to be. History had seen its share of unlikely alliances, forged under any number of unlikely circumstances, but, in this case, what could be proven?

Not a blamed thing.

He was shown to the door and onto the veranda, where the lady of the house was serving his men coffee from a tray. With one look at Hume's face, it seemed apparent the story would end here, at this lonely ranch on the East Frio River. Kings's trail, if there had been one to begin with, had gone cold, and there was nothing left for the rangers to do but ride back to headquarters and report that fact.

The Jacksons watched them go in silence. Finally, with the riders fading into the distance, the major seemed to recover from a trance. His voice was gentle as he held Martha closer and kissed the top of her head.

"Proud of ya, sweetheart. Handled yourself well, past couple days."

Her sigh was a shuddering release, as though she had been holding her breath throughout the rangers' entire stay, but she quickly composed herself and drew straighter. "I only pray God they make it safely."

"They will."

"How can you be sure, Art?"

"The man's a survivor, Martha. Keepin' our daughter safe between here and California'll be easy as pie for him. And remember, John said he'd go along with 'em, least till they're out of Texas."

"But they didn't *find* him here," she persisted. "They'll keep hunting him, won't they?"

Jackson shook his head and said with as much confidence as he could muster, "If they were a week late in thinkin' he was still here, he might as well be dead. They'll never see his dust. Not now."

Behind them, one of the hounds bawled, and then the other joined in. The Elías girls, likely teasing them in some way, shrieked with delight. All around, the shadows were growing long and thin, which meant Titus and Fernando should be getting back from finishing their fence work at any time. With his hand on her hip, Arthur Jackson turned his wife and prodded her ahead of him into the house. It was warm within, and there was the pleasant sound of food cooking on the skillet, accompanied by Oralia's soft Spanish singing.

Oh, yes. The major was sure of it. The initial strangeness of Belle's absence would wear off over the next several days, and Martha's spirits would lift again.

After all, there might be news of grandchildren not far down the road.

CHAPTER 24

It was a wintry and cloud-scudded afternoon in the Sacramento Valley when Mr. and Mrs. Gabriel Kings stepped off the Southern Pacific steamer from San Francisco. It was just about the middle of February 1879, and they disembarked in anonymity, indistinguishable from the rest of the passengers. There was, to the new bride's great relief, no reception committee of marshals or Pinkerton detectives to receive them, but she would have to endure another anxious half hour of waiting on the station bench while her husband arranged accommodations for their horses. It was an impressive string, all branded with a linked "AJ" on their left hips, consisting of three mares—two bays and a sorrel—and a splendid pair of stallions, John Reb and a younger, submissive blue-roan.

"You in the horse business?" the hostler couldn't help but ask.

Clean-shaven below a black derby and wearing a vested suit of gray, Gabriel Kings nodded and said, "Plan to be."

There might have been over a thousand miles separating him now from Texas, and perhaps three hundred from the nearest site of some past heist, but he still was not fully at ease. Since his final departure from the Jackson ranch, he had yet to shake hands with a man or hold a gaze for more than a few seconds. He still feared recognition, though he'd taken steps to alter his appearance. The one unchanging facet was the ivory-handled Peacemaker on his hip, just inside the skirt of his jacket.

Belle had the other secreted in her purse.

The hostler informed him their stock would be held at the J Street stable. Kings paid for two days' board in advance, then turned from the corral and headed back to the platform. He signaled one of the porters and spit out half-truths as the fellow asked how long he intended to stay in Sacramento, what plans he might have.

Eventually Belle hurried across to stand by him, and the questions came to an end. They linked arms—a handsome, if somber-faced, couple—and waited while the baggage car was unloaded. The porter tussled three steamer trunks and a weighty wooden chest onto a pushcart, and, when all was squared away, they followed him to the front of the depot.

Kings noticed a man standing near the edge of the platform. He wore the dark-blue frock coat, seven-pointed badge, and dome-crowned cap of a city policeman. With his wife clinging to his left side, it took all of Kings's strength to keep his right hand from moving toward his gun. But as they went by, the copper lost interest and carried on with his people watching. Kings felt Belle's grip loosen on his arm.

Kings tipped the porter, then hailed a horse-drawn cab and asked to be taken to the city's best hotel. On the ride in, Kings saw firsthand that the tales of Sacramento's riches were all true. Belle, whose experience with cities was limited, stared with girlish wonder as they traversed the paved streets, passing gas-powered streetlamps, brick buildings, and all the finest trappings made possible by the discovery of gold here decades before.

"Ever see anything like this?" Kings murmured into her ear, knowing full well she hadn't. A gust of wind lifted a wisp of blonde hair showing beneath her bonnet, and, as she turned her face toward his, her smile was wide and her dimples deep. He marveled again at what strange luck had spared him a dozen deaths and won him this woman. At the same time, he wondered what penance he might yet have to pay, but she stifled those thoughts for the time being with a huddle and a kiss.

"No," she said, "but I believe I could get used to it right quick."

The cab came to a stop outside the Western Hotel on the bustling intersection of Second and K Streets, and, as soon as the luggage was unloaded onto another cart, they entered the elegant lobby. Plush carpets decorated the gleaming hardwood floor, a central common area was appointed with leather furniture, and the walls and ceiling had been painted with frescoes depicting nature and wildlife.

Belle watched as Kings leaned over the register and signed "Mr. & Mrs. John Aubrey." He ordered a tub and hot water for the room. The desk clerk sent a brass key and a complimentary newspaper across the marble counter, and the Aubreys, with the bellhop, rode a black birdcage of an elevator to the third and uppermost floor.

While Belle stood on the balcony, gazing out over the city, Kings stacked their trunks in the closet, choosing for the foundation the wooden chest that held the means by which he hoped to purchase the meadow he hadn't been able to forget. In the chest there was roughly $150,000 in notes, greenbacks, and coin. Not counted was Yeager's half of the Justicia job, which was hidden below folded pants in a separate trunk.

Would that portion ever be delivered? It was one of many questions that had occupied Kings's thoughts for the last month or so. Had Andy outrun the posse, or had they overtaken him? Had he frozen to death between New Mexico and distant Clinch Mountain? It was Kings's hope that his old friend might still get the chance to breed racehorses, which he'd mentioned once. If so, there could be a future yet for Gabriel Kings and Andy Yeager. A legitimate one.

But that was a question for tomorrow. It was time to focus on tonight.

Kings removed his hat and coat, unbuckled his gunbelt, and dumped it on the bed. Almost on cue, there came a knock at the door. Belle came in from the brisk evening air to see a pair of bellmen labor in and out, lopsidedly transferring a copper tub and four buckets of hot water from the hallway. When it was done, the same bellhop who had carried their luggage up to the room waited while Kings peeled a few dollars from his roll.

"Here you go, friend. Say, where's the best eatin' in the city?"

The man considered the question for a moment before going on to list a number of fine restaurants and their locations. He made sure, when he could think of no more, to add, "And just so you know, sir, the Western itself offers meals for its guests, dollar-and-a-half a plate."

"Obliged."

Time to go, the bellhop turned toward the door, and as he did he caught a glimpse of the newspaper on the dresser. He indicated it and asked eagerly, "You been keepin' track of that story, Mr. Aubrey?"

Kings glanced at the broadsheet. "Ain't had a chance to look at it. What's the story?"

The bellhop stepped into the hall and started to backpedal toward the elevator. "I won't spoil it for you, sir," he called back, "but do take a gander when you can. You and the missus have a nice night."

When Kings rounded back into the room he saw Belle staring down at the paper with one hand cupped over her mouth. He read the headline over her shoulder.

HUNT FOR GABRIEL KINGS CALLED TO AN END

He suddenly felt weak and wondered at it. At his lowest, he had always imagined that this moment—this fantastical day he knew would never come—would generate an overpowering rush of elation. He'd imagined he would rent the skies, whatever skies he happened to be under, with a rebel yell and pierce the clouds with gunshots. But now his throat felt dry and constricted, and he had trouble catching his breath. Why?

Unable to stand, he sat down on the bed, then sank backward onto the mattress, bedsprings creaking under his weight. His left hand touched the cool grip of his Peacemaker. Moving slowly, his fingers skittered over the screws in the frame, over the hand-tooled leather of its holster. He pushed the belt off the bed, and it clouted the floor like a judge's gavel.

None would sound for him now, it seemed. The article, he would later read, reported that the Avenging Angels were no more, that their chief had evaded capture at the hands of former Governor Richard Hubbard's specially conscripted posse. It went on to say that, although the gang was defeated and the posse disbanded, the man might still be at large, and the public ought to remain vigilant.

But the article was wrong on that score.

Gabriel Kings *was* dead.

John Aubrey felt the nearness of his wife's body as she joined him on the bed and hid in his one-armed embrace. Coal-oil light shone golden-white off her flaxen hair, and he could suddenly breathe again.

He breathed deep.

ABOUT THE AUTHOR

Born and raised in El Centro, California, **Michael Dukes** always wanted to be a storyteller, almost as long as he has loved American history, and that of the Old West in particular. A 2012 graduate of San Diego Christian College, Michael worked as a journalist for the *Imperial Valley Press*, covering sports, education, and agriculture over a period of three years. *The Avenging Angels* is his debut novel. His favorite pursuits include spending time with his family, messing with his dogs, and exploring the countryside with his wife, Elise. He currently resides in the San Diego area.

The employees of Five Star Publishing hope you have enjoyed this book.

Our Five Star novels explore little-known chapters from America's history, stories told from unique perspectives that will entertain a broad range of readers.

Other Five Star books are available at your local library, bookstore, all major book distributors, and directly from Five Star/Gale.

Connect with Five Star Publishing

Visit us on Facebook:
https://www.facebook.com/FiveStarCengage

Email:
FiveStar@cengage.com

For information about titles and placing orders:
(800) 223-1244
gale.orders@cengage.com

To share your comments, write to us:
Five Star Publishing
Attn: Publisher
10 Water St., Suite 310
Waterville, ME 04901